Readers Love K.L. Hiers

Acsquidentally in Love

"Hiers rolls worldbuilding mythology, delicious flirting, erotic scenes, and detective work into a breezy and sensual LGBTQ paranormal romance."

—*Library Journal*

Kraken My Heart

"This is a really good series. It is one that is worth reading over again, just for the fun of it."

—Love Bytes Book Reviews

Just Calamarried

"Sloane and Loch are so crazy in love that you can feel it."

—Virginia Lee Book Reviews

By K.L. HIERS

SUCKER FOR LOVE MYSTERIES
Acsquidentally In Love
Kraken My Heart
Head Over Tentacles
Nautilus Than Perfect
Just Calamarried
Our Shellfish Desires
Insquidious Devotion

Published by DREAMSPINNER PRESS
www.dreamspinnerpress.com

INSQUIDIOUS DEVOTION

K.L. HIERS

DREAMSPINNER PRESS

Published by
DREAMSPINNER PRESS

5032 Capital Circle SW, Suite 2, PMB# 279, Tallahassee, FL 32305-7886 USA
www.dreamspinnerpress.com

Insquidious Devotion
© 2022 K.L. Hiers

Cover Art
© 2022 Tiferet Design
http://www.tiferetdesign.com
Cover content is for illustrative purposes only and any person depicted on the cover is a model.

Trade Paperback ISBN: 978-1-64108-458-1
Digital ISBN: 978-1-64108-457-4
Trade Paperback published November 2022
v. 1.0

Printed in the United States of America

CHAPTER 1.

"SO," SLOANE drawled, his hands on his hips as he stared his husband and daughter down, "what have we learned today?"

"Ah! I know this one!" Loch grinned. "Not to make crème brûlée when you're home."

Pandora, their infant daughter, gurgled in what appeared to be agreement.

"No." Sloane shook his head.

"Hmm." Loch frowned. "Not to make crème brûlée while you're sleeping?"

"We have learned to make crème brûlée *never*."

Part of the kitchen was still smoking—the perils of a god and a little demigoddess trying to cook together were many.

"I was able to put out the flames," Loch complained, "and the damage to the cabinets can easily be repaired."

"And what about our daughter? She could have been burned!"

"Ah! I have recently discovered that Pandora is quite fond of fire." Loch tilted his head. "As in, I discovered this about ten minutes before you woke up from your nap. Hmm, and there was something else I was going to tell you...."

Pandora wiggled out of Loch's lap where they'd been cuddling on the sofa, and she waddled over to Sloane. Although she wasn't quite four months old, she was as big as a one-year-old, had two front teeth right on top, and she could walk quite well. She had curly red hair like Loch, but her eyes were brown like Sloane's.

She also had Sloane's very thick eyebrows, brows that Loch often described as luscious, beautiful, legendary, and a plethora of other exciting adjectives.

Sloane bent over to pick Pandora up, but he immediately recoiled when her hands burst into flames. "By all the gods!"

Pandora giggled and waved her flaming hands excitedly.

"No! Young lady! Absolutely not!" Sloane grabbed Pandora around her middle and blew out her hands, quickly checking them for any sign of injury.

Fussing, Pandora swatted at Sloane.

"Ah, that was the other thing I meant to tell you!" Loch grinned sheepishly. "She is also quite flame-resistant."

"Seriously?" Sloane groaned. "We were already worried about babyproofing, and now we need to fireproof too?"

Pandora's hands were warm but otherwise seemed fine.

Sloane knew that life with an old god was going to be interesting, but he could have never prepared himself for the adventure of raising a child together.

Especially a child who had tentacles like her father and a penchant for mischief.

And fire now, apparently.

"Oh, my beautiful husband. Fear not." Loch waved his hand at the kitchen, and all evidence of the fiery disaster vanished. He stood to join Sloane and hugged him with Pandora between them, wrapping them up with a thick bundle of grayish-blue tentacles.

Pandora grabbed for one of the tentacles, her hands morphing into long purple tentacles of her own and curling around Loch's. She immediately pulled his tentacle into her mouth and began to gnaw on it.

"I will cast fire protection wards all over the apartment," Loch promised. "Nothing will catch fire here again, I swear to you."

"Probably should have done that a while ago." Sloane smirked.

Loch gasped. "Is that a slight directed at my cooking ability?"

"Just a tiny one."

"Hmmph."

Sloane leaned his forehead against Loch's, cuddling Pandora as he said, "Seriously. I just worry. Being a new parent is hard enough without having to freak out every ten minutes that she's learned some new kind of magic. What if she opens a portal?"

"Then we will go find her." Loch smiled. "She does have a watchman's spell on her, you know."

"What if she tries to summon bees?"

"You don't summon bees," Loch soothed. "You have to ask for their assistance in smiting your enemies. We've been over this before, my sweet husband."

Sloane groaned.

"I am Azaethoth the Lesser. I am an ancient, handsome, and powerful god. You are a Starkiller with the most gorgeous, luscious eyebrows in the universe. We have saved the world countless times and defeated many demented members of my family. I love you, and I know we can do anything together." Loch kissed Sloane's brow firmly. "Even this."

Sloane's heart fluttered, and he actually felt a little bit better.

They'd been through worse, after all.

Crazy cultists, murderous gods, and even that one time Loch lost his body at the post office.

"Thank you." Sloane kissed Loch sweetly. "You're right."

"I know."

"She's growing so freakin' fast and getting into absolutely everything, not to mention also terrifying me at every turn. But—" Sloane took a deep breath. "—we can totally do this."

"Of course we can." Loch beamed. "We can—ow!" He pouted, pulling the tentacle Pandora had been mouthing on away. "Hey! That is not for eating."

"What happened?" Sloane asked.

"She bit me." Loch sighed. "She has more teeth."

"Already?" Sloane tried to peek into Pandora's mouth.

Pandora grinned and offered a flash of a few shiny little teeth peeking out from her bottom gums to match the two on top.

"Well, then." Sloane cradled Pandora against his chest and kissed her cheeks. "I guess that means it's time to work on getting some baby food, huh?"

"Ah! I will prepare our daughter's sustenance, thank you." Loch turned up his nose. "Say what you will about my culinary abilities, but I am more than capable of providing for her."

"Uh-huh." Sloane headed into the kitchen. It still smelled a little burnt. He reached into the fridge to grab a bottle of formula, a special godly variety that Loch's mother, Urilith, made for them.

"You doubt me?" Loch followed him, pouting now.

"Only a tiny bit." Sloane chuckled as he heated up the bottle with a swipe of his thumb. "I think it's very sweet, but are you really sure you can do all that? She's probably going to eat a lot, isn't she?"

"Most likely, based on her exponential growth, but it will not be a problem." Loch grinned.

"Because you're a god?"

"Yes, because I'm a god."

Sloane rolled his eyes and offered the bottle to Pandora, cooing, "Your daddy is very silly. Don't worry. I'll get you some baby food from the store."

"Oh! How you wound me!" Loch clutched his chest.

Sloane's cell phone rang.

"I'll make it up to you." Sloane scrambled to reach into his pocket while holding Pandora and the bottle.

"Here." Loch gently took her from Sloane as he chided, "Your father is a cruel, cruel man. Don't ever forget that, my darling spawn."

Pandora gurgled in reply.

Sloane chuckled as he retrieved his phone from his pocket. "Beaumont Investigations, how may I help you?"

"Hey, Sloane!" Milo Evans's voice greeted him.

"Hey, Milo!"

Milo was Sloane's best friend from college and former coworker at the Archersville Police Department. Milo's girlfriend, Lynnette, was expecting their first child any day now. They were a few of the small group of people who knew that Loch was actually a god and the true nature of Pandora's birth.

The exclusive circle was affectionately known as the Super Secret Sage Club. They knew that the Sagittarian faith had been right all along, and that while some of the old gods were still deep asleep in the dreaming in Zebulon, some were here on Aeon with them.

Sloane was married to one, of course, and he'd met many members of Loch's family. Loch's mother, uncle, and sister were all quite sane, but his brothers....

That was a different story.

"Everything okay?" Sloane asked. "How's Lynnette? Ready to pop yet?"

"Yeah!" Milo laughed. "She's okay! Super huge and beautiful and ready. Technically she's not due until next week, but I think she's ready to send our new kiddo an eviction notice. How are you and the rest of the godly brood? How's my little Panda Bear?"

"Oh, you know. The usual." Sloane glanced back at Loch and Pandora with a smile. "Setting fires, trying to burn down the apartment. Ah, and Panda has more teeth now. We're up to four."

"Already? Sheesh!" Milo laughed. "She's gonna be headed off to college soon!"

"Right? It's crazy." Sloane didn't mind having a casual chat with Milo, but it was a little odd for him to be calling in the middle of the day while he was at work. "So, what's up?"

"Yeah. Uh." Milo's voice dropped to a conspiratorial whisper. "We have got some high-level weirdness going on down here. Like, definite cultist-type shenanigans."

Sloane's stomach flopped. "Seriously?" He frowned at Loch and put the phone on speaker. "What's going on?"

"Chase and Merrick had this super freaky case a while back where one of the cultists drowned in the alley behind Dead to Rites. Like, drowned in salt water. From the ocean."

"Okay, yeah. I remember Chase saying something about that when we were looking for Nathaniel Ware. Dead to Rites was one of the places that Nathaniel's sister told us to go look for him at."

"Right. Well, that drowning case went cold, but then it happened again."

"Another drowning?"

"Yeah. Last week. And well, then it happened again just today."

Loch's brow creased with concern, and he asked loudly, "Were there any butlers in the vicinity?"

"Uh, no," Milo replied. "Look, we think it's Daisy."

"Daisy?" Sloane echoed.

Daisy Lopez used to be a forensic tech at the AVPD with Milo, and she had secretly been a member of a cult dedicated to Salgumel, Loch's father and the god of dreams. Salgumel had gone mad in his dreaming, and the cult's aim was to wake him up and remake the world into one where the old gods would rule again—by destroying it.

And the cultists weren't alone.

There were old gods who wanted Salgumel to rise so they could reclaim what they'd lost.

Sloane and the other members of the Sages Club had already defeated two of Salgumel's sons, Loch's older brothers, for having the same nefarious desires as the cult. It was how Sloane had become a Starkiller, having been given a sword of pure starlight from Great Azaethoth himself, to strike the gods down and save the world.

But every time was getting harder.

The cult was growing, and they had no idea when any of them would strike next. They didn't know how many gods were in league with

Loch's brothers, but they had to plan for the worst. After the cult's last attempt to wake Salgumel had failed, Daisy had vanished along with Jeff Martin, the cult's leader.

If she was back, that meant nothing but trouble.

"Yeah," Milo confirmed. "The newest victim drowned in a hotel, and we got a pretty clean shot of her going into the room and never leaving. I'm, like, 98 percent sure it's her. Chase and Merrick think so too."

Detectives Elwood Q. Chase and Benjamin Merrick were also members of their little Sage club. Chase was mortal, but Merrick was actually Gordoth, the Sagittarian god of justice and Loch's uncle. Like Loch, Merrick used a mortal body as his vessel to hide in plain sight from the world.

They were partners at the AVPD and in their personal life, Chase having been quite proud of himself for taking "the Untouched" title from Merrick a few months ago.

"Any idea how she's making people… drown?" Sloane asked.

"No clue." Milo sighed. "We were kinda hoping you could swing down here and take a peek? Use that magical, ahem, starlight of yours and see if you got any ideas?"

"We will be expecting a consulting fee," Loch declared. "We no longer accept personal checks unless you have two forms of identification."

"Wait, wait." Sloane scoffed. "We can't go anywhere. What are we gonna do with our little Panda Bear, huh? We can't take her with us, and we can't exactly drop her off at a normal day care center."

"Why?"

Sloane stared at Loch.

"Oh yes, right." Loch grinned. "Tiny demigoddess with tentacles who likes fire in a world where most people assume the old gods are myths and sudden evidence to the contrary might cause mass panic?"

"Yes."

Pandora giggled, and she then pulled off her bottle to coo, "Mafff panic!"

Sloane resisted the urge to slap his own forehead.

"Holy crap!" Milo gasped. "Was that Panda? Sweet little Panda Bear? Did she just talk?"

"Yes. Yes, she did." Sloane didn't know whether to be proud or mortified by Pandora's very first words.

"No mass panic, young spawn," Loch chided, one of his tentacles playfully booping her nose. "That is decidedly frowned upon in this house."

"Mafff panic!" Pandora declared as she swatted back at Loch's tentacle. "Maff panic, maff panic!"

"Ah! I know! I shall summon my sister!" Loch nodded. "She is more than capable of watching over our tiny godly spawn."

"Well...." Sloane reached over to pet Pandora's curls.

He had barely left her side since she was born—other than quick naps, quick runs to the store, and even quicker quickies with Loch—and he remained hesitant to leave her. If the cult was back, however, he knew they needed to help.

Fate of the world and all that.

"All right," Sloane said. "As soon as Gal gets here, we'll come. Just text me the address, okay, Milo?"

"Cool!" Milo replied. "Will do! See you guys soon!"

"Bye." Sloane hung up with a sigh. There was a knot of dread in his stomach, but he did his best to ignore it. "Well, here we go again."

"Go?" Loch asked. "Where are we going?"

"Going on another crazy adventure." Sloane kept playing with Pandora's hair. "Taking time off from working cases and being here at home has been... really nice."

"The midday naps spoiled you, didn't they?"

"They sure did." Sloane chuckled. "Could almost pretend everything was okay, you know?"

"Well, even though we haven't seen the cultists or any of my wayward relatives plotting, we know they're still out there."

"I guess there was a part of me that hoped they'd just give up, as silly as that is. They've been so quiet... which now that I think about it has me more worried."

"Why, my sweet mate?"

"Because it means they've probably been working on something big." Sloane grimaced. "Like drowning people. Why? What possible purpose could that serve?"

"I don't know, but we will figure it out."

"Maff panic," Pandora chimed in.

"And you!" Sloane laughed, grinning down at her. "You, little lady, are the most perfect and wonderful thing in the world. I'd much rather be here with you, dealing with fires and whatever else you decide to get into."

"Maffff panic!"

"She's talking. How is she already talking?" Sloane scooped her up from Loch's arms, cradling her against his chest as he gave her back the bottle. "I swear that we're gonna blink and she's gonna be a teenager."

"That is certainly a possibility," Loch mused, "but unlikely."

Pandora jerked her head away from the bottle and cried loudly.

"Aw, baby girl," Sloane cooed. "Hey. Hey, what's the matter?" He tried to give her the bottle again, but she pushed it away with a frantic wail.

"Oh, little spawn!" Loch fussed over Pandora with his tentacles, trying to comfort her to no avail. "What can we do, hmm? What's wrong?"

Pandora grabbed one of Loch's tentacles and promptly chomped on it.

"Ow." Loch clenched his teeth together as he grumbled, "I am hardly an expert, but I do believe she might be hungry."

"But she won't take her bottle," Sloane protested.

"Flesh! She hungers for flesh!"

There was a knock at the door.

"Gods, I hope that's Galgareth." Sloane passed Pandora over to Loch. "Here."

"Ah yes." Loch made another pained face. "Put her closer to the source of nourishment. Good idea."

Sloane hurried over to the door and then opened it, sighing in relief when it was indeed Galgareth. "Hey! Thank you so much for coming so quickly! And for knocking."

Galgareth was in her usual vessel, a teenager named Toby who liked piercings and dyeing his hair funky colors. It was purple and neon green currently, and he had a new ring in his eyebrow to accompany the ones in his lip and nose.

"Of course I knocked!" Galgareth grinned. "Who knows what kind of debaucherous things you two might be up to?" She embraced Sloane. "Mm, it's good to see you!"

"Good to see you too." Sloane happily returned the hug. "How are you? How's Toby?"

"Toby's good!" Galgareth gestured to her face. "Got a new piece of metal stabbed into his flesh to celebrate his birthday! He's seventeen now!"

"Happy Birthday, Toby!" Sloane always found it a little weird to talk to Toby since Galgareth was always in control of his body, but he didn't want to be rude.

After all, he wasn't like with Loch or Merrick, whose vessels were empty. Toby was a very devout follower of Galgareth and offered himself willingly whenever she came to Aeon.

"That's marvelous. Wonderful." Loch pouted miserably. "Can someone please assist me? Our spawn is attempting to digest me."

Pandora had a very firm grip on Loch's tentacle and was gnawing away.

"Oh!" Galgareth snapped her fingers. "I bet she's teething."

"You think so?" Sloane shut the door, frowning. "She did just have two new ones pop up, but she was born with teeth too. I didn't even think about that."

"Where's the bracelet Uncle Yeris gave you for a wedding present?" Galgareth asked. "It was made of amber. That'll work perfectly!"

Loch held out his hand, and the bracelet appeared. "Ah, you mean this one?"

"Yes!" Galgareth took the bracelet and gave it to Pandora, urging her to take a nibble. "Here, little one. Try having a chew on this, hmm?"

Pandora's eyes widened, and she released Loch's tentacle to eagerly accept the bracelet.

Quickly retracting his tentacle, Loch took a step back and groaned in relief. "Oh yes. Thank you."

"I put a little smidge of healing magic on it," Galgareth said, smiling reassuringly. "That plus the amber should ease the ache."

"Goddess of serendipity, huh?" Sloane grinned. "Of course you'd remember the one magical thing we have that's perfect for teething."

"Don't forget I'm also the goddess of love and night too." Galgareth held her head high.

"We may want to find a substitute for her," Loch warned, carrying Pandora over to the small bassinet beside the couch to lay her down.

"Why?" Sloane followed to help tuck her in. "She seems to like it. Do we really want to upset a happy baby?"

"The bracelet carries my uncle's blessing." Loch stared at Sloane expectantly. "Protects whoever wears it from drowning?"

"Are you guys planning a beach trip soon?" Galgareth quirked her brows.

"No, but the case we're being called in on?" Sloane turned toward her. "All the victims are drowning."

"And Rose was spotted, right?"

"Rose?" Sloane frowned.

"Rose, Tulip, Lily…." Loch shrugged. "It's a flower."

"Daisy," Sloane corrected patiently. "Her name is Daisy, and yes, she was seen with the last victim."

"Here." Galgareth's tentacles appeared, and she touched both Sloane and Loch on their foreheads. "A quick blessing for luck."

"Thank you, Gal." Sloane rubbed his forehead. He happened to glance at Galgareth's shirt, and he saw something familiar in the colorful pattern.

The design was a wild sunburst, and there were words woven in between the waving rays of multicolored light.

"What's on your shirt?" Sloane tilted his head. "Well, what's on Toby's shirt?"

"Do you like it?" Galgareth laughed. "Another birthday present from some boutique clothing store in downtown Archersville."

"The words. Is that… godstongue?"

"Yes! I haven't had a chance to read it all yet, but I believe it's a blessing for Salgumel."

"And they just slapped it on a shirt?" Sloane shook his head. "That's horrible."

"Trust me." Galgareth smiled sadly. "Seeing a sacred prayer to my father plastered all over uppity mortal merchandise isn't exactly my idea of reverent either, but maybe it's a good thing."

"How?" Loch wrinkled his nose. "Are we getting a cut of the profits?"

"Well no, but if people want to know what their shirt says, they might start learning about the old ways to find out." Galgareth's smile brightened. "It might be enough to spark someone's interest and lead them to the gods."

"Conversion through fashion, huh?" Sloane grinned.

"You never know." Galgareth joined Sloane and Loch by the bassinet, and she leaned down to nuzzle Pandora. "Maybe this little one will even have her own worshippers one day, huh?"

"Mmm, yeah." Sloane chuckled to himself. "Anyone looking for help to start a large fire can call on Pandora, goddess of spontaneous combustion."

"That is not her official title," Loch scolded. "We haven't had her naming ceremony yet."

"It was a joke."

"Don't you two have a crime scene or something to go to?" Galgareth politely reminded them.

"Right." Sloane fiddled with Pandora's blankets again, watching her chew away on the amber bracelet. "Okay, she still has that bottle over there on the counter, and the formula Urilith made is in the cabinet by the fridge, and—"

"Sloane," Galgareth cut in. "I've got her, okay?" She smiled warmly. "Goddess, remember?"

"Yes. Sorry." Sloane bowed his head to kiss Pandora's forehead. "Be good for your Auntie Gal, okay?"

"Maff panic," Pandora whispered through a mouthful of bracelet.

"No mass panic. No."

"Mafff?"

"No."

When Pandora pouted, she looked just like Loch.

"We'll be back soon, I promise." Sloane kissed her a few more times before finally pulling away. "Okay. I'm good, we're going. Lemme just grab my coat."

Loch cuddled Pandora with his tentacles and gave her a kiss. "Don't fret, my little one. Daddy and Dad will be back in no time to cuddle you, love all over you, teach you how to flambé—"

"No flambéing!" Sloane rolled his eyes as he put on his coat.

"Go on! Both of you!" Galgareth shooed Sloane and Loch toward the door. "Have fun at the crime scene!"

"Oh yeah," Sloane grumbled. "It's gonna be a real hoot."

The address Milo had texted was for a hotel near the university, and Sloane drove there with his stomach churning. Loch had taken Sloane's phone, claiming he wanted to play a game, but he was instead scrolling through Sloane's text messages.

"Lochlain has invited us over to feast with him and Robert for Dhankes," Loch was saying. "You have not answered him."

Lochlain Fields was Lynnette's brother, and it was his murder that first summoned Loch down to Aeon to seek justice. After his resurrection, courtesy of Great Azaethoth, Lynnette made a ghoul copy of Lochlain's body for Loch to use. Lochlain was a talented thief, and his husband, Robert, was a fence and broker for illegal magical items.

"I did so," Sloane protested. "I told him I'd get back to him."

"Which is not an answer."

"It's literally the first of October. We have all month to figure it out." Sloane glanced at Loch, and he frowned when he saw Loch swiping around more. "Now what are you doing?"

"You haven't spoken to Fred in almost two weeks. We should send him a message and check on his penis."

"We should not do that," Sloane replied firmly. "I'm sure him and Ell are doing just fine."

Thief and best friend to Lochlain, Fred was a ghoul. While the secrets of true necromancy had been lost to the world—the miracle of Lochlain's resurrection aside—it was possible to bind someone's soul to a copy of their body before they died. The practice was rare, highly illegal, and ghouls had the unfortunate tendency to rot.

This created the need for ghoul doctors like Fred's boyfriend, Ell, who specialized in powerful magic designed to preserve and increase a ghoul body's longevity. It wasn't clear how exactly a ghoul could be intimate with another person, but Sloane had long decided that it was none of his business.

Loch, however, disagreed.

"But he's a ghoul. Things... fall off."

"I'm aware."

"But how do they mate? How?"

"However they want. Stop being weird."

"Hmmph." Loch typed something.

"You better not be texting him about his penis."

"I am... texting him about something else." Loch poked at the screen.

Sloane stopped at a red light and put the car in park. He then reached over to grab his phone. "Stop! Right now!"

Loch twisted away, using his tentacles to push Sloane back as he typed faster. "I'm almost done!"

"Oh, I swear by all the gods I'm going to kick your ass if you send him something about his dick—"

Loch cackled, and he easily kept Sloane's swinging arms at bay with his many tentacles. "Just a few more words… hmmm, how do you spell 'engorged'? The automatic correction is failing me."

"Dead!" Sloane laughed at the sheer ridiculousness of fighting a god over what was certainly a very lewd text message. "You're so dead!"

"It keeps trying to spell 'enforced.' Hmm. Oh, I know—"

"Loch, quit! Right now—" Sloane gasped as the car lurched forward.

"Hey!" Loch braced himself against the dash.

The car was still moving—no, it was being *lifted*—until the front grill was parallel to the street and hovering several yards up in the air. The only things keeping Sloane from falling into the windshield were his seat belt and a bundle of Loch's tentacles.

"Loch!" Sloane exclaimed. "What the—"

"This is very rude!" Loch griped.

Sloane watched in horror as something stepped into view in front of the windshield. It was massive, horrible, too many eyes, and way too many legs, but wait….

No.

Too many *tentacles*.

It was a god.

CHAPTER 2.

"IT'S A god!" Sloane shouted.

"Not everything with tentacles is automatically a god," Loch scolded. He then stared at the monster picking up the car, and he corrected himself, "Okay, but that probably is."

"Loch!" Sloane watched the street get farther and farther away as the car continued to lift into the air. "If we drop from way up here—"

"Hold on!" Loch braced his feet against the dashboard, freeing himself from his seat belt and unbuckling Sloane's. His tentacles curled tighter around Sloane, and he shattered the windshield with a thought.

Sloane clung to Loch, closing his eyes and putting up a shield of starlight around them. "Go, go, go!"

"Going!" Loch leaped out of the car through the broken windshield and landed safely on the street, cradling Sloane against his chest. He turned so they could look at the monster holding the car.

It was at least twenty feet tall, a giant amorphous blob covered in hundreds of red eyes, with multiple tentacles peeking out from all over its slimy bright orange flesh. It reminded Sloane of a rotting pumpkin, both from the gooey texture and strange orange color.

The people around them were fleeing their cars, abandoning them right there in the middle of the street, screaming as they ran away from the giant beast. Horns honked away, brakes squealed as several cars slammed into each other down the block, and the frantic wail of sirens pierced the air.

It was absolute chaos.

The mass panic that Sloane had long feared was right here, happening now. He could see people taking pictures and video with their phones even as they ran, and months of trying to keep the secret of the old gods' existence was all going to pot in seconds.

Loch set Sloane down and stepped in front of him, yelling up at the god, "Hey! Cousin Cleus? Is that you?"

"Who?" Sloane blinked.

"My third cousin, Cleus, twice removed, on my mother's side." Loch firmly planted his hands on his hips and stalked forward to confront the monstrous god. "Cousin Cleus, you put that car down right now! This is Azaethoth the Lesser, brother of Tollmathan, Gronoch, Xhorlas, and—"

Cleus, if that's in fact who it was, roared and promptly smashed Loch with the car.

"Loch!" Sloane screamed. "No!"

The entire front end of the car had crumpled like paper, and there was no immediate sign of Loch trapped beneath it. Sloane knew Loch was immortal, but he could still be hurt, and the vessel he lived in couldn't have possibly survived being crushed like that.

Sloane prayed that Loch was all right and focused his magic into a large shield to hold on his arm. Deflecting Cleus's swinging tentacles with the shield, he dropped his other hand by his side to summon a sword of starlight. The surge of power burned his palm, and he gritted his teeth and fought through the pain to form the massive blade.

Even as his heart pounded with dread, he stared up unflinchingly at Cleus.

"Hey! Cleus!" Sloane shouted. "You'd better stop this right now because you clearly do not know who you are fucking with!"

"I second that!" Loch's muffled voice called out.

"Loch!" Sloane stared at the wreckage in disbelief.

The car tore right in half as a magnificent dragon burst forth from beneath it, and Sloane's heart stopped at the wondrous sight. The dragon had a long neck, huge glittering wings, and tentacles at his chin and tail. He was lean, with thick hind legs, and when he roared, the very pavement quaked.

This was Azaethoth the Lesser, in all of his glory….

Whose back foot was stuck in what was left of the car.

Loch growled, shaking his leg frantically, and then the wreckage went flying off into a storefront. It busted through the windows and caused a new barrage of frantic screaming. He ducked his head. "Oops."

"Oh, for fuck's sake!" Sloane groaned.

"It was an accident!"

"Where's your body?"

"Hmm. I think what was left of it was squished to the car."

"Shit! Look out!"

Loch turned just in time to catch another car being hurled at them, batting it away with a swing of his powerful tail. The car crashed into the building across from them, and glass rained down on the streets. "Accident! Also an accident!"

Sloane raised his shield to protect himself from the broken glass, cringing as Cleus roared loud enough to shake the ground beneath his feet. "Loch! We have to get out of here!" He looked around at the people still trying to run away from the battle. "It's not safe—"

"Wretched cousin! Starkiller!" Cleus bellowed. "You are both doomed!" His tentacles shot out, grabbing Loch's neck and one of his legs.

Loch roared in reply, and he let loose a stream of prismatic fire from his mouth, scorching the tentacles holding him. He stomped through a bus stop, frantically trying to break free.

Sloane wove through the cars to keep up, squeezing the hilt of his sword as he prepared to swing. He went for the tentacles holding Loch's leg, and the starlight blade sliced right through Cleus's godly flesh.

As tentacles burned and fell away, dozens more took their place, seemingly without end, from Cleus's slick flesh. The new tentacles coiled around Loch's legs and neck, squeezing hard enough to draw blood.

Loch whipped his long neck around to blow more fire directly at Cleus, but Cleus didn't seem affected.

Sloane kept cutting through Cleus's tentacles to free Loch, but there was no way to get through them all. He turned his attention to attacking Cleus directly, and he jumped up on the hood of an abandoned car to gain some ground. He flung the sword as hard as he could, cheering when the blade sunk into one of Cleus's eyes and made him howl in pain.

"Ha! Take that, you donkey!" Loch shouted triumphantly.

Already summoning a new sword, Sloane called out, "Cleus! Stop this now! No one else has to get hurt! I've killed two gods, and I don't want to make it three, but you're leaving me no choice here!"

"Never… not until he comes…!" Cleus snarled, and his bodily mass lunged forward, consuming the car Sloane was standing on. "He will be with us… soon."

Sloane slashed at Cleus's blobby flesh, but he was losing too much ground and had to stumble back onto the trunk of the car. "He who? Salgumel, right? Real original!"

"It is getting a bit old!" Loch called out with a snort, blasting another bundle of tentacles binding his legs. "We have a big family! You think they'd get bored and try waking up somebody else!"

Sloane swung the sword over his head for another strike, but Cleus's tentacles grabbed his wrist. The very touch of his orange flesh burned, and Sloane cried out, losing the sword. "Shit, shit, shit!"

"Sloane!" Loch squirmed against the tentacles trapping him, roaring in frustration.

"AVPD!" a very firm voice shouted. "You are under arrest for destruction of property, both public and private, using unlicensed magic to terrorize and create panic, and for willfully blocking an intersection!"

"I don't think he gives two flyin' fucks!" another voice chimed in. "Have you noticed that he's *eating* a car right now?"

"Felony vandalism as well!"

Sloane whipped his head around, grinning when he saw Detectives Chase and Merrick racing toward them on foot.

Merrick vanished behind an abandoned van, and a giant winged dragon with empty eyes and thick tentacles emerged. This was Gordoth, Merrick's true form, and he wasn't quite as tall as Loch, but he was thicker, with big horns and powerful front arms. His lower half was a mass of tentacles, and he moved like a snake, slithering forward at lightning speed.

Merrick attacked Cleus with unbridled ferocity, clawing at his eyes and using his tentacles to rip Cleus's tentacles away from Loch. As soon as Loch was free, he launched himself at Cleus to tear at him too.

Sloane scrambled out of the way, back down on the street, and nearly ran right into Chase. "Hey! What are you doing here?"

"Dispatch called in all available units, and I quote, because a fucking monster was messing up cars on Glen Eden Avenue!" Chase replied hurriedly. "We were still at the crime scene down on Messer Road, just two blocks up. Traffic is fucked, so we've been hoofin' it the whole way." He wheezed for breath. "What in the actual fuck is going on?"

"That's Cleus! One of Loch's cousins! He just attacked us while we were sitting at the light!"

"Looks like he's gettin' his ass kicked right about now." Chase nodded toward the fight.

Loch and Merrick had Cleus on the run, the two of them able to keep up with Cleus's never-ending supply of tentacles and destroy them before either of them could be overwhelmed again. Cleus was bleeding from some of his eyes and his giant mouth, and he was retreating down the street.

"The rest of the AVPD is gonna be here any minute." Chase pulled at the brim of his fedora and groaned. "I don't even know what in the fuck we're gonna tell them."

"The old gods are real?" Sloane cringed. "Surprise?"

"Oh yeah, sure. That'll work out great. Yeah, the chief will love—"

"Shit! Chase!" Sloane raised his shield as a piece of shrapnel from a wrecked car came flying their way. He held the shield with both hands, struggling under the weight of what may have been a door panel.

"Fuck me!" Chase grabbed Sloane's arms to help power the shield. It was only a small spark of fire magic, but it was enough to tip the wreckage away from them.

Sloane backed away from the heap of metal as it slammed into the ground. "Shit. We have got to get out of here."

As Cleus attempted to flee, he was tearing cars and telephone poles—whatever he could grab—into bits and throwing them at Loch and Merrick to keep them back. His would-be missiles were hitting the buildings around them, the sidewalk, and….

An awning over a restaurant patio where several people were cowering beneath.

Oh fuck.

"Chase!" Sloane ran as fast as he could toward the patio, and he could see the awning giving way from the weight of a car's front end that had landed on top of it. "Shit! Come on! They're gonna get crushed!"

"Fuck, fuck, fuck!" Chase chanted as he tried to keep up. "Hey! Outta the way! You guys! Hey, get outta there!"

The people hiding were either too scared to move or couldn't hear the warning. Sloane knew they were too far away, but they had to try. They just had to.

The support beams of the awning made an awful sound as they gave way, and the people beneath it all screamed.

"No!" Sloane cried.

But the awning didn't fall. The car didn't crush anyone. It remained suspended in the air, held up by…

Glimmering, translucent tentacles.

A white-haired young man in a trench coat was standing there now, looking quite annoyed as he shouted at the people, "Hey! You idiots! Time to run now!"

"Alexander!" Sloane shouted joyously. "Rota! You're here!"

Hello, Starkiller, Rota's voice rumbled inside Sloane's head. Out loud so everyone could hear him, he said, "Ah, and Detective Chase. Hello."

Alexander was the white-haired young man, and Rota was the soul of an old god who had been bound to him in much the same way ghouls were made—except Alexander had nearly died during the agonizing procedure, and though he was Silenced, with no natural magic of his own, he now commanded Rota's godly power.

As soon as the people were clear, Alexander let the awning and wreckage collapse. He glared at them as they fled in terror, shouting after them, "Yeah! You're welcome! Assholes."

"Boy, are we glad to see you!" Chase grabbed Alexander in what looked to be a very uncomfortable hug. "Where's Ollie?"

"Back home." Alexander grunted. "Safe."

"What are you guys doing here?" Sloane asked.

It's all over the television, Rota replied earnestly. *The news reports are quite frantic. We wanted to help.*

"Ollie told me to," Alexander drawled.

"I'll be sure to tell him thank you!" Sloane glanced back to Loch and Merrick when he heard a loud crash, and he grimaced when he saw Loch tumbling into the side of a truck. "We have got to get this fight out of the city before anyone gets hurt."

"One giant portal coming right up." Alexander started toward the battle. "We'll get him into another world, and then you can go all Starkiller on his ass, all right?" He paused, smirking over his shoulder at Sloane. "Unless you're not in the mood to take a life?"

Sloane hated how his face burned at the comment, and he replied firmly, "I'll do what has to be done."

"Just checking, Starkiller."

You are so rude! Rota scolded. *Be nice. We came here to help.*

"You came here to help," Alexander countered. "I came here so Ollie wouldn't make me sleep on the couch."

The first wave of police backup had finally arrived, though they had to park at the other end of the block because of the abandoned cars and advance on foot. Their approach was rather timid, understandably so against monstrous gods, but they had their guns drawn and offensive spells at the ready.

"Ah fuck!" Chase said when he saw them. "Hey, Sloane. Go do your thing and get those guys outta here. I'm gonna go stall 'em!"

"Are you sure?" Sloane frowned.

"What the fuck am I gonna do against a god?" Chase's smile was strained. "Go. Kick that fucker's ass, okay? Make sure Merry comes back in one piece or I'm gonna kick your ass, got it?"

"Got it!" Sloane started back across the street after Alexander. "Good luck, Chase!"

"Yeah! Blessings of the gods and all that shit!" Chase grimaced. "We're gonna need it!"

Sloane broke into a sprint when he saw a massive portal opening up beneath Merrick and Cleus, and the resulting vortex sucked them both in. Alexander was standing right on the edge, and he waved before he dove in, vanishing into the hole with a faint shimmer of Rota's giant mass trailing behind him.

"Shit, shit!" Sloane shouted. "Loch!"

Loch was being pulled in as well, but he turned when he heard Sloane calling for him. He whipped out his tentacled tail to grab him. "Hold on, my sweet mate!"

Sloane hugged Loch's tail and closed his eyes, his stomach lurching as they dropped into the portal. Loch's wings came around Sloane, holding him against his chest. It was over in only a matter of seconds, but Sloane was still nauseated by the time they reached solid ground.

"Ugh." Sloane looked around to find Alexander had brought them to an endless field.

It was a world between worlds, one of thousands of tiny pocket dimensions that existed between the fabric of Aeon, Xenon, and Zebulon. Many of these worlds had been created by the old gods for worship or as private sanctuaries.

From personal experience, Sloane also knew this included places to have wild tentacle orgies.

This was one Sloane had visited before when he and Alexander and Rota were not exactly friends.

It was a battleground.

Cleus had recovered from the fall, and he now found himself surrounded by Loch, Merrick, Alexander, and Rota. Rota purposefully made himself visible for a second, a powerful behemoth that towered over them all, built like a gorilla and covered in big spikes, as if to show Cleus what he was truly up against.

Sloane stood out in front of Loch, raising his arms to summon a shield and the sword of starlight. He breathed through the familiar throb of pain from taking on so much power, and he glared up at Cleus. "Stand down! Now!"

"Doomed," Cleus roared, his endless tentacles writhing all around him. "All of you.... Starkiller.... Azaethoth the Lesser.... Gordoth the Untouched... ugh... and the abomination...."

Alexander flipped Cleus off.

"When he comes, none of you... will be able to stand against him," Cleus growled on. "Not even your little sword... will be enough...."

"My brother's dreaming will not be disturbed," Merrick snarled. "We will stop you."

"Brother...?" Cleus actually seemed confused, and then he laughed. "Fools. You're doomed.... You're doomed! You know nothing. That is why you're all—"

"Doomed?" Alexander snapped. "Yeah, for fuck's sake, we get it. We're all fuckin' doomed, blah blah blah. Holy fuck, say something else already." He looked to Sloane. "Can you please stab him now?"

"Wait." Sloane narrowed his eyes. "Cleus! Please! We don't have to do this! Stop this now!"

"No!" Cleus's tentacles shot forward. "All will rise for the end! All will rise!"

Loch swept his tail in front of Cleus's tentacles, snapping his teeth on them and ripping them apart. Merrick lunged next, and he sunk his claws into Cleus's eyes. Rota was with them, guided by Alexander, and he tore into Cleus's tentacles without mercy. Orange goo was weeping from Cleus's wounds, but every destroyed tentacle was quickly replaced.

Sloane was right there with them, swinging his sword and cutting the tentacles away as fast as he could. He managed to get in a few direct strikes to Cleus's flesh, making him howl in agony, but something strange was happening.

Cleus was getting bigger.

He swelled like a balloon, and his pained cries soon turned into peels of hysterical laughter. He was so bulbous and round, and his skin was drawn so tightly that it was shiny. His tentacles stopped growing, and now he was a big smooth ball.

It was almost funny in a way, because Sloane swore as he swung his sword over his head that Cleus looked like he was going to—

Cleus exploded in a blast of guts and orange goop, his fleshy bits raining down over everyone in a wave of wet, hot slime.

Sloane lost the sword instantly, frozen in place and trying not to gag. He was absolutely soaked, and he had no idea what had just happened. He cringed, praying that he could open his mouth to speak without tasting the gunk on his face. "The... fuck?"

"Well." Alexander wiped the slime from his face with a scowl, trying to shake it off his hand. "That was fucking disgusting."

"My sweet husband!" Loch was beside Sloane in a second, and his tentacles spiraled out to pat over him from head to toe. "Are you hurt?"

"No." Sloane tried to smile. "I'm just... very sticky." He cringed. "And okay, ow, it kinda burns."

"Here." Loch bowed his head, and the thick slime evaporated off Sloane. "Is that better, my darling?"

"Yes. Thank you." Sloane was grateful to be clean of the gunk, but he swore Loch had missed some in his ears. "What the hell happened?" He stared at the empty space where Cleus had just been. "Did he.... Did I... pop... him?"

"If you are asking if you killed him, no, I do not believe so." Merrick shook his head to rid himself of the goo, and he then nodded at the ground. "This was merely Cleus's cowardly way of escaping us. Behold."

Sloane followed where Merrick was gesturing, and he saw big globs of slime crawling down into the soil. "What is Cleus the god of?"

"Pageantry, dissection, and regeneration," Rota said, using his outside voice so everyone could hear him. "He can destroy himself and regenerate from almost nothing."

"Oh, that's just great."

"He cheated." Loch huffed in annoyance and flapped his wings, casting away the last of the slime.

Some of it hit Alexander, who had just finished his own de-sliming, and he fixed Loch with a death stare.

Loch pretended not to notice.

"Cleus is said to have a vulnerable inner core deep within his body," Merrick said quickly. "It may be the only way to truly destroy him."

"Like a Tootsie Roll Pop?" Loch asked.

Merrick cocked his head. "I… I suppose so, yes."

Alexander scowled and reached into his coat for a cigarette, bringing over one of Rota's tentacles to help him light it.

You said you were quitting, Rota fussed.

"I said I was going to cut back, and this is the second damn time I've been covered in someone's fuckin' guts." Alexander puffed defiantly. "I'm having a cigarette."

Sloane pressed his blistered hands together to heal them, and he smiled as Loch's tentacles curled around his wrists to boost the spell. He frowned at the burns left behind on Loch's glittering skin, watching them close much more slowly than he would have liked. "Are you okay?"

"I'm fine, my sweet husband." Loch cuddled close, wrapping his tail around Sloane and nuzzling the top of his head. "I will heal. And you? Are you well?"

"I'm okay," Sloane promised. "Worried. I don't like how Cleus laughed about that brother comment."

"What comment?"

"When Gordoth said his brother's dreaming would not be disturbed," Alexander drawled. "Cleus launched into his little doomed speech again, remember? Implying we're wrong about who Cleus is trying to wake up."

"But if not Salgumel, then who?" Sloane asked, hating how the question hung unanswered. "Well, shit."

"We need to head back." Merrick sighed. "We still have a crime scene to investigate, and I am sure Chase is having a difficult time explaining my empty vessel. And, well, everything else."

"But at least you didn't leave it at a post office!" Loch said cheerfully.

"Wow." Alexander rolled his eyes. "Not touching that one." He saluted Sloane. "Been fun. Total blast. We're leaving now."

"Wait, that's it?" Sloane frowned. "What if Cleus attacks the city again?"

We will come, Rota swore.

Alexander jerked as if he'd been nudged, and he grumbled, "Yeah, whatever. We'll come."

"Thank you." Sloane waved. "Say hi to Ollie for me."

"Whatever." Alexander rolled his eyes again and vanished through a portal.

"I don't think he likes me," Loch mused.

"I don't think he likes anyone." Sloane smirked. "Well, except Rota and Ollie."

"It is very unfair, since I let him give you tongue—"

"Oh gods, not *this* again."

"I am going to return now as well," Merrick interjected. "There will be many questions that I do not yet know how to answer." His empty eyes moved to Sloane. "You may want to create a glamour for yourself until I know what is going on."

"Why?" Sloane quirked a brow.

"Because there is likely lots of photographic and video evidence of you fighting an old god with a giant sword of starlight."

"Shit. Yeah."

"It is only a matter of time before you are identified, and the AVPD will want to speak with you. We need to come up with a plan to maintain our cover."

Sloane grimaced. "I mean, it's kinda too late, isn't it? All those people saw Cleus. And you. And Loch."

"Ah! But this is not my fault!" Loch protested. "My vessel was involuntarily crushed by a car."

"Great Azaethoth's will trumps the laws of mortal men." Merrick bowed his head. "If he wanted us to walk Aeon again and make ourselves known, he would have awakened himself by now. As much as it troubles me to be dishonest with my superiors, we must try to hide the truth of what happened."

"How the hell are we gonna do that?" Sloane scoffed.

"I do not know."

Sloane groaned loudly. "We have Daisy running around doing gods know what with the cult, people drowning all over the place, and an actual old god terrorizing the city. This is insane."

"I am aware that it seems difficult, but we shall persevere," Merrick insisted.

"I absolutely agree." Loch held his head high. "As long as my beautiful Starkiller and I are together, we can do anything."

"I hope so, Azzath." Merrick bumped his forehead against Loch's. "I will contact you once I have more information about the current situation. Stay safe."

"You too, Uncle."

"Do not forget your glamour," Merrick warned Sloane. "Your face is… very distinct."

"I am going to take that as a compliment, thank you." Sloane snorted, waving farewell as Merrick ported away. "Well, crap. I guess we should go back too. The city is probably a mess right now, and I want to check on Panda and Gal."

"I have already alerted Galgareth of the situation, and all is well with our spawn," Loch soothed. "There is one tiny problem with returning, however."

"What? What's wrong?"

"Since my poor vessel has been crushed, I only have one option for returning to Aeon."

"Wait. Why are you smiling like that?"

"Because this option is so very perfect, my sweet mate. It's discreet, and oh, we've actually done it before. And, as I recall, it was very fun."

"Oh no."

"Oh *yes*."

CHAPTER 3.

"THIS IS so stupid," Sloane grumbled. "This is a stupid idea."

What else would you have me do, beautiful husband? Loch's voice asked inside Sloane's head. *I cannot walk around as a magnificent and stunning dragon. People might notice.*

"You'd better not do anything. You had better behave yourself in there."

Loch gasped. *When have I ever not?*

"Oh, just every single day of your life."

Not having his usual vessel to hide in, Loch needed a willing body to possess. The only one available was Sloane's, of course, and Loch was all too happy to hitch a ride with him. He allowed Sloane to remain in control, but they both knew he could take over whenever he wanted to.

That's preposterous, Loch complained. *I'm a very responsible god now. I'm a husband and a father.*

"Yeah, let's talk about how you became a father." Sloane smirked. "How did that happen again?"

Okay, but since then. I've grown.

Sloane was sitting at a coffee shop within walking distance of the crime scene. He hadn't heard from Merrick or Chase yet, but he'd gone ahead and created a simple glamour spell to make himself into a young blond. He sat in the corner with his phone to his ear so he didn't look insane talking to himself.

Just look at me now! Loch continued in protest. *The old and less mature version of myself would have already been touching your most delicate parts by now. But see, I can and will behave myself despite the luscious temptation that is your body.*

"Why couldn't you just fix your vessel?" Sloane asked. "I've seen you repair it before."

There's a fine line between a light thumping from a dumpster and being crushed into the pavement with a car by an angry god.

"I guess we need to ask Lynnette to make you another one. I really hope she's feeling up to it." Sloane heard his phone beep.

Is that my uncle?

"No, it's Gal." Sloane swiped over the screen, and he smiled when he saw it was a picture. "Aww."

It was a selfie shot of Gal sitting on the couch with Pandora in her lap, cradled in a nest of lavender tentacles.

After attempting a small fire and biting me a few times, we had applesauce, and now we're taking a nap, the accompanying text read. *Hope you guys are okay!*

Our spawn is so precious, Loch cooed. *Although I am going to have some words with my sister about her first meal being processed sauce of apples from a jar.*

"Technically, I would say her first meal was you."

Hmm. I suppose that's true. And I am organic and free of pesticides.

Sloane chuckled, sending a quick text back, thanking Gal and letting her know they were still waiting to hear from Merrick and Chase. He happened to scroll down to check his other messages, and he scowled when he saw what Loch had sent to Fred.

Hi this is totally Sloane here and definitely not anyone else! Just wanted to see if your 8==D was okay! I am always here to discuss your 8==D needs for mating. Goodbye my friend!

Fred had not replied.

"Seriously?" Sloane put his phone back to his ear. "You sent Fred dick emojis?"

I was very concerned about his penis. He is our friend, is he not?

"Yes, but how about we don't ask our friends about their private parts, okay?"

Hmmph. What else am I supposed to talk about, then?

"Anything but that." Sloane turned his head when two women sat behind him and started talking excitedly.

"Did you see it?" one was asking. "It's crazy! It was one of those god guys messing everything up! Like, like for real!"

"No way," argued the other. "All of that is totally fake."

Sloane casually glanced around the coffee shop, and he noticed almost everyone was either on their phones or pointing up at the TV on the wall, where the news was rehashing the battle.

A very pixelated image of himself standing on top of a car with the sword of starlight popped up on the big screen.

Even though Sloane was glamoured, he instinctively tried to duck down.

Oh! Look! You're on the television! Loch sounded very impressed. *You look sort of fuzzy, hmm, but still quite handsome.*

"Thank you," Sloane mumbled, trying to shield his face and stare down at the table.

But where am I? Aren't they going to show me?

"I'm sure they will."

Hmmph. They had better.

Behind them, the two women were still chatting away, and it was impossible to avoid their conversation with as loudly as they were talking.

"Come on," pleaded the first. "You can't tell me that you don't see it."

"What I see is a really nice but very fake video," the other replied. "It had to be some guy in a suit using forced perspective."

"There's no way it was just someone in a suit! There were three of them!"

"Look at that guy!" The other woman gestured to the TV, where Sloane's fuzzy picture was still on screen. "He's an actor. He's that one guy from that thing. So this is all probably a stunt for a new movie or something."

"Hey, I'm serious!" The first woman was getting upset. "Don't you ever wonder? Don't you think that just maybe—"

"You know those stupid old gods aren't real."

Sloane hated how those words cut into him, echoes of the insults he suffered many times as a child when Lucian kids would cruelly tease him over his family's faith. He took a deep breath and did his best to ignore the familiar rage being ignited.

Loch, however, did not.

"Stupid?" Loch snapped, suddenly seizing control of Sloane's body and whirling around to glare at the offending woman.

Loch! No, no, no! Sloane pleaded.

The woman blinked in surprise, but she was quick to confirm, "Yeah. Stupid. They're ugly and stupid, they're all made up, and anyone who believes in them is stupid too."

"Oh really?" Loch seethed.

Azaethoth the Lesser, I love you, but I swear by all the gods that if you don't give me back control of my body—

"Yeah, really!" the woman barked back.

—I will not mate with you for an entire month!

Loch smacked the table in frustration, clearly struggling to keep his temper restrained as he announced, "Yes! That is what I thought you said! I was just confirming it. Confirming what I thought it was that you said. For no reason."

"Ugh. Whatever." The woman rolled her eyes disgustedly, and then she took a long, noisy slurp of her iced coffee.

There. Thank you. Sloane sighed. *Now just turn back around. There you go. Nice and easy.*

Loch was about halfway around to facing the other way before he stopped to snap back at her, "But for the record, your face is stupid, your hair is stupid, and I put toilet water in your stupid coffee."

The woman spat out the mouthful she'd just sipped and squealed in horror. "What?"

"I'm so very sorry! Heh-heh, just a bad joke!" Sloane now had control of his body and jumped to his feet. "I am really sure there's no toilet water in your coffee! I'm so sorry!"

"What is wrong with you?" she screeched.

Sloane raced to the door and bolted outside, snarling, "Loch! How could you?"

Oh! Easy! I summoned water from the commode and then—

"By all the gods!" Sloane wished Loch had a body so he could strangle him right then, speed-walking along the sidewalk to put as much distance between them and the coffee shop as he could.

I know you wanted me to behave, and I will very much miss the lovely sounds you make when I fill you with my seed over the next month, but she made me angry. I am a god. I may be a tad irresponsible, but I am not stupid. I am not… make-believe.

"I know." Sloane's heart twisted in sympathy, and he let his anger fade. "I'm sorry. I can't imagine how difficult it is for you. I mean, I told you how I used to get picked on for being a Sage. So I do know what it's like to be made fun of. It hurts."

Yes. Yes, it does. Loch sighed sadly. *This is the first time I feel like I truly understand why so many of my family long for the return of the old ways. Not that I have any inclination to destroy the world or anything… but in that moment, I wanted to prove her wrong.*

"I get it." Sloane had slowed down, aimlessly walking along with his phone back to his ear. "It's what they want to do. To prove the whole world wrong. Maybe that's why Cleus chose to attack us out in the open."

Oh?

"If the gods want more followers, showing people that they exist is a pretty good way to round some up."

Hmm....

"Have you been hearing any more prayers than usual?"

Not yet, but I believe the news station was identifying me as the "sexy dragon" and not by my proper name.

Sloane laughed.

Loch summoned a tentacle out of sight beneath Sloane's jacket to gently squeeze his arm inside his sleeve. *I am sorry. Sincerely.*

Reaching up as if he was scratching an itch, Sloane discreetly returned the loving squeeze. "It's okay. I'm still a little mad at you... I mean, toilet water?" He grinned. "Really?"

I flushed before I summoned the water. Does that help?

"Eh. A little."

I love you.

"I love you too."

Does this mean you're still going to withhold the sweet bliss of your body from me for an entire month?

"Mmm, strong maybe." Sloane heard his phone beep. "Hey, Milo texted me." He paused to read. "Merrick wants us to meet Milo over at the crime scene while he and Chase work the mess over on Glen Eden. Our code name is... H.P. Macaroni?"

Is that the name of our new disguise? Because I do not like it.

"Well, Merrick is right. You saw the news. People from the AVPD might recognize me, and they damn sure know my name."

I suppose you can't tell them you just so happen to own a sword of starlight and wanted to help, hmm?

"Probably not."

May I pick a new disguise? I don't like you as a blond.

"No." Sloane changed direction, heading toward the hotel where the crime scene was located. It wasn't too far of a walk, but he couldn't help but lament, "Damn, I miss my car."

It was a very nice car. We shall mourn its loss.

"Mm, and the loss of your body. Damn, I forgot to ask Lynnette about that." Sloane swiped back to his texts to send her a quick message. "Hope she can whip you up a new one soon."

Indeed. While I do love this quality time together, this is not how I prefer to enjoy being inside of you.

"Agreed."

So, still waiting a month for mating...?

"Hmm. More likely the more you ask me."

Sloane didn't know how it was possible, but yet again, he could feel Loch pouting.

As H.P. Macaroni, Sloane was granted access to enter the crime scene at the hotel. It was an executive suite on the tenth floor. Although he got some funny looks from a few officers, no one questioned his presence since he was there with Detective Merrick's blessing.

Milo was waiting for him inside the suite, and he smiled wide when Sloane walked in. "Hey! Special consultant Macaroni! Good to see you!"

Sloane shook Milo's hand, leaning in close to whisper, "This name was your idea, wasn't it?"

"What? I think it's funny!" Milo whispered back. "Where is, uh, your partner?"

Sloane tapped his chest. "Along for the ride since his ride got, ahem, wrecked."

"Oh, right."

Hello, Milo, Loch intoned politely, speaking so that Milo could hear him too. *How is my second favorite new Sage doing?*

"Second favorite?" Milo frowned.

The first being my spawn, obviously.

"Right!" Milo grinned wide. "Hey, I'm good! I don't mind being second to little Panda Bear!" He cleared his throat and spoke at normal volume as he said, "So, our victim is Daniel Wallace, in town for a business conference. He works for a company that fabricates liners for swimming pools."

"And he drowned?" Sloane made a face. "That's some horrible irony there."

"Right?"

Sloane glanced around the suite. It was clean, modern, and there was no sign of a guest staying here except an open suitcase on the rumpled bed and a soda can by the television.

Oh, and Mr. Wallace, of course. He was on the floor by the bed, and he was covered with a sheet.

"Any connection to the other victims?" Sloane headed over to Mr. Wallace and grabbed the corner of the sheet for a quick peek.

Mr. Wallace was frozen in a position of terror, his hands clawing at his throat and his mouth and eyes wide open.

No wonder he was covered up.

"None that we can find," Milo replied. "The first victim from a few months back was Clyde Wynette, one of the cultist perps from the shoe factory shooting Chase and Merrick were on. Second was a woman who worked at a fancy nail salon uptown."

Raising his hand and positioning his index finger and thumb to resemble half of a triangle, Sloane cast a perception spell to look over Mr. Wallace's body. Through his fingers, he could see...

Well, not a lot, unfortunately.

Sloane could detect the salinity from the salt water the poor man had drowned in, and a hint of a glamour spell that was probably used to hide some razor burn. He also noted that the carpet was mostly dry around Mr. Wallace, and he wondered—

What's that? Loch asked.

"What?" Sloane whispered back.

That. That ugly thing. There on his wrist.

Sloane saw a leather bracelet with a swirling design, and there was an odd glimmer, though very faint. "Look at you, my little detective."

I am a genius, it's true. I find all the clues. Loch was preening. *Now tell me what I found.*

"Not sure yet." Sloane glanced back at Milo. "What do you have on this bracelet?"

"Uh." Milo referred to his clipboard. "He bought it yesterday. We inventoried the receipt already as part of his personal effects. Why?"

"Might be nothing. Might be something." Sloane carefully removed the bracelet and then covered Mr. Wallace back up. Through the gaze of his perception spell, the faint glimmer was limited to the ink used to print the design on the leather.

It was a design he had seen before.

"Huh." Sloane frowned. "I've seen this. Just today, actually."

"Yeah?" Milo perked up. "Where?"

"Galgareth was wearing this same design on a T-shirt." Sloane tried to remember. "She said Toby got it at some boutique for his birthday.

Some trendy place putting godstongue on fancy wares to make a quick buck. Or at least that's what I thought."

The glimmer in the ink was prismatic, every color and none at the same time.

That's right! Loch declared. *We don't think that anymore.* He paused. *What do we think now?*

"We think that's godly magic in this ink, and we really wanna know what this says now." Sloane had the oddest urge to trace the swirls in the design, but he instead encased the bracelet in a protective bubble of starlight.

"I can send a pic to Ollie," Milo offered.

"Please." Sloane passed the bracelet over to Milo. "I know this probably sounds crazy, but be careful. We don't know what this does yet."

"Okay." Milo held the bracelet out away from himself as if it might explode.

"Don't suppose you can access the case files for the other two victims?"

"Depends. What are you looking for?"

"Anything else with that design." Sloane shook his head. "With certain godly things literally running up and down the street, it might be worth looking into. Probably not a coincidence."

Milo took a picture of the bracelet with his phone and typed on the screen. "Okay, sending it over to Ollie, and I requested a copy of the personal effects from the other victims from dispatch. Hopefully they can pass it along fast."

"Don't suppose you remember anything?"

"No. And I worked those scenes too. Sorry." Milo grinned sheepishly. "There's been a lot of crazy stuff in between then and now. Plus caring for my massively pregnant girlfriend and trying to remember exactly what kinda chips and ice cream she wants? My brain can only hold so much."

"It's okay. Really." Sloane looked back around the hotel room. "I just messaged her, actually. About, you know, a new… vehicle."

A vessel for me, Loch clarified.

"She might be sleeping," Milo said. "I'll check on her in a bit and see what she can do, ahem, to help you acquire that new vehicle."

Much appreciated, dear mortal.

Sloane walked around the hotel room, checked the bathroom and closets, and found nothing else of interest except all the towels were missing. The place was clean. He returned to Milo, asking, "Anything?"

"Not yet." Milo shrugged. "Dispatch is dragging their butts on connecting me with someone who can upload the photos. Look, I can just go back to the office after this and send them to you myself."

"That would be great. Thank you, Milo."

"Sure, dude! Find anything else while you were poking around?"

"Any idea what happened to all the towels?"

"Towels? Oh! Right, right. Yeah, no. No clue." Milo shrugged. "We checked with housekeeping, but they said the room was fully stocked when Mr. Wallace checked in."

Never mind that. Loch huffed. *What about my new vessel? Has your mate responded yet?*

"No." Milo shook his head. "Sorry, your godliness. She's probably still napping. But I swear I will make it a priority. After the evidence thing. You know, or I could do it before. Uh, I don't wanna be disrespectful or anger you—"

"You're not gonna anger him," Sloane soothed.

Hmmph. Loch snorted. *He is right to fear me.*

"It's totally fine," Sloane insisted. "Loch can keep hanging out with me for a little while longer. If you hear from Lynnette before I do, just ask her to text me back, please."

"All right, cool." Milo gave a big thumbs-up.

"Where's that receipt at? The one for the bracelet?"

"Got it right here." Milo plucked an evidence bag out of his kit and offered it to Sloane for his inspection. "Some place called Sagely Wisdom."

"Cute." Sloane rolled his eyes and made note of the address.

"It's right next to that frilly adult store. You know, the one with the clerks wearing suits and stuff, and they never have porn playing?"

Adult store? Loch immediately perked up.

"Yeah," Milo said. "Drusilla's." He lowered his voice. "They make, uh, you know, the custom toys. You guys got some gift certificates for them? You know, from your wedding?"

Loch seized control of Sloane's body and walked him toward the door.

"Wait, wait!" Sloane laughed, trying to force his legs to turn back around. "Hey, Milo! Just, uh! Call me whenever you got something!"

"Will do!"

"Slow down!" Sloane whispered urgently as Loch dragged them outside. "What's the big hurry?"

The hurry is that you have never allowed me inside an adult store, and I am not missing this opportunity! Loch said. *We must go now!*

"We can go after we visit the boutique," Sloane argued. He managed to wrestle one of his arms away from Loch to put his phone to his ear to keep up their conversation discreetly. "We're on a case, remember? Really important? Your, uh, cousin just wrecked a whole bunch of stuff?"

Indeed! And who helped stop him, hmm? Me. I deserve a reward, and I want to go to the adult store.

"I swear we will go right after."

Hmmph. Fine. I will be responsible and accept your ridiculous demands.

"Thank you."

Meanie.

Sloane snorted. "Mm, very mature. Can I have control of my body back now?"

I suppose.

"We got a little bit of a walk ahead of us." Sloane glanced at his phone just to make sure he hadn't missed a notification. "Damn car."

We can get another, my sweet husband. Never fear.

"Trying not to. I hope Merrick and Chase are having better luck than us."

We found good clues, did we not? The design is very suspicious.

"It is. I just wish we knew what it said. I mean, obvious choice is that it's a prayer or something for Salgumel."

He is quite popular these days.

"Yeah, with the cultists." Sloane sighed. "They're definitely crazy enough to test something out on one of their own, but I don't know. I know a few words for Salgumel, and that didn't look right."

The salt water could mean Yeris. My uncle? Or any of the other oceanic inclined deities.

"Maybe." Sloane's stomach decided to twist up again. "I just have this really weird, really bad feeling."

All will be well, my sweet husband.

"I hope so."

Sloane had to struggle against Loch's grip on his body to keep him from bolting into the adult store, because of course they had to pass it before getting to Sagely Wisdom. He managed to stay in control, although he was out of breath by the time he stepped inside.

Sagely Wisdom was bright, clean, and trendy techno music played through big speakers on the walls. It was full of clothing racks, shining glass cases, and Sloane hated it immediately.

He recognized the strange swirling design from the crime scene on the shirts near the front, and that wasn't all. He saw binding symbols like the ones used for ghouls on hoodies and sweaters, the crest of Great Azaethoth's horns on magnets, and the Sage's cross was plastered all over everything, from socks to panties to coffee mugs.

Sloane froze, struggling to take it all in.

Sloane.... Loch's voice was choked up.

"I know."

All of this felt wrong.

"Hi there!" the cashier greeted them with a friendly smile. "Welcome to Sagely Wisdom! Let me know if you need help finding anything!"

Sloane waved but said nothing, still pretending to be on his phone as he walked around the store. He raised his hand as if checking a price tag on a shirt, but he was casting a perception spell to check out the designs.

Like with the bracelet, all the items with the swirling design had the godly glimmer. The rest appeared normal, though it still wasn't any less weird to see such sacred images slapped all over merchandise. This was somehow worse than the hideous Halloween decorations Sloane would see put up year after year with cartoonish caricatures of the gods.

They want sixty dollars for that shirt? Loch scoffed. *That's the real crime here.*

"It's certainly something," Sloane mumbled. "Just hang on. I gotta call you back."

Wait, is that a signal? Are you going to go talk to that mortal clerk? Good! Because I have some questions of my own!

"Later, okay? Talk to you soon." Sloane put his phone back in his pocket, and he offered a charming smile as he approached the cashier. "Hey there! Do you have a second?"

"Of course!" She smiled politely. Her name tag said Olivia. "What can I help you with?"

Sloane discreetly flicked his hand for a truth spell, playing it off as reaching for one of the magnets next to the register. "So, all of these designs are Sagittarian, right?"

"Yes, sir!"

"Can you tell me what they mean? Like, that one at the front with all the swirls?"

"Yes, sir. That's one of our most popular designs! It's a love spell designed to draw in your one true love."

Sloane doubted that very much, but the truth spell detected no dishonesty. Which probably meant that Oliva here had been told that, and therefore she believed it to be the truth.

"Okay, we both know that's ridiculous," Loch said, taking over Sloane's voice. "How about you tell us how you sleep at night, profiting off someone else's faith? Hmm?"

"Wh-what?" Olivia stammered. "We're, we're not! The owners are Sages! They use all the proceeds to fund their coven!"

"Oh! A likely story! Tell me, young mortal. Have you felt the urge to commit any murders lately?"

Loch! What are you doing? Sloane snarled inside his head.

"I'm handling this," Loch argued. "Now, where was I? Ah yes! When you killed Mr. Wallace, did you feel any regret? Yes or no?"

"Mrs. Patty!" Olivia shouted, backing away from behind the counter and scrambling toward the rear of the store. "Mrs. Patty! This guy is talking crazy!"

Now look what you've done. Sloane groaned. *They might call the police!*

"We are the police," Loch said firmly.

"No, we're not," Sloane countered, sighing in relief as Loch allowed him to take the wheel again.

An older woman had emerged from the back room to comfort Olivia, and she glared at Sloane. There was something about her face that gave Sloane pause, and he immediately raised his hand for a perception spell.

The older woman was wearing a glamour.

Is that Tulip? Loch gasped.

"Daisy," Sloane corrected out loud before he realized what he'd said.

The older woman's eyes widened when she heard her name, and she was not alone. Coming out from the back behind her was another familiar face.

Jeff Martin, the leader of the cultists.

CHAPTER 4.

"TULIP DAISY! Jeff Martin!" Loch declared in Sloane's voice. "You are under arrest!"

We can't arrest anyone! We're not cops! Sloane complained.

It was a bit of a surprise to see Jeff standing there, especially since he'd reportedly lost a leg to a portal.

Jeff seemed confused, but once he raised his own perception spell at Sloane, he groaned in recognition. "Really? You idiots again?" He murmured a quick spell and promptly launched a giant wave of fire at Sloane.

Daisy bolted into the back, and Olivia screamed and scrambled to get out of the way.

Loch's tentacles unraveled from Sloane's body to deflect the fire, knocking it into a display of shirts that immediately caught flame. He ran toward Jeff, snarling, "If I can't put him under arrest, then I am going to put him beneath my foot very, very aggressively!"

Jeff threw up another spell, some sort of wall to stop Loch from coming after him, and he fled into the back room after Daisy.

Loch destroyed the barrier with a smack of his tentacle and surged forward to give chase.

Olivia was screaming, suddenly trapped by the blaze of clothing. The fire was spreading quickly, and it would certainly consume the store in moments.

Loch! The clerk! Sloane cried. *Turn around!*

Loch whined. "But I wanna put him beneath my foot and stomp up and down!" He glanced back, groaning when he saw Olivia in obvious distress. "Fine. I will be the handsome hero and save the mortal."

Thank you!

A twirl of Loch's tentacle extinguished the flames, and he hurried over to help Olivia stand. "Are you all right, little mortal?"

Olivia was wide-eyed and trembling. "I... I...."

"Perfect! Goodbye now!" Loch spun around and then launched himself into the back room.

It was full of boxes, a computer station with a giant printer, and a workspace that appeared to be used for making the various products the store was selling.

There was no sign of Daisy or Jeff.

Loch found a rear exit that opened into an alley behind the store, and there was still nothing.

No portal trail, no nothing. Sloane sighed.

"Perhaps they fled in a car?" Loch suggested. "Like the one we used to have so long ago."

Maybe. Well, shit.

Sloane's phone rang.

"Ah! A phone call!" Loch eagerly answered it. "Hello? Beaumont Investigations, happy to investigate all your investigative needs!"

He'd pressed the wrong button and answered it on speaker, Chase's voice asking worriedly, "Sloane? Is that you? You sound fuckin' weird."

"It is probably my nephew," Merrick said from somewhere close by. "He is still, ahem, hitching a ride."

"It is indeed! Hello, Uncle!" Loch exclaimed.

Sloane took back control and fixed the phone, putting it to his ear as he said, "Sloane here. Hey, where are you guys?"

"Heading to Sagely Wisdom," Chase replied. "Milo said you guys were headed over, and we just got reports of a fire. That you guys?"

"Not us. Jeff Martin and Daisy were just here. Think they fled on foot or in a car? No portal trace, but they're both gone."

"Fuckity fuck fuck." Chase sighed haggardly. "We'll be right there."

"Hey, what's going on with the scene downtown?"

"Ugh." Chase sounded particularly nauseated. "We got construction crews trying to clean up the damage with a bunch of our guys barricading everything off, and oh, you know, just every nutjob in town trying to crawl right through to get a look at what a god did."

"Allegedly," Merrick added.

"We've also been told that several Lucian churches are being overloaded trying to keep all their people calm, and the not-crazy local Sagittarian covens are getting overwhelmed too. We had a small riot, some looting, and someone let a damn goat loose in the middle of a grocery store to honor the gods. It's fuckin' nuts."

"Wow." Sloane grimaced. "Great. Awesome. We'll wait for you guys here." He walked back inside through the storage room toward the front of the store. "Only person left is a cashier, a young woman named Olivia."

Olivia was frozen right where Loch and Sloane had left her, still apparently in shock. She lifted her head to stare at Sloane. "What... what's going on?"

"I'm on the phone with the AVPD right now," Sloane said, hoping that he sounded comforting. "They're coming, okay? Are you all right?"

"O-okay. I'm okay." Olivia ducked her head back down and hugged her knees to her chest.

"She with Jeffy boy and Daisy?" Chase asked hesitantly.

"I don't think so, but you never know." Sloane tried to keep his expression neutral since Olivia was only a few feet away.

"Sit tight," Chase said. "On our way."

"See you soon." Sloane hung up and then turned back to Olivia. "Hey, are you really all right? Are you hurt?"

Olivia shook her head. "I... I'm okay. I... I just... I don't understand what's going on."

"Your employer is not who she says she is." Sloane struggled to find the right words. He wasn't sure how much he should say, fearful of upsetting her more. "I'm sorry you had to see all that, but I'm really glad you're okay."

"Are you a cop?"

"Private investigator." Sloane offered a kind smile. "Everything is gonna be okay, I promise. The cops will be here soon." He turned away to give Olivia some space, but he was stopped by her hand on his arm.

"Thank you." Her eyes were red and full of tears. "For saving me."

"Of course." Sloane smiled again. He waited for her to let go so he could take a few steps back, sucking in a deep breath and trying to calm the anxiety bubbling up beneath his skin. His stomach was twisting on itself again, and he didn't like any of this.

The chaos Chase was describing was exactly the sort of mass panic Sloane had always hoped to avoid. But now there was little any of them could do except try to contain it and hope it would be over soon. Sloane knew what it was like to not believe and then have your world turned upside down learning the truth of the gods.

Even having been raised by Sages, it had been quite a shock.

He couldn't imagine how hard it was for Lucians.

Or any of the other faiths, for that matter. With the lone exception of the Tauri, a well-established polytheistic faith whose deities were mirrors of Sagittarian gods save for the names, Sloane didn't anticipate any of the world's faithful taking this revelation well. The majority of the public were going to be angry, upset, and afraid.

And angry, scared people in large numbers were very, very dangerous.

What's the matter, sweet husband? Loch asked. *Your stomach is making awful sounds.*

Just worried, Sloane replied in his thoughts. *Archersville is just the start, you know. This is only going to get worse. And I wonder if that's part of Cleus's plan.*

To terrify everyone and cause the mass panic?

Yeah.

Loch discreetly slid a tentacle beneath Sloane's shirt and stroked his chest, hovering over his heart. *It's all right. All will be well, I promise.*

Sloane squeezed Loch's tentacle. *I really hope so.* He noticed Oliva staring at him, and he asked, "Hey? Do you need something?"

Olivia's troubled expression had given way to something like awe, and she hesitated before speaking. "Did you.... Did I really see that?"

Sloane tensed. "What do you think you saw, exactly?"

"It probably sounds crazy, but I think... I think you had tentacles."

Sloane forced a smile while he screamed inside his head. *Oh shit, shit, shit—*

The front doors busted open, and Merrick and Chase came charging in. They had their guns drawn and looked ready to take on a whole army. Sloane had never been so happy to see them and made a mental note to thank Galgareth for her serendipitous blessings.

"Hey, AVPD!" Chase shouted, his wide eyes taking in the burned section of merchandise and Olivia huddled on the floor. He frowned at Sloane and squinted. "Who the fuck are you?"

"Uh." Sloane had almost forgotten that he was glamoured.

Hello, my name is Azaethoth the Lesser, and I'm fantastic, Loch said sweetly. *This is my husband, Sloane, who really loves it when I put my tentacles in his—*

"Right, got it." Chase cleared his throat and put his weapon away. "Sl—Smoane. Smoane Momont. Yup. That's you."

Merrick sighed audibly.

"How about me and you go have a little chat, Smoane, and uh, my partner will talk to—" Chase smiled at Olivia. "Olivia, right?"

"Y-yes," Olivia said quietly. "Olivia Harker."

"Hi. I'm Detective Chase, and this is Detective Merrick. He's gonna take real good care of you, okay?"

"Hi." Merrick smiled in what may have been an attempt to be friendly. "Can you please give me a detailed report of the violent events that transpired here?"

"Be easy, okay," Chase muttered under his breath. He jerked his head for Sloane to join him in the back room. As soon as they were alone, he pinched the bridge of his nose and asked, "So, uh, what the fuck happened?"

Sloane ran back through the events with Chase, trying to be as detailed as possible. After Merrick was done talking with Olivia, he found them, and Sloane had to go through what had happened again for him.

"That is not helpful," Merrick said flatly when Sloane was done repeating the story.

"You're telling me." Sloane grimaced. "All this does is confirm that Daisy and Jeff are back and definitely involved with selling these magical designs. I don't suppose Olivia was more useful?"

"No. She has only been working here for a few weeks, knew Daisy as Mrs. Patty, and she claims to have never seen Mr. Martin before today." Merrick's nose wrinkled. "Paramedics have taken her to be treated for minor smoke inhalation and shock."

"Did she say anything else about the man with the beautiful tentacles who rescued her?" Loch asked urgently in Sloane's voice.

"She now believes she imagined that, and I suggest we allow her to maintain that illusion."

"Hmmph."

Sloane's phone beeped, and he saw it was a text from Lynnette. "Ah, hey. Lynnette says if we give her two orders of peanut sesame noodles, she'll make Loch a new vehicle in—" He gasped as Loch suddenly pulled out of him and vanished. "Oh by all the gods."

"What is wrong?" Merrick frowned.

"If you get any reports of a dragon robbing a Thai place, it's your nephew." Sloane rubbed his forehead. "What is the AVPD saying about all this? Or are they still trying to maintain an illusion too?"

"The official statement says that we are investigating the event. Nothing more."

"Which is not very calming to a city currently on the edge of freakin' the fuck out," Chase said. "Cops included. Everybody on the force we've talked to is as nervous as a bunch of long-tailed cats in a room full of rocking chairs. Except the chairs are fuckin' gods."

"Why would a long-tailed cat be in a room of rocking chairs?" Merrick wondered out loud.

While Chase tried to explain the finer points of idioms to his beloved partner, Sloane turned his attention to the workspace, raising his hands for a perception spell.

There were tiny splatters of godly essence all over the table, the counter, and even inside the big printer. He checked the boxes and found they were full of finished merchandise. Like in the store, only the products with the swirling design had the godly glimmer in the ink.

"Anything?" Merrick asked.

"They were definitely using the godly essence in the ink to print that one swirly design," Sloane replied. "But we don't know the source of the essence or what the design is for."

"What about ol' fuckin' pumpkin pie explodey face?" Chase suggested. "Couldn't the godly juice be his?"

"Cleus? Perhaps." Merrick's bright eyes focused on a corner of the table. "It appears to be quite diluted, so it is difficult to be certain."

Sloane rummaged around some of the drawers by the computer and found tiny funnels, pipettes, and dozens of printer cartridges. "Well, whatever they were using, they had enough of a supply to keep filling cartridges. They must have…."

There was a bottle.

It was a small plastic bottle, and it was full of godly essence. The most shocking part, however, was that Sloane had seen this particular bottle before.

"Holy fuck." Sloane inhaled sharply.

"What is the matter?" Merrick came over to see what the fuss was.

"This bottle." Sloane pulled the lid off to reveal it had an attached bubble wand. "Holy *fuck*."

"What's that?" Chase squinted. "One of them bubble things they give away at weddings?"

"Not just any wedding." Sloane took a deep breath. "This is from Robert and Lochlain's wedding. You see, there was this little girl, and Loch—"

"Ah! I hear my name!" Loch popped up beside Sloane with a grin. He was in a new body now, eagerly pulling Sloane in for a kiss, and he was naked. "Missed me so much that you had to start talking about me, hmm?"

"Loch!" Sloane nearly dropped the bottle.

Chase politely turned away, coughing loudly. "Maybe you shoulda grabbed some clothes? Just a thought?"

"Yes. Clothing." Loch looked around and immediately went to the boxes of merchandise to poke around.

"The bottle," Merrick said, getting right back on track, and not put off by his naked nephew running around in the slightest.

"Right." Sloane held the bottle up. "At the wedding, there was this little girl who ran out of bubbles—"

"I taught her to summon bees!" Loch sounded very proud.

"Fuck, yes, that too. But he enchanted this bottle so that it would never run out of bubbles." Sloane put the lid back on and handed it to Merrick. "Somehow Jeff and Daisy got it, and I bet this is what they've been using to make the magic ink."

"All they needed was one small sample to create an infinite quantity." Merrick scowled as he looked the bottle over.

"Well, that's good, ain't it?" Chase asked.

"How?"

"Well, what we were talking about before," Chase explained. "Worst-case scenarios, and one of them being that Jeffy boy and his buddies were working directly with a god. I mean, that would explain how they were makin' all this, right?"

"I am not following."

"We thought the only way they could have so much godly spunk was because they were in cahoots with a god. But if they had this magical bottle, all they needed was a tiny bit, so…." Chase waved his hand expectantly.

"They still needed an initial source," Merrick drawled.

"They could have gotten it from an artifact," Sloane suggested. "Lots of old Sagittarian items floating around out there on the black market, right?"

"Except there was literally a god walking down Glen Eden."
Merrick shook his head. "No. I believe that the cultists and Cleus are
working together now. They have the same goals, and it was only a
matter of time before one found the other useful in some way to initiate
cooperation."

"Party pooper," Chase teased halfheartedly.

Sloane knew Merrick was probably right, but he really wished he
wasn't. Fighting gods and cultists was hard enough on their own, but
knowing they were probably teaming up now did not sound like a good
time at all.

Loch had found a purple crop-top shirt and matching sweats, each
stamped with a colorful assortment of wards. He threw his arm around
Sloane's shoulders, asking cheerfully, "What have I missed?"

"Your little bubble trick is being used to mass produce godly ink to
create magical designs."

"Mmm. Is that bad?"

"Considering that the designs are being made by the cultists and
everyone we've found with one has drowned, probably really bad."

"The wards you are wearing...." Merrick trailed off, and he
suddenly headed to the boxes Loch had found his outfit in.

"There's no more purple left!" Loch warned.

"What's wrong, Merry?" Chase watched as Merrick tore into the
boxes. "Hey, yo, what's going on?"

"The wards on Azzath's ensemble are Babbeth's wards of protection
for a new grave. This?" Merrick held up a coffee mug. "A spell invoking
Chandraleth for removing a hangnail." A pair of panties. "This one is a
spell in my own godstongue for rendering all manner of veritas spells
impotent." A magnet. "And this? One of Bestrath's prayers to reduce the
fattening properties of food on Dhankes."

"That's a weird bunch of stuff." Chase whistled. "Except okay, let's
talk about that last one. Does it only work on Dhankes or—"

"Later." Merrick kept digging. "Though I cannot identify all of
them, I can say with absolute certainty that they are very old."

"Why would they be using such random magic?" Chase frowned.

"Well, Olivia said the owners were Sages, and we know now it's Jeff
and Daisy." Sloane shrugged. "Practically nobody can read godstongue
these days. They probably picked wards or whatever looked nice to slap
on T-shirts, figuring people would believe whatever they told them."

"The age of these spells is what concerns me," Merrick said. "These likely came from an ancient grimoire, and I am worried what else they may have found. I have examined the questionable swirling design again, and I now feel certain that it is not written for Salgumel."

"No?" Sloane gulped. "Then… who?"

"I do not know." Merrick's brow creased, and he sighed. "I can only now assume that it's for a minor deity I am not familiar with, but it may be in Great Azaethoth's own tongue."

"Could it be, like, fan mail?" Chase asked. "You know, like written for Salgumel but in Great Azaethoth's mumbo jumbo?"

"Possible, but not very likely. The only thing I am certain of is that the swirling pattern is meant to entice a tactile response."

"What?"

"He means it makes you want to touch it," Sloane explained kindly.

There was a barrage of beeps as everyone's phone suddenly went off at the same time. It was a text from Milo. Sloane was the quickest, and he read it out loud: "Confirmed swirling design on two vics. Keychain and shirt."

"So, all three victims had that swirly shit on them? Swirly shit that makes you want to touch it, and then what?" Chase grunted. "You fuckin' drown?"

Sloane's stomach dropped. "I need to call Galgareth right now."

"The shirt." Loch's eyes widened. "You don't think she would—"

"I know she's a very smart goddess, but she needs to get rid of that shirt." Sloane dialed Toby's number, waiting anxiously for her to pick up.

"Hey!" Galgareth answered cheerfully. "Everything okay? More godly relations attack the city yet?"

"No, but please listen," Sloane said quickly. "This is going to sound crazy, but you need to take off your shirt right now."

"Excuse me?"

"Listen. The design. All three drowning victims had it on them in some way. There's some sort of old magic at work here, and you need to take it off immediately. Grab something from our closet, I don't care, but get rid of that shirt."

"O-okay." Galgareth sounded worried. "Boom. Done. It's off. I can destroy it if you think that would be safest. I'll burn it—" There was an audible *thwoom* sound. "Oh, well. Pandora just incinerated it for me. Aww, good girl! You knew that icky shirt had to go, didn't you?"

Sloane could hear Pandora gurgling happily, and he slid his hand over his face. He tried not to smile. "Great. That's good."

"So Toby somehow bought a magical drowning shirt?"

"Sagely Wisdom, the boutique he got it from? It's apparently a front for the cultists. We're still not sure what they were up to, but they were making some kind of god ink to print that design with."

"And you don't know what it says?"

"We've got Ollie translating it for us—"

"Wait, wait, wait!" Galgareth exclaimed. "This design is connected to people drowning and you sent it over to the one guy who can read anything he sees?"

Sloane paused. "I am now starting to see that may have been a terrible idea."

"Might wanna go handle that. Just in case."

"Thanks, Gal! Talk to you later!" Sloane hung up and then scrambled to find Ollie's contact information.

"Hey, hey, what's wrong now?" Chase asked. "Is it something about Ollie?"

"So, we just sent that design over to Ollie? The very design that might be making people drown, and, as Galgareth so helpfully pointed out, we sent it to the one person we know for sure can read it."

"Ah! I can fix this!" Loch vanished.

"What the fuck is he doing?" Chase demanded.

"I have no idea." Sloane smiled wryly. "You just kinda learn to go with it."

"But Ollie will be okay?"

"I'll call him." Sloane dialed, but after several rings, the call went to voicemail. He left a brief message and sent a text as well.

Chase tried him too, and his expression was grim when he also couldn't make contact.

"Hey," Sloane soothed, "maybe he's just busy with Rota and Alexander. He might not have even had a chance to look at the damn thing yet."

"If we do believe the design to be that dangerous, we must inform the public," Merrick said. "This store has been open for months. There is no telling how many people have purchased tainted wares from here."

"But there's still only been three drownings so far, right?" Sloane tried to be hopeful. "Maybe only certain batches of merchandise are potent enough to be harmful."

"While that may be true, we still have an obligation to protect the people of the city."

"Oh. Sure. This will be great." Chase took his hat off so he could rake his fingers through his long hair. "Already got old gods running up and down the damn street eating cars and shit. How about a pair of panties that can kill you? Sure!"

"I did not see the design in question on any panties," Merrick informed him shortly.

"I'll make the call," Chase grumbled as he headed back into the store with his phone in hand.

Just as Sloane sat at the computer, Loch reappeared. His shirt was gone. "Shit! Hey! Where did you go?"

"First of all," Loch said, "our spawn is very upset with me."

"Why?"

"Because I stole the amber bracelet from her," Loch replied.

"The one from Yeris," Sloane realized. "Oh, good thinking!" He grimaced. "Panda got mad?"

"She set my shirt on fire. She's getting really good at it."

"What bracelet is this?" Merrick asked.

"It was a wedding gift from Yeris," Sloane explained. "Protects whoever wears it from drowning."

"Which is why I thought it would be an excellent idea to give it to Ollie!" Loch said. "He did not seem very excited about the gift, but maybe he will appreciate it later. I also tried to tell Alexander and Rota about Jeff Martin being seen again, since they're very keen to find him, but they also did not seem pleased."

"What happened?"

"It was hard to tell exactly." Loch looked thoughtful. "But I believe Ollie was mating with Alexander while Rota was mating with both of them—"

"By all the gods." Sloane tried to hold in a laugh.

"Tentacles, so many tentacles—"

"Do you just know when people are having sex? Is that a secret godly superpower you have?"

Loch scratched his chin. "Perhaps it is…."

"Hey, I got some not real great fuckin' news," Chase announced as he came back in. He paused, staring at Loch. "Why are you naked again?"

"Ah. Because of fire." Loch looked down. "And I am only half-naked, technically."

"What is the not real great news?" Merrick demanded, his tone indicating that his patience was thin.

"The powers that be in the AVPD don't wanna make any public statement about the fuckin' swirly shit until we can confirm that it's what killed the victims," Chase replied. "Everybody is losing their minds over the Great Pumpkin tearin' up the street, and they claim they don't wanna create any additional panic."

"But more people might die!" Sloane protested.

"Hey, I know." Chase sighed. "They ain't budgin' until we know for sure. So it's up to Ollie to figure out what the fuck that thing is and what it's doin' to people." His brow furrowed. "Did you guys talk to him yet? Is he okay?"

"He's fine. Loch saw him and gave him a magical bracelet that'll keep him from drowning just in case. He's been, uh, busy. We might need to encourage him to, ahem, get on translating and off of Alexander."

"And Rota," Loch happily chimed in. "Although I do believe Alexander was more on him. It was sort of hard to be sure—"

"I'll handle it," Chase cut in. "We gotta finish up here, and then our beloved captain wants us to work on tracking down ol' Jeffy boy. I'll make sure we get up with Ollie, all right? As soon as possible. Even if I gotta go turn a water hose on 'em myself."

"All right." Sloane took a deep breath and tried to ignore the sinking in his chest. "What do you need us to do?"

"Stay close and maintain an open line of communication," Merrick replied. "If Cleus shows up again, we will need you ready for battle."

"You got it." Sloane nodded. "Let us know if anything else comes up."

"Before we take our leave, here." Loch handed a section of beads over to Chase.

"The fuck is this?" Chase blinked in surprise. "Usually you're taking shit from me, not giving me somethin'."

"It is a portion of the bracelet of Yeris. I thought it would be wise to share its enchantment with you and my sweet husband since you are both squishy mortals and may be in danger of magical drowning."

Chase tipped his hat. "Me and my squishy bits are much obliged." He checked his pocket. "Huh. And what do you know? My badge is even still here."

"I've matured. I'm a father now."

"Come on, mature father." Sloane smiled. "Let's go home."

They said their farewells to Chase and Merrick, and then they headed out to the sidewalk after Sloane put his glamour back on and Loch helped himself to a new T-shirt. This one was bright green and had what Sloane thought to be a blessing for Urilith.

"So," Sloane said. "No Jeff, no Cleus, and no other leads. How about a nice godly portal home? I miss Panda Bear, and I don't feel like walking."

"What if I had an idea to be helpful?" Loch asked with a bat of his eyes.

"An idea? For the case?"

"You were upset that the AVPD is not going to make public how dangerous that magical design is. I happen to know where we can find a large quantity of the tainted merchandise still available for purchase to the public at another location. We can remove said merchandise and make the city a little safer."

"Wow! Yeah!" Sloane grinned. "That would be awesome. Maybe we can't do anything about the people who have already bought stuff, but we can stop more from getting sold."

"Are you pleased, my beautiful Starkiller?"

"Very pleased."

"Pleased enough to reconsider not mating with me for a month?"

Sloane laughed. "Aw, Loch. You and I both know I couldn't go a month without tasting your sweet godly flesh."

Loch beamed. "I knew it all along."

"So, where is this place?"

"Ah, it is very close." Loch's smile turned wicked.

"How close?" Sloane frowned suspiciously.

"Oh, very close. Right next door."

"You don't mean—"

"Oh yes, my sweet husband. We are going to the *adult store*."

CHAPTER 5.

"WHILE I was making myself not naked, I happened to find an invoice for a very large amount of clothing sold to the adult store," Loch explained cheerfully. "I do believe my sister's blessing is working well."

"Wait, where exactly did you find this invoice?" Sloane asked.

"In the cash register."

"Why were you… never mind."

"I was removing the cash."

"Loch!" Sloane groaned.

"We need it to purchase the dangerous items, do we not? Or were you going to spend our own hard-earned moneys, hmm?"

"Fine." Sloane didn't want to argue. "Let's just buy everything with the stupid swirly design and go home, okay?"

Loch looped his arm with Sloane's, smiling knowingly. "You miss our spawn, hmm?"

"Yeah, I do." Sloane leaned into Loch. "Maybe it's silly, but I really do miss her." He smirked. "And I'm also slightly concerned about what else she might try to set on fire."

"Fear not, my beloved mate," Loch soothed. "Galgareth can handle anything our sweet little spawn attempts to incinerate, I promise."

"I know." Sloane rubbed Loch's arm as they stood in front of the doors of Drusilla's. "As fast as Panda is growing now, I guess I just worry we're going to miss something. That I am going to miss something. And I don't want to miss anything. Even if it is more fire."

"I understand." Loch kissed Sloane's cheek. "But it's perfectly all right if you do."

"Oh?"

"The mere fact that you are concerned for those lost moments means a lot, sweet Starkiller." Loch's smile was a little sad. "Trust me."

"Are you okay?" Sloane urged Loch away from the doors so they could talk for a few more moments without blocking the entry.

"Okay with what?" Loch sighed loudly and rolled his eyes. "That you're cruelly threatening to withhold the perfectly delicious muscular hold of your innermost places? That you would deny me the brilliant flavor of your sweet reproductive nectar? That you—"

"Hey. Seriously." Sloane poked him. "Stop deflecting."

"You and I both know I only pretend to understand what that word means."

"You know that if you ever need to talk about anything, I'm here for you. I mean it. Even if it's about Salgumel. *Especially* if it's about him. Yes, he's a god, but he's your father too, and I know he hasn't exactly been a great one."

"I am okay," Loch promised. "I appreciate that very much, my darling mate. This is never easy for me. This is...." He turned away, an alien look of confusion and mourning on his handsome face.

Loch was always so confident—even for a god—and to see him appear so uncertain was troubling.

"I'm here." Sloane touched Loch's cheek. "I love you."

"And I love you, my sweet husband." Loch's brow furrowed. "I had a father who cared very little about what he was and was not present for. I believe, in my heart, that if he'd made an effort... that I might feel differently about him."

Sloane knew Loch had a very complicated relationship with Salgumel—having a father who was absolutely insane and would destroy the world if he ever woke up was hard enough, but it was even tougher when said father hadn't exactly been an active parent.

"I'm sorry," Sloane said. "Really. I can't imagine—"

"Could we discuss this later?" Loch asked, his minty eyes swirling with more than a hint of despair. "I would like to focus on possible theft and the untold delights of finally entering the adult store."

"Yeah, of course." Sloane squeezed Loch's hand. "We can talk about it whenever you want."

Loch's lip twitched as if he was resisting a smart comment. He kept whatever it was to himself and kissed Sloane. "Thank you. Now!" He grinned, as sly and daring as ever, declaring, "To the adult store!"

Sloane let Loch take the lead, and he tried not to laugh at the exuberant way Loch nearly tore the door off its hinges before dragging him in.

Drusilla's was well lit, clean, and honestly didn't look much different than Sagely Wisdom except for the type of merchandise being offered. There were tidy shelves neatly stocked with a variety of toys and accessories, and clothing racks filled with everything from skimpy lingerie to raunchy novelty T-shirts.

A sophisticated kiosk with a computer filled a corner near the register, the sign hanging above it promising to fulfill potential customers' every need. The menu posted below indicated it was for designing custom dildos.

Sloane blushed when he saw there was—what else—a tentacle option.

"This… this is it?" Loch appeared heartbroken as he whipped his head back and forth to look all around. "Where is the leather? The sex swings? The whips and chains?"

"I'm not sure." Sloane tried not to smile.

"Hello! Welcome to Drusilla's!" A young man in a suit greeted them from behind the counter. "Is there something I can help you gentlemen with?"

"Oh, yes there is." Loch hurried right back over. "First, I need to know where your fetish wares are located. And secondly, I will need to purchase any and all inventory you received from Sagely Wisdom. And thirdly…." He glanced at the kiosk. "I shall require an in-depth tutorial of how to operate *that*."

Sloane snorted out a laugh, distracted enough by Loch's litany of demands that he didn't hear someone stepping up behind him.

"I must say," a purring voice declared, "I much prefer you as a brunet, Mr. Beaumont."

Sloane didn't have to turn around to know who it was. He sighed. "Hello, Stoker."

Sullivan Stoker was a notorious gangster and crime lord who ran a hidden world in Archersville where descendants of the everlasting races lived—monstrous beings that the gods had created before mortals. Alexander, Rota, and Ollie had seen it before, and they'd told Sloane the most fantastic stories of the people who lived there.

They were free to be themselves without having to rely on glamour magic to hide their horns, claws, tails, or whatever else they might have that would potentially freak out the public. This kindness, of course, came with a price, because Stoker was a businessman first and foremost.

A very mysterious, very powerful, and frustratingly handsome businessman.

Oh, and he was definitely not human.

"To what do I owe the honor of this visit? Your divine marriage not so divine?" Stoker was almost grinning. "Or are you just here to spice things up?"

"This place is yours?" Sloane scoffed.

"I own many businesses, Mr. Beaumont."

"I'm sure you heard about what happened," Sloane said flatly. "The, uh, little rampage on Glen Eden?"

"Indeed. What does that have to do with your charming husband grabbing armfuls of lingerie?"

"Did you actually look at any of that stuff?"

"I don't spend a lot of time looking at panties." Stoker winked. "Perhaps I just haven't met the right model."

"There's godstongue all over them. The swirling design Loch is going after? It's been found on three drowning victims."

Stoker's mirthful expression finally cracked. "Oh?"

"Yeah. They all drowned in salt water."

"Are you so sure about that?"

"What do you mean?"

Stoker was looking over Sloane's shoulder at Loch, and there was something strained in his expression. It was more than unusual to see the smooth gangster appear rattled.

"What are you talking about, Stoker?" Sloane pressed.

"Let me guess. Our Salgumel-enthusiastic fan club was making these?"

"Yeah, how did you—"

"Because our dear mutual friend Jeff Martin reached out to me to procure some unusual items a few weeks ago. Some not-so-legal items of a godly nature, as he very much wanted a sample of divine essence."

"Hey!" Sloane snapped. "You said you would call me if you ever had anything on Jeff!"

"While I would love to have a reason to call you and hear your enchanting voice, it seemed pointless when Mr. Martin didn't agree to the terms of purchase. We never made a deal. Now I know why. He found his own source."

"Cleus." Sloane scowled.

"Most likely."

"Wait a damn second." Sloane narrowed his eyes. "Are you telling me you didn't know Jeff was right next door to you, makin' all that crap?"

"No." Stoker met Sloane's fierce gaze without flinching. "Drusilla's is a recent acquisition. I was not the owner when those items were purchased. This is actually my first visit to this location. Feel free to ask the staff if you don't believe me."

"I just might." Sloane crossed his arms. "You still should have called me when you talked to Jeff."

"And tell you what exactly? That we discussed a deal that never materialized?" Stoker raised his brow. "We don't have these chats in person over coffee and cake, Mr. Beaumont. I would have had nothing useful to share."

"You could have set up some sort of fake deal! You could have given us a chance to catch him and finally arrest him!"

"And risk my reputation by giving potential customers the idea that I work with the police? I think not."

"Whatever." Sloane turned to check on Loch, finding him still pulling clothes down off shelves and dragging them to the register. He looked back to Stoker. "Do you know what that spell is? What it does?"

"Run along with your husband, Mr. Beaumont," Stoker replied. "Expect a call from me. Soon. Oh, and take the lingerie, no charge."

"You didn't answer my question."

"If you do feel an inkling of desire to try some on, may I suggest red?"

"If you know what it is and people get hurt because you didn't tell me, I am going to poke you full of holes with my sword. And no, that is not any kind of innuendo. I will actually stab you."

"Of that I have no doubt. If I knew what it was, I would tell you."

"Ugh." Sloane rolled his eyes. "Goodbye, Stoker. You have been useless and confusing. As usual."

"Remember to pick up when I call you later."

"I hope your stupid cat is still green."

"Always a pleasure, Mr. Beaumont."

Loch had just finished stacking the last of the Sagely Wisdom clothing on the counter when Sloane joined him. "Ah! Husband! There you are! I was wondering…." He sneered when he saw Stoker. "Oh, it's *you*."

"Hello," Stoker said with dripping sweetness. "I was just having a nice chat with your husband. You know how much I enjoy spending time with him."

"Hi, Stoker. I hope your cat is still an obnoxious green color."

"Did you know he said the very same thing to me just a moment ago?"

"Did he also say that he hopes your inside bits fall out and become outside bits in a very painful manner?"

"You're adorable." Stoker nodded at the clerk. "They'll be taking all of this, free of charge."

"Yes, sir," the clerk replied as he hastily tried to pack it all into bags. "Right away."

Sloane rubbed his hands over his face. His head was hurting. He wanted to get home, see Pandora, and try to sort out what to do next. He didn't trust that Stoker's intentions were purely motivated, but he did want to believe that he would help.

After all, the end of the world wouldn't be profitable, so Stoker had as much to lose as any of them.

"Oh, there's no need for wasting those silly bags." Loch batted his eyes. "Please allow me—"

"Loch," Sloane warned.

Anything could happen.

Fire, flood, intestinal braiding.

The clothing exploded into a giant cloud of lime green glitter. Heaps of it poured over the counter and onto the floor, and Stoker was absolutely covered in it. No one else seemed to have been hit, and Sloane knew that was entirely intentional.

"You have yourself a lovely, shiny day," Loch declared. "I think that just about settles things. Oh, but wait!" He looked longingly at the dildo kiosk. "Maybe just one quick—"

"Get out." The entire building rumbled as Stoker slowly wiped off his face and glared at the state of his suit. "Now."

"Been fun! See you later!" Sloane grabbed Loch's arm and steered him to the door.

"But I want to create a dildo!" Loch protested. "I can make one with a pulsating head and up to five vibrating settings! How neat is that?"

"Next time, okay?" Sloane dragged Loch outside and kept them walking until they were down the block.

"Are you mad at me, my sweet mate?" Loch asked. "I know you detest my violent shenanigans, so I thought this would be more suitable."

"It was fine. I'm very proud of you." Sloane couldn't help but laugh now, and he appreciated the levity. "It was actually kinda epic. You glitter-bombed Stoker."

"I did indeed."

"Chase will love this."

"Shall I go tell him? We can easily return to the horrible clothing store."

Sloane looked back, taking note of additional police vehicles parked out front. "No, it looks like they're busy. Plus I don't wanna walk back by Drusilla's right now. I'll just text Chase and tell him what Stoker said."

"Mm." Loch pulled out a tube of red lip balm from his pocket to apply to his lips. "And the glitter. Don't forget to tell him about the glitter."

"Where did you get that?" Sloane eyed the tube.

"From the adult store. It's called Pecker Up, and it tastes like strawberries."

"It's also shaped like… never mind." Sloane finished his text to Chase, trying not to laugh.

"Would you like a taste, my sweet husband? It's very reminiscent of the artificially flavored lubricant you enjoyed so much."

"Later." Sloane put his phone in his pocket and reached for Loch's hand. "Can you take us home?"

"Of course, my beloved." Loch stepped around the corner into an alley so they would not be seen and ported them right home.

They appeared in the middle of the living room to find Galgareth stretched out on the couch and Pandora fast asleep in her bassinet. Nothing seemed amiss, except Sloane could definitely smell something burnt.

"Hey!" Galgareth whispered as she waved. She tilted her head at Sloane.

"Hey! Yeah, I know." Sloane removed the glamour and tiptoed to the bassinet to check on Pandora. "Sorry we took so long. It's been crazy."

"Yeah, I know." Galgareth sat up. "Toby showed me social media on his phone, and you guys are all over it."

"Hence the glamour."

"That's what I figured."

"Has she been okay?" Sloane adjusted Pandora's blankets and gently brushed her curls back from her face. Seeing her sleeping so peacefully was the perfect balm for his worries, and he drew back his hand so he wouldn't risk disturbing her.

"She was wonderful. Other than, you know, the fires."

"Fires?" Sloane blinked. "As in… more than one?"

"Oh, hey, nothing I couldn't handle!" Galgareth cleared her throat. "So, uh, what's the latest?"

"I made a glitter bomb," Loch said proudly. He stood beside Sloane at the bassinet, one of his tentacles unfurling to sweetly nuzzle Pandora's cheek. She cooed but didn't otherwise stir.

"Why exactly did you make a glitter bomb?" Galgareth asked.

"Stoker," Sloane replied with a roll of his eyes. "We found out that Sagely Wisdom had sold a bunch of their tainted inventory to the store right next to them—"

"An *adult* store," Loch chimed in. "Disappointing. No swings."

"—and it just so happened that Stoker owns it. He claims he didn't know about the merchandise or Jeff and Daisy working out of there, but he said he was gonna help."

"That was before the glitter."

"Well, hopefully he doesn't change his mind." Sloane leaned against Loch and sighed. "The way he looked at the design? I swear he recognized it."

"We should bomb him with more glitter until he answers."

"So, there's no sign of Jeff, Daisy, or Cleus," Galgareth said slowly, "and we still don't know what the design is for?"

"No. We haven't heard back from Ollie yet." Sloane checked his phone. "And nothing new from Chase and Merrick. They're still over at the crime scene at Sagely Wisdom, and they're gonna try to talk to Stoker too. I guess for now we're stuck."

"Do you need me to hang around?"

"If that's okay? I'm not sure when something might come up next."

"Totally fine!" Galgareth smiled. "I just gotta take Toby over to crash a party real quick."

"A party?" Loch's interest was immediately piqued.

"It's something his parents have been planning for a few weeks now, and they even missed his piano recital because of it." Galgareth huffed. "So I decided we're going to make it extra special for them, those jerks."

"I have found that glitter bombs are quite effective."

Galgareth laughed. "We'll keep that in mind!" She hugged Loch and then Sloane, promising, "If you guys need anything, just call me!"

"We will. Thank you so much again for watching Panda." Sloane hugged her back.

"Aww, of course!" Galgareth grinned. "Happy to! I love hanging out with my beautiful little niece. You guys take care. Love you!"

"And we love you, Sister." Loch offered his arm to walk her to the door. "Now, when it comes to glitter, I really do think a fine grade is best...."

Sloane sat on the couch and peeked inside the bassinet, watching Pandora still sleeping soundly. He didn't want to wake her, but he couldn't resist reaching in to pet her hair again. "Hey, little girl. Missed you today. Your daddy is very proud of the glitter mess he made. I think you would have liked it."

Pandora wiggled and yawned, revealing two more front teeth that hadn't been there before.

"Wow." Sloane smiled. "You really are growing up super fast, huh? Crap. I hate I missed it... but hey, you got more teeth coming, right? I'll be here for those, sweet girl."

Panda seemed to smile, and she drifted back off with another little yawn.

"So." Loch came strolling back with a purposeful sway in his hips. "We're alone."

"Panda is right here." Sloane smirked, immediately recognizing what Loch was up to with that provocative swagger. "So no, we're not technically alone."

"She is fast asleep, and someone said they couldn't possibly go a month without tasting, and I quote, my sweet godly flesh."

"Daughter. Right here. Asleep."

"Have I not been very mature today? Do I not deserve some kind of reward for my good behavior?"

"Hmm. Maybe." Sloane pretended to think. "I want a shower first. I still feel kinda gross from having your cousin explode all over me."

Loch grinned.

"Shut up." Sloane rolled his eyes, doing his best to resist laughing. "Look, I wanna take a shower, and then we need to figure out lunch. Did you see Panda has two more little teeth now? That's six now. Gotta come up with something for her to eat too."

"I shall prepare a most wondrous feast for us all to enjoy." Loch held his head high. "I believe I have finally found a recipe that will make you produce the *Moan*."

"The Moan?" Sloane got up to head to the bathroom, stopping along the way to hang up his coat and put his phone on the charger by their bed. "Is this the moan from our wedding? The one you haven't let me forget because I liked your mom's cake so much?"

"Yes, that is the one."

Sloane got undressed and threw the rest of his clothing in the bathroom hamper, unsurprised when Loch groped his bottom as he bent over to turn on the shower. He playfully smacked him away, adjusting the temperature. "Get in here with me and I'll make all the moans you want."

"I was already planning to, but it is not the same." Loch sighed haggardly.

"No?" Sloane stepped into the water and immediately went for the soap to start washing up.

"No, it is not." Loch was magically naked in a snap, and he joined Sloane, whipping the shower curtain closed with a huff. "Your cries of pleasure when I'm inside of you are to be expected. I'm a god."

"Really?" Sloane teased. "I hadn't noticed."

"To have you make the Moan with my culinary skills has been an elusive prize, but it is one that I am securing today." Loch's tentacles unfurled from his arms where they normally lay hidden as thick scars, taking the soap from Sloane and lathering up. "You just wait, sweet husband."

"Oh, I'm waiting." Sloane closed his eyes as Loch's soapy tentacles scrubbed over his body, paying particular attention between his legs. The slick friction over his cock was good, and he could already feel himself being stretched open by Loch's magic. "Mmm, waiting... so patiently."

Loch pressed close, mouthing along Sloane's neck as one of his tentacles rubbed between Sloane's cheeks.

Sloane knew by the slick touch that it was one of the tentacles used for mating—one of the smaller ones that could both give and receive, but not the massive *tentacock*. That thing was a god in its own right, and just the thought of being stretched open on it made Sloane's cock ache.

Loch pushed his tentacle inside Sloane, holding him close and kissing his way over to his lips. More of his tentacles curled around Sloane's hips and legs, and Loch kissed him sweetly as he pinned him against the shower wall.

Sloane went willingly, hugging Loch's neck tight. He loved the slow, deep thrust of the tentacle inside his hole, and there was truly no greater bliss than making love with the god he adored. He was full, hot, and his entire body was alight with cascades of sensation.

He knew they didn't have much time, since Pandora would likely wake up from her nap at any moment, and the sense of urgency made the passion hotter and more intense. Sloane wanted to come fast, and he pulled at Loch's hair impatiently.

"Ah-ah," Loch tutted, sending more of his tentacles to pin Sloane's hands above his head. He slid his hands into Sloane's hair, brushing his lips over Sloane's as he teased, "We're taking our time, my love. Relax... and let me take care of you."

Sloane tried to protest but was silenced by a passionate kiss. He struggled against Loch's tentacles for the sheer thrill of it, and he groaned as Loch fucked him harder, faster, hitting impossibly deep places inside of him. Sloane's feet weren't touching the ground now, his entire body suspended in the powerful hold of Loch's tentacles.

He let himself relax, giving over to Loch's incredible talents, and he lost track of how many times he climaxed. Loch could keep one orgasm going right into another, over and over, until Sloane was a sobbing blissful mess and all of his muscles turned into goo. Loch filled him with his hot load, whispering beautiful things in his ear and kissing him senseless for what felt like hours.

It was absolute perfection, and the pleasure was so overwhelming that Sloane thought he might actually pass out. But Loch was right there, guiding him back to sanity with sweet kisses and warm touches, never letting go for a second. When Sloane's feet finally came back down, he had to lean on Loch for support, and he grinned dopily from ear to ear.

"Wow," he said, still trying to catch his breath and waiting for his head to stop spinning.

"Better?" Loch asked smugly.

"Mmm, much better." Sloane laughed. "You're amazing."

"Oh, I know."

"And I'm definitely hungry now."

"Ah, another problem I can easily solve." Loch took Sloane's hands and helped him step out of the shower.

"Too bad you can't solve this case," Sloane lamented as he grabbed a towel to dry off. His legs still felt a little wobbly, and he groaned as he stretched his back. "Damn."

"There are no butlers in the vicinity, so no, not yet." Loch was dried and dressed in a fresh change of clothes in a blink, and he took the towel from Sloane to help finish patting him down.

"I feel like I'm missing something. It's like when I was pregnant and couldn't figure out why the angle of that gunshot wound was so off." Sloane headed into their bedroom for some sweats and a T-shirt, deciding that they were probably not going anywhere else for the day. "Like there's something right in front of me, and I can't see what it is."

"Well, right now, I'm in front of you." Loch waggled his brows. "And I am about to cook for you and our spawn, and you shall make the Moan. You will find yourself in such a perfect state of euphoria that your brain will seize in pleasure and you shall solve the case immediately."

Sloane chuckled. "Oh? I guess we'll see, huh?"

"Oh yes. Oh yes, we will."

"I love you." Sloane did his best not to laugh at Loch's extremely serious expression.

"And I love you, my beautiful husband." Loch nuzzled Sloane's cheek, wrapping him up in several thick tentacles. "So very much."

Sloane hugged him back, sighing contentedly. It wasn't often they got to spend any time together like this now, and even the pleasure of a simple embrace was a rare treat. It was so nice just to be held, and maybe they could finally talk about Loch's father—

Sloane's phone rang.

"Dammit." Sloane grabbed it from the charger and answered it on speaker when he saw it was Ollie. "Hey, Ollie! Got some news for us?"

"Hey!" Ollie said. "I sure do! And I got Uncle Elwood and Merrick on here too. I did the swirly thing translation, and I wanted to tell you all at the same time, okay?"

"Okay, what is it?"

"It's not good. Like really, really not good. Like, it's the totally way opposite of good."

"Come on." Sloane snorted. "Is it another prayer to wake up Salgumel? We already kinda know it's not gonna be great, but—"

"It's the death song of the Kindress."

CHAPTER 6.

"THE WHAT?" Sloane didn't think he'd heard Ollie right.

He couldn't have.

"The. Death. Song. Of. The. Kindress." Ollie repeated each word carefully. "The true firstborn of Great Azaethoth. The one that, like, most Sages don't even believe is real. That guy. Person. God. Thing."

"Look." Alexander's voice came on the line. "Ollie read it twice just to be sure. It's a stupid poem about how the Kindress dies."

"Drowning in Great Azaethoth's tears?"

"Not just Great Azaethoth's. According to this, he also drowns in his own."

"What?"

"The Kindress is trapped in an endless cycle of death and rebirth, right?" Alexander drawled. "This is saying when he dies—"

"Can we have a review for the new members of the class?" Chase piped up. "Still gettin' the hang of all this very important Sage stuff."

Alexander grunted in annoyance.

"I gotcha, Uncle Elwood!" Ollie said cheerfully. "So, most Sages believe Great Azaethoth's very first kids were the twins, Etheril and Xarapharos, but it was really the Kindress."

"The star baby," Chase recalled. "Okay, got it. But then he dies, right? Before he even takes his first breath?"

"Yup. Big bummer, so Great Azaethoth brings him back. Cool, right? Except not cool, because Great Azaethoth was still fucked-up from having his very first kid die in his arms, or whatever, that the pain corrupts the Kindress. Kindress goes way crazy, so Great Azaethoth has to kill him, but he just can't live without his baby, so he brings him back, only for that same grief and probably some fuckin' guilt from murdering said baby to corrupt the Kindress again, and the shit starts all over."

"Wow." Chase coughed. "Yup. Got it. And the tears bit?"

"It's how Great Azaethoth kills the Kindress," Alexander cut back in. "By drowning it in his tears. But the song whatever bullshit is about the Kindress and his despair, knowing he will always fail Great Azaethoth no matter how hard he tries to not be corrupted, and it says he also drowns in his own tears."

"Fuck," Sloane whispered.

"He blames himself for not knowing how to love Great Azaethoth enough to overcome it—"

"Not knowing how to love period!" Ollie corrected.

"Whatever." Alexander's eye roll was audible. "Not knowing how to love who or whatever, he dies, drowning in his tears and Great Azaethoth's to finish him off. And that's what the spell does. It feeds off despair and makes you drown in your own tears like he does."

"I have never heard that part of the story," Merrick said firmly. "How can we be certain of its authenticity?"

"I'd say all them people drowning makes it pretty authentic," Chase muttered. "Milo can confirm whether or not the salt water we got from the victims coulda been tears. At the very least, this is fuckin' proof that the spell is dangerous, so we can get on the damn horn with the captain and get this to the press."

"We must be careful," Merrick warned. "People are already very upset—"

"Pretty sure having a pair of panties that might kill you is pretty fuckin' upsetting."

"It's only dangerous if you're already all sad," Ollie said, pausing to belch. "Mm, excuse me. Sorry. Right, it's only dangerous if you're sad. Then it makes you wanna touch it, and when you do, you magically read the dumb poem, and then, oh look, you drown."

"But why?" Sloane blurted out.

Silence.

"What's the point of killing all those people?" Sloane asked out loud, more for himself than anyone else as he tried to work through the possibilities. "It doesn't have anything to do with Salgumel."

"Perhaps this is what Cleus meant by his mysterious comment about it not being my brother," Merrick said. "Their new target may be the Kindress itself."

"Okay, got it, but again, why?" Sloane pressed. "Isn't the Kindress supposed to be a bit on the unstable side? He tries to destroy the universe when he gets corrupted, not just the world."

"Until we actually catch Jeffy or Daisy, there ain't no way to know for sure," Chase said, "but maybe this is like one of them 'usin' a chainsaw when you need a hammer' type situations."

Once again, there was a collective silence.

"Hear me out!" Chase exclaimed. "The cultists have been trying everything to wake up Sally, right? And every time, it's failed. We screwed over their painting thing and that totem thing, and that time they tried to sacrifice Ollie—"

"Technically, Oleander's death was part of the painting thing—" Merrick tried to correct him.

"Okay, whatever! But look! Maybe they decided to try somethin' they think we can't mess up. Maybe they think we can't stop them since they got so many of those shirts out there already."

"How many have they sold?" Sloane asked urgently.

Chase sighed. "Over two thousand."

"Shit."

"They did not keep a very accurate inventory," Merrick said gravely, "but based on the orders of blank T-shirts we found compared to current stock left in the store, that is our best guess."

"You guys have got to get this out to the press. Somebody. Anybody." Sloane glanced up at Loch. "People have to know and get rid of these damn things as soon as possible."

"If the spell is designed to work on people's grief and despair, the sudden appearance of an old god may trigger just that," Loch said quietly, reaching out to take Sloane's hand.

"If the cultists and Cleus are conspiring together, that may very well have been their plan," Merrick said, a touch of worry in his usually calm tone. "Spread the merchandise, have Cleus make his appearance to cause panic, and reap in the deaths of thousands from this wretched spell."

"Yeah, I hate to ask again, but I've also been drinking." Ollie hiccupped. "Did we already cover the why part for all of that?"

"Oh."

"Alexander and I have examined countless books of magic," Rota's voice rumbled through the speaker, "and we have never seen anything like this before. I know not of any spell that would require such a volume of mortal tears."

"But hey! Wait! There's that weird place!" Ollie exclaimed. "The one Stoker knew about!"

"Umbriech's Glen," Rota recalled. "It was a world with a stream once filled with tears not shed at funerals. We found it while we were trying to locate my body."

"And it was all messed up. Like, totally messed up."

"What about it?" Sloane remembered hearing the story of the strange broken world from Alexander and Rota before, but he didn't understand why Ollie was bringing it up.

"Stoker knew about that weird shit none of us had ever heard of," Ollie explained. "Maybe he knows something about this."

"He was supposed to call you with some kinda information, wasn't he, Sloane?" Chase asked.

Loch made a face.

"Yeah, he was," Sloane confirmed, "but I haven't heard from him. I guess you guys didn't get anything from him?"

"He was gone by the time me and Merry got over there." Chase chuckled. "There was a shit-ton of glitter all over the place, though. Any idea how that happened? Or was that Loch's, uh, little surprise to Stoker that Sloane told us about?"

"It sounds like the work of a genius," Loch declared.

"Well, my genius nephew, we may need you to play nicely with Stoker." Merrick let out a long sigh. "If he potentially has information we require that may help us stop whatever the cultists and Cleus are planning, we must... cooperate... with him." It didn't sound like that was easy for Merrick to say. "So please, no more tricks."

Loch crossed his arms.

"I can hear you pouting, Azzath."

"Fine. No more tricks. Starting now." Loch tilted his head. "Maybe."

"We'll talk to Stoker," Sloane said. "If I don't hear anything from him by tonight, I'll call him myself."

Pandora cried suddenly, loud and shrill, and there was the distinct smell of smoke coming from the living room.

"I will go check on her." Loch dipped out of the bedroom.

"Everything all right?" Chase asked worriedly.

"Just the many adventures of raising a tiny demigoddess." Sloane laughed, grimacing next when he heard Loch fussing— something about flame-retardant blankets. "Uh, so I think I'm gonna go."

"Go ahead. Let us know if you hear somethin' from Stoker. I'm gonna talk to Milo about the saltwater thing, and then me and Merry are gonna get the press goin', see if we can get some of these damn evil-ass swirly shirts out of circulation."

"Sounds good."

"What are we going to do?" Ollie asked in a not-so-hushed whisper.

"Going to bed," Alexander replied dryly. "I'm tired."

"Tired? Or, like, *tired*? Like sexy tired?"

"Shut up," Alexander grumbled.

"We will check our books again," Rota said. "There may be something we missed that might help us discover the intent behind this strange spell."

"Before I sober up, I'll look too," Ollie added. "See if the ol' starsight can kick up anything useful. Maybe get a lead on where Jefahfah and Daisy are hiding out."

"We *are* very interested in having a personal chat with Jeff," Alexander said. "If any of you find something before we do, let us know."

"All right, we will. Thanks, guys. Talk to you all later." Sloane hung up and headed into the living room to see if Loch had taken care of Pandora's latest fiery accident.

He was pleasantly surprised to see them on the floor together in front of the couch, playing with a bunch of blocks and Loch's old teething ring. Whatever had been on fire was fixed, though Sloane was starting to think that the burned smell was going to be a regular occurrence in their home from now on.

"Everything okay?" Sloane asked cautiously.

"Yes. Everything is fine," Loch assured him. "Our spawn has been changed, given more milk, and I put out the fire."

"What was it this time?" Sloane flopped on the couch behind them.

"Ah, her blankets were the offending article."

"Fffending!" Pandora exclaimed as she collided two blocks together. Her eyes widened at the resulting sound, and she continued to smack them into one another repeatedly. "Fend, fend, fend!"

"Thank you." Sloane watched Pandora playing, and he wondered if she had grown more since her nap or if he was imagining things. "Chase and Merrick are going to get the word out about the design, Rota is gonna try to find out more about what the spell is for, and Ollie is gonna use his starsight to help too."

"What about Alexander? Is he not contributing?"

"I think he's either trying to get laid or take a nap."

"Ah, both are worthy diversions."

Pandora was still slamming the blocks together, and she was getting so excited that her hands were turning into tentacles.

Sloane did his best to ignore the banging and rubbed his hands over his face. "I hate just sitting here. We don't have any leads, nowhere to go, and nothing to do."

"We could always go searching the worlds between worlds again?" Loch carefully removed one of the blocks from Pandora's tentacles and replaced it with the teething ring.

She banged it against the block she still had, seemingly satisfied with the new quieter rattling sound, and continued on without protest.

"We've been searching them for months and months," Sloane replied. "All of us have. There's just too many to check unless you happen to know where ol' cousin Cleus liked to hang out."

"Afraid not."

"What about Asta?" Sloane perked up.

"The Asran prince?" Loch grimaced. "What about him?"

"The Asra are still pretty concerned with what's going on here on Aeon, right? And Asta knew about the world ending before with Gronoch's conduit plan. Maybe they know something we don't."

"I don't exactly have 'horrible filthy cat creature' on speed dial."

"Cat, cat, cat!" Pandora exclaimed in time with her toy smacking.

"He did tell us that we have an IOU with the royal family," Sloane pointed out. "There's got to be a way to cash that in."

"Are you very sure?" Loch wrinkled his nose.

"Yes. We need all the help we can get." Sloane smirked. "Unless you want me to go ahead and try calling Stoker?"

"Cat prince it is."

"Thought so."

Loch smooched Pandora's forehead, teasing, "Sorry, but Daddy has to go find paper so he can write a note to a stinky cat creature."

"Cat!" Pandora repeated with wide eyes. "Cat, cat, cat, cat!"

"Seems like she has a new favorite word." Sloane chuckled as he slid onto the floor to take Loch's place. He stacked a few blocks for Pandora to knock over, glancing back to see what Loch was doing.

Loch had removed the notepad from their fridge and was scribbling away. Judging by the very pleased smirk he had, it was probably not a very nice message.

"What are you writing, exactly?" Sloane asked.

"Fear not, my beautiful husband." Loch batted his eyes. "I am being extremely mature and diplomatic."

"I don't believe you."

"Hmmph." Loch ripped the paper from the pad with a flourish. "It's rude of you to undermine me in front of our spawn."

Sloane whispered dramatically to Pandora, "Your daddy is a very silly god." He heard noise and looked back to see Loch picking through the fridge. "Now what are you doing?"

"Messages should be sent in bottles." Loch snapped his fingers and the note vanished. He held up a bottle he'd taken from the fridge and snapped again, making it vanish. "There! It has been delivered to the front gates of the Asran palace in Xenon. I think. Either that or inside a bathroom."

"Did you have to use a ketchup bottle?"

"I thought the red label was very festive."

"You could have at least washed it out first."

"Pfft. Details." Loch swept his hands over the counter. "Now, I do believe you and our spawn were craving the finest meal in all of the land, yes? Something rare and wonderful to sate your rabid hunger?"

"As long as rare and wonderful is small goddess approved."

"Oh, prepare yourself for a feast like no other." Loch grinned. "It is going to be a meal you never forget."

It seemed that Pandora got her penchant for fire from Loch if the wailing of the smoke alarm was anything to go by. Refusing to give up, Loch kept right on cooking. He never used magic when he cooked, determined to prepare meals using only mortal culinary skills he learned from television.

Sloane kept Pandora entertained, turning on some cartoons for her while they continued to play with her blocks. When she grew bored of that, he took her into the kitchen to watch Loch cook for a little while. It was nice to spend time together as a family, and his heart fluttered when Loch set Pandora on his shoulders so she could have a front-row seat while he finished getting their lunch ready.

Loch's latest creation was hand-rolled cheese ravioli with sage brown butter sauce and walnuts. The fire had been the first failed round of sauce, but Loch was confident he had still been able to create a moan-inducing quality dish.

Sloane was starving, but he waited to eat until Pandora was settled in her new high chair with a few cut-up bits of ravioli to nibble on. He hadn't expected that they would need the high chair quite this soon, and he wondered what else they should go ahead and get ready for.

Potty training? Learning the alphabet? By all the gods, how soon would she have to start school?

It was all happening so fast, and his thoughts were suddenly spiraling as he sat down beside her at the table. He watched her squeeze a bite of ravioli in between her fingers, and he used his phone to snap a picture of her adorably entranced expression.

This messy moment of exploration felt important, and the urge to capture it before it passed him by was strong—like so many others he might have already missed and didn't even know. He was struck by a strange surge of guilt for not being there to see Pandora get those new teeth, to see how powerful her fire magic had gotten, and....

Loch was watching him intently.

"What?"

"I'm preparing myself to hear the Moan," Loch replied.

"Sorry." Sloane chuckled and put his phone down.

"What's wrong, sweet husband? Are you worried about your moans being so loud that they upset our spawn?"

"No." Sloane resisted the urge to roll his eyes. "Was just thinking about what we're missing when we're out there trying to save the world."

"Ah." Loch extended a tentacle to curl around Sloane's arm. "Such as the presence of her new teeth and her growing vocabulary?"

"Yeah. I mean, what do we tell her when she's older? Sorry, Daddy and Dad don't totally remember what your first word was because we were out fighting an old god?"

"That is precisely what we tell her, but her first word was mass panic. I remember." Loch beamed. "We have the rest of our lives together to spoil her positively rotten to make up for any of the time we miss making sure there's a world here to spoil her in."

Pandora had discovered she could smash the raviolis into her tray, and she laughed excitedly. She had both hands firmly plastering the pasta into a paste, and she had never looked happier.

"Yeah." Sloane smiled as he watched her. "It doesn't help that she's growing up so fast."

"But not yet grown enough to fully appreciate my culinary prowess," Loch observed. "I am still pleased that she seems to enjoy the firm texture of my pasta."

"You're supposed to eat it, sweetie," Sloane said to her, trying to urge her to take a bite. He took a forkful from his own plate to show her, and he almost forgot to moan. "Mmm-hmmm, that is really good!"

Loch pursed his lips.

"What?" Sloane grinned. "It really is good! I love the rich, nutty sauce, and the filling is freakin' delicious."

"That *grunt* was barely passable as a cry of pleasure."

"Ah, come on. I was distracted trying to show our baby girl how to actually eat food." Sloane glanced at her. "You know, instead of smearing it into her hair."

"Perhaps she is trying to absorb the nutrients through her hair follicles?" Loch mused.

"At least she looks like she's having fun." Sloane chuckled and picked up his phone again to snap a few gloriously messy shots. "Do you like that, silly girl? Hmm? Is that fun?"

Pandora laughed and immediately slapped more of the pasta paste into her hair and over her face.

"I do not believe that is the best way to enjoy your meal," Loch scolded her playfully.

Sloane attempted to clean Pandora up as quickly as she was making a mess and was promptly rewarded with some mushed-up ravioli on his face. "Mm, thank you."

Pandora clapped, and Sloane swore her laughter was the absolute best sound in the world.

Loch's stifled giggles were a close second.

"Ha, yes, very funny." Sloane wiped off his cheek. "I'm glad you're both happy. But I'm going to eat my food now. Daddy can get gooped."

"Is this not a special moment you would have been sad to miss?" Loch used one of his tentacles to get a glob Sloane had missed on his chin.

"No, it absolutely is." Sloane took another bite of the ravioli from his plate and made sure to groan appreciatively. "This is amazing. Really. And it's our first meal as a family."

"It is indeed." Loch carefully navigated a bit of pasta into Pandora's mouth that she immediately spit back out.

"Just think. We'll have her first Dhankes in just a few weeks."

"Not to mention the anniversary of when we first met."

"My parents' death day. Lochlain's death day." Sloane paused. "I'm not sure if it counts, since he got resurrected."

"Probably not. Hmm." Loch took a moment to reflect before exclaiming, "Oh! And then there's the anniversary of the first time I was inside of your sweet mortal body and gave you all of my mating tentacles. I already know how I want to celebrate that."

"More mating?"

"Naturally. I will ravage you on a bed of fallen stars while the universe shudders around us from the force of your orgasmic ecstasy. We're going to have a very busy autumn."

"Mm, very."

Loch tried again to feed Pandora, frowning when she spat it out like before. "Does it count as our first family meal if she's not actually eating it?"

"Hang on, I'm not giving up yet." Sloane tried next with his fork, waving it back and forth before offering it to her. "Come on, baby girl. I believe in you. You are going to eat this pasta, oh yes you are."

Pandora's eyes widened, and she gurgled curiously.

"Yes, come on, baby girl," Sloane urged. "Eat the nommy pasta."

She opened her mouth to take the bite, chewed it, and swallowed it. She then opened her mouth for more, smacking her hands on her tray.

"Yeah, there we go!" Sloane eagerly gave her another piece. "Yes! Parenting win!"

"Maybe she is old enough to appreciate my cooking," Loch mused. "She might just need a more interactive experience. I may look at securing a hibachi grill."

"How about no?"

"She likes fire. It could be fun. I can show her how to make the very good chicken."

"You say fun, I say horribly dangerous." Sloane smirked. "But I do think it's sweet that you wanna teach her to cook." He leaned over to kiss Loch's cheek. "You're an incredible father, Azaethoth the Lesser."

Loch's expression softened, and his smile was nearly bashful. "Thank you. I… I am trying. I want to be better than my father was. I want to be there when Pandora needs me. I want to help her find her way as a goddess. I want her to be happy, loved, and if anyone so much as harms a single hair on her precious beautiful head, I will make ladder braids with their lower intestinal tract."

"Well, then I think you're already a better father than Salgumel ever was," Sloane said firmly. "Because you care so much. We both do. That's what is going to make us kickass parents."

"I believe we already are." Loch smirked. "After all, the very reason you stress out over missing time with our spawn is because you care."

"Yeah, I know. And I know I need to stop and just be happy and make the most of the time we do have together with her." Sloane frowned as an old pain came rushing to the forefront of his mind. "I guess it's because I wish I'd had more time with my parents. I start thinking about all the times I went to my room to play instead of hanging out with them, all the things I missed with them…."

"Oh, my darling husband." Loch frowned. "You couldn't have known what was going to happen to them."

"I know." Sloane blinked away a few hot tears that were threatening to spill over. "It's been almost twenty years now, and gods, I still miss them so much."

"You will see them again," Loch promised. "We can still visit them whenever you'd like. We can even take Pandora with us so we can tell them about her many wonderful accomplishments. Like learning how to cook with a hibachi grill."

Sloane laughed. "Oh no."

"Oh yes."

"I'm still not sure—" Sloane flinched as Pandora rejected her most recent offering by setting it on fire and flinging it over his head. "Okay, yeah, definitely no hibachi cooking."

"Maybe for her birthday." Loch quickly extinguished the flaming pasta. He fussed at Pandora, scolding, "No, little one. No making fires with your food!" He sent a few tentacles over to check Sloane. "Are you all right? Are you singed? That came very close to your beautiful brows."

"I'm totally fine. Thank you." Sloane took Loch's hand. "Thank you for everything. For making me smile, for putting out fires, for always loving me so damn much, and you know, being pretty damn amazing in general. I really couldn't do this without you."

"Nor I you, my beautiful mate." Loch smiled adoringly and kissed Sloane's hand. "I love you more than there are stars in the skies of all the worlds here and beyond."

"I love you too." Sloane squeezed Loch's hand, his chest flooded with a wonderful warmth. "Now let's see if we can get through lunch without anything else getting burned, shall we?"

"Burrrrn weee! Burn weee!" Pandora cheered excitedly and clapped her gooey hands together. "Burnnn and maff panic!"

"Or not."

As it turned out, there was only one more fire, and it came when Loch went to pull Pandora out of her high chair to clean her up. The flames were extinguished, the high chair was fixed, and Pandora went down for a nap in her room.

Starting fires was apparently quite draining.

The rest of the afternoon was uneventful. Sloane and Loch gave Pandora a much-needed bath, played lots of games, and nothing else burst into flames until she got cranky about bedtime. It was a small fire, thankfully, and Loch soothed her to sleep by rocking her in his tentacles. Even though Sloane knew there were multiple dangers looming over their heads, he had been happy to spend the day with his family.

Maybe it was because of those dangers that he wanted to make these hours count—especially not knowing when and if Cleus might attack again or whatever potential disaster might befall them or the city.

He hadn't heard anything from Stoker, though Chase and Merrick checked in often to keep them posted about the investigation. There wasn't anything new to report until well after Pandora was in bed for the night, when Chase told them that the mayor would be holding a press conference soon about the dangerous design.

Loch and Sloane got settled on the couch to watch, and Sloane turned the TV on to the news.

"How long do we have until the program begins?" Loch asked, side-eyeing Sloane with a grin.

"Not enough time for mating, if that's what you're thinking." Sloane playfully poked his side. "You can wait until after it's over, I promise."

"Can I, though? Really?"

"Yes. I believe in you." Sloane had muted the TV, but he turned the sound back on when he saw what looked like a forensic sketch of someone very familiar.

Himself.

"—the AVPD is still actively searching for a man they say may be going by the name of Smoane Momont," the reporter was saying. "Eyewitnesses believe he is the unidentified man from the viral video that allegedly shows him battling Sagittarian gods."

A video clip played of Sloane leaping onto a car with his sword of starlight before cutting back to the reporter.

Sloane cringed.

"You look very handsome," Loch whispered loudly.

"Thank you," Sloane mumbled.

"—additional witnesses at a local coffee shop claim they were accosted by a man with a similar build and black jacket as the one seen in the footage. He allegedly tainted a drink with sewer water for insulting Sagittarian gods. Authorities believe he may be using glamours—"

Sloane narrowed his eyes at Loch.

"Ah! The news lies!" Loch smiled sweetly. "It was clean toilet water, not sewer water."

Sloane's phone rang, and he cursed lightly as he dug it out of his pocket. He took a deep breath and answered, "Beaumont Investigations, how may I help you?"

"Don't you mean, *Momont* Investigations?" Stoker's purring voice teased.

"Hi, Stoker." Sloane sighed. "What's up?"

"I have something for you, Mr. Beaumont."

"And what's that?"

"A dead body."

CHAPTER 7.

"And oh, some fashion advice as well," Stoker continued, chuckling low. "I very much enjoyed your television debut, but perhaps you should consider changing up your wardrobe and not just that handsome face when you don a glamour, hmm?"

"Wait, what's this about a dead body?" Sloane demanded as he put the call on speaker so Loch could hear Stoker as well. He grabbed the remote to mute the TV again. "I thought you were working on figuring out what the deal is with that swirling design."

"Don't be coy." Stoker snorted. "You already know it's the death song of the Kindress, thanks to Ollie."

"He told you?"

"Yes. Imagine my surprise. In the future, I would very much appreciate if the flow of information was more consistent between us—"

"Like the consistent flow of beautiful, shining glitter?" Loch suggested.

"Yeah, this is real cute coming from the guy who never gives us a straight answer to anything," Sloane mumbled. "Send him more glitter, Loch."

"Mr. Beaumont, Azaethoth, please." Stoker sounded like he was smiling. "I do believe the severity of our current circumstances calls for a bit of cooperation, don't you?"

"No," Loch replied flatly.

Sloane hated to admit it, but he knew Stoker was right. They needed all the help they could get right now, even if he didn't trust Stoker as far as he could throw him.

"Fine, yes." Sloane huffed. "We'll keep you in the loop with all the Super Secret Sage stuff, okay?"

"Thank you," Stoker said. "Now as much as I enjoy our darling little chats, that is not why I'm calling you."

"Right," Sloane said. "What's this about a body—"

"Is it because you're still picking all that glitter out of your bodily crevices?" Loch asked gleefully. "Did you find the batch between your toes yet?"

"Hush now, the grown-ups are talking," Stoker scolded. "Although, if Mr. Beaumont wants to check for me, I wouldn't mind undressing for a very thorough bodily examination—"

"Ohhh, next time I'll make sure to summon an entire dumpster full of glitter and shove it right up—"

"Hey, hey!" Sloane patted Loch's shoulder. "Remember what we just talked about? About cooperating? Play nice."

Loch scowled. "I am playing nice. I just want to play nice with his organs and a dumpster full of glitter."

"Charming," Stoker drawled.

"And you!" Sloane snapped at Stoker. "Quit screwing around with your weird flirting crap and just tell me what you called to tell me already. Where is this dead body? Because I haven't heard anything from Chase or—"

"Oh, I'm not calling the AVPD," Stoker cut right in.

"And why is that?"

"Because the victim is one of my people," Stoker replied. "My, ahem, unique people."

"Right. People who aren't supposed to exist." Sloane sighed. "You know I'm still gonna have to tell Chase and Merrick about this."

"As long as it's on a very unofficial basis. I'm sure you understand."

"All right. We'll be down there as soon as we can."

"I'll be waiting."

Sloane hung up with a groan.

"So much for hot sensual mating after the press conference," Loch lamented.

"Shit, the press conference." Sloane quickly unmuted the television to see how much they'd missed.

"—again emphasize the danger that these garments may possess," the mayor was saying. "We are asking any citizen who may have purchased one to surrender it immediately. No questions asked. Safe drop locations are being set up at the AVPD, here at city hall, and the Archersville Library. We will also have counselors available if you feel that you might be in crisis or at risk after purchasing one of these items.

"Now, I know I've talked a lot about the Sagittarian religion tonight, a faith we all seem to be talking about more and more lately, but I am not asking anyone to surrender their personal or spiritual convictions. I am only asking for you to do the right thing, to help do your part and step up to fight against evil magic by turning over these cursed items, and that should be something we can all agree on no matter what we believe. Together we can overcome this terrible threat and keep both our beloved city and one another safe. Thank you."

"Meh." Loch shrugged. "Nice enough speech, I suppose. But I didn't vote for him."

"You can't vote," Sloane reminded him. "You don't technically exist."

"That's hurtful."

"Mr. Mayor!" a young reporter shouted. "Are we not going to discuss the obvious conspiracy at work here?"

The mayor shook his head. "Please, if anyone else would like—"

"No!" The young reporter refused to back down. "It was leaked last month that your office worked to suppress statements from Hugh Barman, the man who was charged with the murder of Deacon Thomas Hills, because he claimed abominations were walking among us. Now we have old gods destroying the city? Cups and T-shirts that are making people hurt themselves? Oh, please. I think that leak was intentional, and all of this is to create a panic for you to profit from for next year's election!"

"Mr. Zabel, we all have questions about what's happening," the mayor calmly retorted. "What were those things? Why—"

"They're gods, sir. Azaethoth the Lesser, the god of thieves, was right there—" Mr. Zabel tried to cut in.

Loch perked up.

"—were they here?" the mayor went on as if he didn't hear Mr. Zabel. "What do they want?"

"If your office is going to try and scare the public into voting for you again," Mr. Zabel snapped, "you should at least know the gods they're doing it with!"

"Who or what is Smoane Momont—"

"Gods, that name." Sloane cringed.

"—and how does he fit into all of this?" The mayor continued to ignore Mr. Zabel. "Please know that my office and the entirety of the

AVPD are doing everything we can to find the truth. To accuse me and my staff of using this tragedy or any other to benefit politically is both disgusting and piss-poor journalism. Excuse me. No further questions."

"Oh, you wouldn't know the truth if it slapped you in the—" Mr. Zabel could be heard shouting before the feed abruptly ended.

"I think I will vote for him after all," Loch said cheerfully. "He is small and angry. Like a little puppy."

"Mayor Penche?" Sloane didn't understand, as the mayor was a large, robust man.

"The one with the mop on his head."

"That was William Zabel," Sloane explained. "He's a tabloid reporter. He writes crazy stuff, like Fish Boy being spotted swimming in the new fountain at the park."

"Oh?"

"Uh-huh. He also likes to show up uninvited to crime scenes. Milo's complained about him before, said he's even tried to swipe evidence and take photos of victims. He's slimy."

"What I'm hearing is that he is very bold and daring."

Sloane rolled his eyes. "You only like him because he recognized you."

"Hmm. That is probably true."

"Can you call your sister and see if she and Toby are done crashing that party? We're gonna need someone to watch Panda."

"Will do, my sweet love." Loch tilted his head, listening to something Sloane could not hear. "Ah, yes. She will be here shortly. From what I understand, the party was a wonderful success. A success, in the sense that it has been thoroughly wrecked."

"Good for her and Toby." Sloane leaned into Loch and snagged a quick kiss. "I'm going to go change."

"Taking Stoker's fashion advice?" Loch wrinkled his nose.

"Heard that part, huh?" Sloane shrugged. "He's right. Unless I want to glamour my whole body, I need to change it up."

"As if that would be a challenge for a beautiful witch of starlight like you."

"Just let me change, okay?" As Sloane shifted forward to get off the couch, a shimmer of magic washed over him and gave him pause. "Loch, what did you do?"

"I provided you with a new glamour. You're welcome."

"What did you do?"

"Mmm, you don't sound very grateful. I think you look very handsome."

Before Sloane could question who or what Loch had glamoured him into, Galgareth appeared in front of the TV and startled him. "Shit! Hi!"

"Hey! Sorry!" Galgareth grinned sheepishly. She was wearing a very expensive-looking tuxedo, and Toby's colorful hair was slicked back. "I figured Pandora would be sleeping, so we decided to just pop in…." She stared at Sloane and then Loch. "Really?"

"Really really." Loch bounced up to his feet. He gave Galgareth a big hug as he said, "Thank you so much for coming. We must be going. Dead body and all waiting for us."

"You're not going to tell me, are you?" Sloane touched his face, and he swore it felt eerily familiar. "Galgareth? What has he done to me?"

Galgareth slid her hand over her mouth and tried to stifle a laugh. "You look great. Love you! Have fun with the dead body!"

"But—"

The apartment vanished, and Sloane was standing on the sidewalk a few yards away from the Velvet Plank, surrounded by waves of people. Loch had put his arm around Sloane to keep him moving forward and avoid getting bumped into by the crowd. It wasn't that late in the evening, so Sloane wasn't too surprised to see so many people out despite it being a weeknight.

The energy in the air, however, was very unexpected and equally unpleasant.

It was tense, restless, he could hear lots of raised voices, and no one sounded happy. He couldn't explain why, but it felt like a fight was about to break out at any moment. He saw an older man get shoulder checked by a younger one trying to squeeze by, and a violent scuffle erupted immediately.

Loch had fortunately managed to teleport them right into the flow of people without anyone noticing, and he quickly steered them away from the scuffle and toward the club.

The Velvet Plank was an old theater that had been converted into an exotic night club. There were big posters for adult entertainers, and rows of Xs filled the glowing marquis. The elaborate carvings of seashells and waves around the doors gave a glimpse into the building's majestic past, but the plywood nailed over them was a stark reminder of its current grim state.

Inside, an athletic man in a glittering thong was gyrating his way down the catwalk that had been built onto the main stage, while other men swung around poles on smaller catwalks flanking either side. Above the main stage were worn reliefs of waves and twisting tentacles, another peek into the theater's former glory. The music was pounding, colorful lights were flashing through the darkness, and there was not an empty seat in the whole place.

This was the first time Sloane had been here at night, and it didn't look much different, except it was harder to see how filthy the floor was. He noticed a giant crack in the middle of the bar, and he wondered what had gone down since he'd been here last.

Stoker was waiting for them there, dressed down in jeans and a neon pink shirt with the Velvet Plank logo on the front. He quirked his brows when he saw Sloane and Loch, and then he snorted. "Cute."

There in the reflection of the mirror behind the bar, Sloane finally saw what Loch had done—he had glamoured Sloane to look just like Loch.

"This isn't exactly what I meant by changing up your look," Stoker drawled. "I have to say, it's definitely a step down—"

"I have made him into a splendid vision of my gorgeous vessel," Loch declared. "Now when you stare at him lustfully, you are in fact staring at me. Enjoy."

"It's a good thing that I can see through glamours very well, so my lustful staring will continue uninhibited."

"What if I remove your eyes? Can your staring be lustful without eyeballs?"

"*Please*. By all means. Go on and try—"

"Would it be inhibiting if I fill your eye sockets with glitter and macaroni?"

"Can we please just go wherever it is we're going?" Sloane sighed loudly. "I'm so not in the mood for you two to have a freakin' pissing contest right now."

"Right to business it is." Stoker waved. "Let's go, then."

Sloane moved to follow Stoker, expecting to be led back to his office or some other part of the club. Instead, the entire theater vanished and they were crowded together in the foyer of a small apartment. There was nothing remarkable about it except the body over on the kitchen floor covered with a sheet.

Stoker was magically dressed in a slick black suit with red pinstripes now, and he strutted over toward the body. With a wave of his hand, the sheet pulled back to reveal a shirtless man who appeared half-human and half-fish.

"His name was Lance Wise," Stoker said briskly. "He was descended from the Vulgora. I had made the announcement about the dangerous merchandise from Sagely Wisdom, but…." He paused to suck a breath in between his teeth. "Lance apparently did not agree with me."

"How so?" Sloane asked as he approached.

"He said the magic was, and I quote, bullshit, and he was going to wear whatever he wanted."

"Seriously?" Sloane blinked. "He's a descendant of a mythical fish race that is not mythical at all, but some swirling design being dangerous was too much for him to believe?"

"My dear Mr. Beaumont, never underestimate any creature's aptitude for ignorance." Stoker massaged his temple absently. "I'd considered Lance a friend, but there was nothing I could say or do to convince him of the risk. And, well, here we are."

Sloane examined Mr. Wise's body with a perception spell and found it was much the same as the other victim at the hotel. Other than clearly not being human, he didn't see anything unusual. "What was he wearing that killed him?"

"A T-shirt," Stoker replied. "I already destroyed it."

Sloane looked at the tile floor around the body and touched it, finding it dry. "Huh. Did you clean up too?"

"Pardon? I'm sorry, I'm having trouble listening to you with your face looking like that. There's just something about it that makes me want to ignore anything you have to say."

"He drowned, right? So where's all the water? Tears? Whatever it is." Sloane glanced over the kitchen cabinets and appliances, and he noticed that the paper towel dispenser was empty. There were also no signs of any dish towels. Not entirely unusual, but Sloane couldn't shake the feeling something was wrong.

He took a step back from the body and clapped his hands, casting a spell to detect the absence of missing objects.

Through the vision of the spell, he could see that two dish towels, the paper towels, and a rug were all missing. The rug would have been right beneath Mr. Wise's body.

And that's when it clicked.

"There were towels missing from the hotel where one of the other victims died, and now this," Sloane said. "Dish towels, the rug. Anything that would have been wet or could have been used to soak up the water from the victims drowning has been taken."

Loch, who had been busy searching through the kitchen cabinets for gods knew what, paused his exploration to clarify, "And by water, you mean tears?"

"Maybe? Kind of a weird thing to gather, isn't it?"

"Depends on what the cultists are using them for, sweet husband."

"Which, of course, we still don't know." Sloane frowned. "These tears wouldn't be magical. At least, I don't think they would be." He rubbed the back of his neck. "We need to let Rota and Ollie know too. Maybe that will help with their spell searching."

"You're certain it's the tears they're after?" Stoker asked quietly. His expression was murky, and if Sloane didn't know better, he'd swear the gangster looked worried.

"Pretty sure. Nothing else is missing. I don't understand how killing these people would help them contact the Kindress or have anything to do with Salgumel, though. The old gods weren't big fans of sacrifice, you know?"

"I may have something that can help." Stoker used his magic to cover the body back up. "Come with me, Mr. Beaumont."

Loch raised a blender he had found as if he was going to hit Stoker with it, eyeing him suspiciously. "And Mr. the Lesser, yes? Mr. the Lesser is coming too?"

"Not you." Stoker managed a familiar smirk. "Where we're going is shielded from gods. My apologies. You can wait for us back at the club."

"And where are we going?" Sloane demanded.

"My home," Stoker replied. "It'll only be for a moment to retrieve a scroll."

"Why don't you just bring the scroll to us?"

"I can't do that, nor can I tell you why."

"Gods, you're annoying." Sloane threw up his hands. "Fine. We'll go look at your stupid scroll, and then you're bringing me right back to Loch. Got it?"

"Of course." Stoker bowed his head.

Loch was not pleased, and he snarled at Stoker. "If you dare—"

"Yes, I know," Stoker drawled. "If I dare offend your beautiful husband, it'll be an eternity of visceral arts and crafts. Lots of glitter, glue, and my organs."

Loch still had the blender raised, and he looked to Sloane expectantly.

"It'll be fine," Sloane promised. "If he so much as looks at me the wrong way, I'll do some intestinal crafts of my own."

Loch lowered the blender and pulled Sloane close, curling a tentacle around his waist. "Hurry back. You know I shouldn't be left unsupervised for very long."

"I know. Don't worry. I'll be back as soon as I can." Sloane kissed his cheek and then turned to Stoker. "Okay. Let's get this over with."

The moment the words left Sloane's lips, the apartment disappeared and he was standing alone in an elaborate indoor garden. He could sense that he was in another world, and yet he was still somehow on Aeon. A quick pass with a perception spell was even more confusing, because it was telling him that he was actually back inside the Velvet Plank.

The pathways here were violet brick, the flowers plentiful and fragrant, and the night sky was visible through a high arched glass ceiling. In the very center of the garden was a large glowing white tree, its branches reaching up toward the glass like arcing lightning bolts frozen in time.

He heard a chirping meow, and he saw a fluffy lime-green cat prancing toward him from one of the paths.

"Hey, Madame Sprinkles." Sloane kneeled down to greet her. "Long time, no see."

Madame Sprinkles paused when Sloane spoke, and her ears went back. She sniffed the air and then hissed loudly, retreating back the way she came.

"Right. Nice to see you too." Sloane snorted, and then he remembered he still looked like Loch, and Loch was, in fact, personally responsible for the cat's unusual green coloring. He sighed and removed the glamour, glancing around the garden expectantly.

He didn't know what was taking Stoker so long to show up, and he caught himself looking back at the tree. He was drawn to it in a way he couldn't explain, and he reached out to touch its trunk. It was warm, firm, and there was powerful old magic coursing through it. The tree's luminous bark grew dark where his hand was, and he watched it slowly light back up once he pulled away.

"It's a Xenon tree," Stoker said, his voice close enough to make Sloane jump.

"For fuck's sake!" Sloane whirled around with an angry hiss. "Hey! A little warning, huh?"

"My apologies, Mr. Beaumont." Stoker was clearly trying to hide a smile. "I did not mean to startle you."

"Yeah, whatever." Sloane pointed at the tree. "Is this the tree from the city park? It really wasn't destroyed, was it? You took it."

"Hmm." Stoker shrugged. "So it appears I did. You look much better, by the way. I'm very glad you removed that wretched glamour."

"And you figured out how to wake it up," Sloane went on, ignoring Stoker's compliments.

"It would seem so."

"There really was a tear between worlds, then," Sloane pressed. "Something tore the veil and made the Xenon tree appear in Archersville. But what?"

"What indeed," Stoker said mysteriously. "A puzzle for another time, I'm afraid." He held up a fragile tattered scroll. "This is what I wanted to show you. It's one of the oldest spells ever written. The godstongue is Great Azaethoth's own, the same dialect as spells for the Kindress were written in."

"Why would anyone want to invoke the Kindress?" Sloane watched as the scroll opened and revealed several long, twisting paragraphs that he recognized as segments of the lethal swirling design.

"The Kindress is very powerful. Being able to bring life to where there is only death would be quite handy."

"But he takes life away too, right?"

"Details." Stoker waved his hand. "Now, I don't know how the cultists or Cleus plan to contact the Kindress, but I do know this.... Umbriech's Glen is the key."

"The world that had the stream full of tears?"

"Yes, tears not shed at funerals. Once upon a time, that stream would overflow with the tears of old gods who never mourned the passing of the Kindress whenever it died. This was called the Great Tide, and the tears would be so great that they would flood over into Babbeth's Orchard. It was said any fruit harvested from the orchard after a Great Tide would be especially potent."

"What does this have to do with everyone drowning?"

"Everything." Stoker offered the scroll for Sloane to inspect. "Mortals would sing the death song of the Kindress and refuse to weep as the gods did in hopes that their unshed tears would join those of the gods in Umbriech's Glen. After a Great Tide, they would gather at Babbeth's Orchard to harvest the fruit to use in special rituals."

Sloane was too afraid of damaging the old scroll to touch it, but he did lean in closer to look it over. "What kinda special rituals?"

"The fruit was often used as an offering to the Kindress himself. Isn't that fun?"

"How do you know all of this?" Sloane narrowed his eyes. "You could be making this crap up."

"Take some pictures with your fancy little phone and send them to Ollie to translate if you don't believe me."

Sloane did just that, snapping several shots as he mumbled, "Let's be real here. I know you're not human. You somehow managed to wake up a Xenon tree, you have all this crazy old magic, not to mention stopping time and all the other freaky stuff I've seen you do." An insane thought came racing to the forefront of his mind, and he blurted out, "Are you the Kindress?"

"Me?" Stoker laughed. "What a charming idea."

"Okay, since you're laughing, I'm guessing that's a no."

"If I was the Kindress, why would I need your help stopping the idiots trying to use me to wake up Salgumel?"

"Fair." Sloane squinted. "But you're still totally not human."

"We may never know."

"Are you ever going to tell me?"

"Mmm, that's getting rather personal, don't you think, Mr. Beaumont?" Stoker rolled up the scroll and made it vanish. "I don't think I'm ready to take our relationship to that level yet."

"Right." Sloane rolled his eyes. "So, the spell. The tears. You think the cultists are trying to get the stream going again to make a freakin' fruit salad for the Kindress?"

"It's a bit more complicated than that, but yes. They may be planning to create an offering to entice the Kindress into waking Salgumel for them."

"Chainsaw for a hammer," Sloane muttered.

"Pardon?"

"Never mind. Can we go now? Unless there was anything else you wanted to tell me?" Sloane looked around the garden, and he had to fight the urge to touch the tree again. "Like explain where the hell we are?"

"I told you, this is my home."

"Your home is a world between worlds that's not actually between anything?"

"Ah, you're so very clever." Stoker smiled fondly. "I do so admire that brilliant intellect of yours. Yes, this is part of my Hidden World, the safe place I created for myself and the descendants of the everlasting people to live."

"Is it really shielded from gods?"

"Maybe. Or maybe I just said that because I wanted to be alone with you."

"Where's the rest of it, then?"

"Interested, are you? I would love to give you the grand tour sometime." Stoker's eyes sparkled, and he gestured toward the pathway closest to them. "I'll go ahead and spoil the best part. That leads right to my bedroom."

"Hard pass." Sloane snorted.

"As you wish, Mr. Beaumont." Stoker bowed politely.

"Now that I know you're done being helpful, let's go."

"And here I was so enjoying your company without the taint of your deplorable mate's presence."

"The longer we're here, the longer my deplorable mate is unattended at your club."

"Fair point."

The garden was gone in a flash, and they were back at the Velvet Plank. Stoker was dressed once more in his T-shirt and jeans, and Sloane could feel that his glamour had been restored. Sloane was impressed that Stoker had somehow been able to portal them here without anyone questioning how they appeared out of thin air.

That, after all, was usually a talent reserved for gods like Loch.

"Let me know if Ollie finds anything that I missed," Stoker was saying. "I'll be in touch."

"Yeah, sure." Sloane offered his hand. "Thank you for your help."

Stoker took Sloane's hand as if he was going to kiss it, but then only shook it instead. "Always a pleasure. Mr. Beaumont."

"Yeah, it's been a real treat." Sloane definitely noticed when Stoker held his hand a little too long, and he politely pulled away. "Have fun with your magical glowing tree."

"Thank you. Your husband is at the bar. You have five minutes to get him out of here. And please, tell him to leave the blender he stole from Mr. Wise's apartment."

"Oh gods."

The sound of an angry shout grabbed their attention, and they turned to see a couple of guys squabbling over a chair near the main stage. Their struggling had collided them with the patrons of another table, and what had started as a small tussle was growing into a free-for-all.

A bouncer was already on his way to intercede, but it was clear that the fight was getting out of control fast. It was the same restless and violent energy Sloane had felt outside earlier, and he wondered what the hell had gotten into everyone tonight.

"Never a dull moment." Stoker turned to leave. "Good night, Mr. Beaumont."

"Hey, wait." Sloane caught Stoker's arm.

"What?" Stoker stared at Sloane's hand, his fierce eyes flicking up to meet Sloane's in questioning. He tensed as if he wanted to push Sloane away, but he was waiting to do so.

"I'm sorry about Mr. Wise," Sloane said urgently. "I know losing someone… isn't easy."

Stoker's face softened, and he smiled. "I appreciate that." He nodded toward the bar. "Go on. Fetch your husband before I think you're getting sweet on me."

"Good night, Stoker." Sloane headed to the bar to find Loch, ducking instinctively as a plastic pitcher went flying over his head.

Loch was serving up lime-green slushie drinks to eager patrons from the pilfered blender, and he didn't appear to be taking any money. He lit up when he saw Sloane, leaving behind the stolen appliance to rush over to him and sweep him into a loving embrace. "Ah! My beautiful husband!"

"Hi!" Sloane couldn't help but laugh from the exuberant greeting, and he squeezed Loch tight. "You know this probably looks really weird. You hugging on yourself?"

"Perhaps, but I don't care. Did Stoker behave? Do I have reason to eviscerate him?"

"He was fine, I promise. Did you have fun while I was gone?"

"I made a new drink. I named it the Revenge of Madame Sprinkles. Catchy, eh?"

"I like it. I'm afraid to ask what's in it."

"You should be."

The music stopped playing abruptly as the fighting spread, forcing the dancers to flee from the stages. People were either trying to get as far away from the brawl as possible or eagerly diving in to join the fray. Several tables got flipped over, and somehow a section of the weathered carpet had caught fire.

"Do you have anything to do with this?" Sloane asked suspiciously. "Maybe something you put in those drinks?"

"Me?" Loch gasped. "As if I would ever do such a thing."

"Uh-huh."

There was a loud crash as a chair came flying through the air and shattered against the floor nearby. The chair had been occupied, and the person sitting in it managed to get to their feet and stumble forward about a yard before collapsing with a groan.

Sloane lifted his hand for a perception spell—just in case Loch wasn't being honest about what he'd put in that blender—but he didn't see any magical influence at work. The surge of anger and anxiety was entirely mortal, and he sighed. He almost wished there was something supernatural at work here.

"What's the matter, my darling husband?" Loch asked.

"Oh nothing." Sloane gestured vaguely at the ongoing chaos. "Just taking in what mass panic actually looks like."

"It looks like a lot of intoxicated people."

"Angry, scared intoxicated people." Sloane ducked as a glass went zooming by. "Shit!"

"Ready to leave, sweet Starkiller?"

"Ready." Sloane cringed. "Let's go home."

CHAPTER 8.

AFTER RELIEVING Galgareth from babysitting duty, Sloane and Loch updated everyone with the new information Stoker had revealed about Umbriech's Glen. Sloane sent the photos of the scroll to Ollie to look over and verify Stoker's story, and Chase and Merrick informed them that there had been three more drowning victims since the press conference had aired.

Including Mr. Wise, that made four new deaths in only a few hours.

Unrest was eating the city alive, and arrests were skyrocketing as the tensions escalated. A riot had broken out at a Lucian church and spilled over into the surrounding streets, culminating with cars being flipped and set ablaze. What Sloane and Loch had seen during their visit to the Velvet Plank was just one small fraction of a city being pushed to the edge, and Chase said that the mayor was now considering a mandatory curfew to curb the violence.

Alexander and Rota volunteered to head right over to Umbriech's Glen to see if they could find anything, and it only took about five minutes for them to report back and say it was empty. If the cultists were planning to do something there with all the tears they were gathering, they hadn't started yet.

Milo joined the group text to inform them that not only did Lynnette now hate pistachio ice cream after he went to five different stores trying to find it, but he also confirmed that the salt water recovered from the victims was indeed their own tears.

While that gave credence to Stoker's story about the ritual for the Kindress, it still didn't give them any clues as to what they should do next.

It left Sloane anxious as he got ready for bed, more than a bit frustrated, and he brushed his teeth hard enough to draw Loch's concern.

"I'm not sure why you feel that your mouth has to be punished so aggressively, my darling husband," Loch said from the bathroom doorway. "What's the matter?"

"Just can't stop thinking." Sloane frowned at his reflection.

"About?"

"Everything."

"Could you be a little more specific?"

"Well, if Stoker is right, then Cleus and the cultists are trying to fill a river full of tears to make some weird-ass fruit to bribe the Kindress into waking up Salgumel."

"Technically, it's a stream."

Sloane ignored him and kept going. "But if that's true, why didn't Alexander and Rota find anything when they went to Umbriech's Glen? Why aren't the tears just, you know, magically transporting themselves there like they used to when they made the Great Tide? And who the fuck is Umbriech?"

"Those are all lovely questions," Loch declared as he strolled up behind Sloane and hugged him. "Of course, I don't know the answers, but they're still very nice questions."

Sloane closed his eyes, trying to enjoy Loch's strong arms and tentacles curling around him. "I'm worried that we have no idea what we're doing, and there's so much at stake. Innocent people are getting hurt, and I feel so helpless."

"Trust that I always know what I'm doing." Loch nuzzled the side of Sloane's neck. "We're going to be fine. Me, you, and our beautiful little spawn. We will figure this out, my darling Starkiller."

Sloane closed his eyes, and he sighed pleasurably as Loch's tentacles massaged his shoulders. In only a few seconds, he was sagging against the sink.

"I have a plan," Loch said confidently. "You'll see."

"Oh?"

"Yes." Loch slid his hands beneath Sloane's shirt, rubbing his belly. "First, I am going to take you to bed. Once you have been thoroughly ravaged, I am going to tuck you in and let you rest... while I finish the laundry and put the dishes away."

"Gods, yeah." Sloane grinned. "And the trash? You'll take that out too?"

"I certainly will."

"Fuck, why is that getting me hot?" Sloane laughed, rocking back into Loch's hands as more tentacles moved over his body. He really was getting turned on, and he groaned softly when Loch's tentacles rubbed his cock through his sweats.

"I do not know, but I will happily continue." Loch mouthed up the side of Sloane's neck, his voice a hot whisper in Sloane's ear as he went on, "I will match all the socks instead of leaving them to languish in that little white basket. I'll dust the entire apartment. The ceiling fans too."

"You're so good to me." Sloane sighed adoringly, his cock growing hard beneath Loch's firm touch. "Mmm, that feels nice."

"Come to bed, and I will make you feel much nicer."

Sloane turned so he could kiss Loch, hugging his neck as Loch's tentacles curled around him. He barely felt his feet leave the ground as Loch carried him to their bed, and he happily drank in the ever-present minty taste of Loch's lips. His clothes vanished, and he murmured curiously when Loch laid him facedown on the bed.

"You've been very busy, my darling husband. Worrying about the world, our city, our family." Loch kneeled on the bed beside Sloane and slid his hands up Sloane's bare back.

A scented oil had materialized, allowing Loch's fingers to glide smoothly against Sloane's skin. The pressure was fantastic, and Sloane let out a happy groan as Loch's tentacles joined in on the action to rub him down.

He hadn't realized how tense he was until Loch was working out a knot that felt like it was the size of a baseball, and he melted into the bed. "Mmm, that's… mmm, that's amazing, Loch."

"I know." Loch was smiling as he kept on massaging Sloane, his tentacles moving down Sloane's hips and thighs to rub there too. "You're rather amazing yourself, my sweet mate."

Sloane's reply was another happy grumble, and he worried that he was in danger of falling asleep. His erection had flagged, though there was residual heat simmering inside him. The massage was wonderful but maybe too relaxing, and he fidgeted as he fought to stay awake.

Perhaps sensing that Sloane was getting a bit sleepy, Loch sent a tentacle to rub right between his cheeks.

"Mm, does that need to be massaged too?" Sloane chuckled.

"Oh yes," Loch said seriously. "It's very tight here. Definitely needs to be rubbed vigorously. We must relieve the tension."

Sloane's laughter faded into a light groan, and his cock stiffened back up from the intense attention. He shifted his hips, savoring the slow stretch as Loch pressed the tip of his tentacle in. Loch's other tentacles were still curling and rubbing all over his body, but Sloane's focus was zeroed in on the one sliding inside of him.

It was hot, wet, and Loch was moving at a crawl, letting Sloane feel every sweet second of the tentacle dragging against his most intimate walls. Sloane grabbed the sheets beneath him, shivering from the intense sensation, and he moaned when a second tentacle pressed against his hole.

"Is this all right, my beautiful love?" Loch had crawled up behind Sloane, and he leaned down to kiss his shoulder. "I want to open you up for me. For all of me."

"Yes," Sloane gasped. "I want it." He arched his back and tried to push into the second tentacle. "Gods, yes, please. Give it to me."

"Mmm, my darling mate…." Loch's voice had a deep purr now, a rumble that seemed to resonate throughout the entire room. "I will. I will give you everything."

Sloane inhaled sharply as the second tentacle penetrated him, the wave of increased pressure leaving him writhing. There was never pain, but the sudden fullness made him ache, and he had to grind his hips down to help relieve it. "Ah, f-fuck…."

"Breathe for me," Loch whispered. "Just breathe for me." He pushed both tentacles as one massive appendage, moving in and out with careful, smooth thrusts.

"Ah… mmm…. Loch!" Sloane nearly shouted and tried to quiet himself down. The last thing he wanted was to wake up Pandora because he was being too loud.

Shaking his head, Loch urged, "No, don't. Go on, my beautiful husband. Let me hear you. I'll make sure our little spawn doesn't stir."

Sloane didn't even question what magic Loch was using to accomplish that, far too relieved to be able to let go and moan frantically as Loch's tentacles fucked him deeper. There were tentacles squeezing his thighs and hips, and more around his arms and slinking beneath his body to caress his chest.

The touches were overwhelming, and Sloane shivered from so much pleasurable contact. His nipples were hard, teased to firmness by the tentacles, and he was flushed and sweating. The tentacles fucking him felt so good, and he was already close to coming.

He knew it would likely be the first climax of many, but he still resisted the temptation to come right away. He loved drawing it out, trying to forestall the inevitable, and he groaned excitedly as Loch twisted the tentacles inside of him to create a burst of wondrous ecstasy. He couldn't stop himself now, coming with a frantic cry and gritting his teeth as Loch fucked through the quick pulses of pleasure.

"There you go," Loch soothed, peppering Sloane's shoulder and neck with little kisses. "There, my gorgeous mate... oh, how I love feeling you quiver around me."

Sloane whimpered in reply, fighting to catch his breath while the tentacles continued to move. Loch had slowed back down, and the lazy thrusting was weirdly relaxing. All he had to do was sag down into the sheets and let Loch worship him, and it was fantastic. "Mmmm, Loch. That's so good."

"Just good, hmm?" Loch teased. "I suppose that means I'll have to try harder." He used the grip of the tentacles to turn Sloane on his side and then got settled down behind him. He hugged Sloane's waist, his tentacles sliding over Sloane's hip and grabbing a hold of the leg he wasn't lying on so it could be stretched toward the ceiling.

"Oh f-fuck!" Sloane jerked, moaning at the new depth the tentacles fucking him could achieve in this position. He arched back, unsure if the noises he was making right now were even human—breathy grunts and strangled cries as he was lost to the sweet pounding inside of him.

"Yes, my darling husband," Loch whispered heatedly. "Yes, take it... take all of it."

Sloane babbled more happy nonsense, and he clung to Loch's arms around him to brace himself. The delicious pressure of another orgasm was building, this one faster than before, and he swore Loch's tentacles were reaching new and unexplored depths. He was full, hot, and he whimpered as each tentacle took turns thrusting inside his hole before twisting together to slam forward as one mass again.

His climax took his breath away, and his leg kicked in the tentacles' grasp. He was overcome with shivers and twitches, and his cock pulsed so many times that he sobbed. Loch came with him, pumping two thick loads inside of him, and prompted Sloane to orgasm again. His vision went nearly white, and he screamed as his entire body shook, ever grateful for Loch's strong grip to hold him tight while he writhed.

"Gods... f-fuck... mmm.... Mmm!" Sloane was certain that the room was spinning, and he struggled to breathe through the waves of blissful sensation. Loch's come was leaking out of him in steady gushes as he continued to thrust, and Sloane wiggled his hips in protest. "Mm, wait. Wait just a second."

"What's the matter, my sweet Starkiller?" Loch ceased immediately, turning Sloane onto his back so he could look at him. "Are you all right?"

"Mmhmm. Just need a second… you know, before my head explodes." Sloane laughed.

Loch smiled and leaned in for a soft kiss. "Did I bring you great pleasure?"

"Oh, such great pleasure," Sloane mumbled. "Very great."

"Do you still desire the rest of me?"

"Gods, yeah." Sloane pulled Loch over on top of him and spread his legs wide for it—the *tentacock*.

The monstrous, giant, knotted tentacle that only had one singular purpose, and that was giving the most exquisite pleasure imaginable. It was laughably big, with a pointed head, thick ribbing along the shaft, and a bulbous knot about eight inches down, and it seemed impossible for any person to take on and live to tell the tale.

But Sloane had, would again, and couldn't wait to have it now.

The other tentacles had left his body, and he clenched just to feel how open and wet he was. He cradled Loch's face, beaming up at him. "I love you."

Loch's eyes turned black, inky pools of shining stars, and he smiled. "I love you too, my beautiful Starkiller."

The first press of Loch's tentacock made Sloane gasp, and he whined as the next thrust made him shudder. The stretch from the tentacock's huge girth was extraordinary, and Sloane grabbed on to Loch's shoulders to ground himself. There wouldn't be pain, there never was, but it was a sense of *feeling* that was so keen it made it hard to think clearly. He lost himself to it, his entire world vanishing except the intimate point of connection between his body and Loch's.

It was searing pressure, intoxicating heat, and waves of tingling pleasure as every nerve inside exploded from the otherworldly stimulation. He was full enough that it ached, and his breath caught as he tried to pant through each deep thrust. The knot was right there, pressing against his hole and seeking entry.

Sloane found he could move his legs freely now, and he hiked them up around Loch's hips. He wanted to be as close as possible, and he wrapped himself around Loch, mirroring how Loch's tentacles were coiled around him. Loch's tentacock was magically wet, and it slid in and out effortlessly, but it was still being stopped from going farther by the thick knot.

Squirming desperately, Sloane pleaded, "Loch, please... I need it...."

"Patience." Loch kissed Sloane's cheek. "Almost, my beloved mate. Almost there."

"Loch... mm... mmm—fuck!" Sloane let out a blissful shout as the knot popped inside. His thighs shook with the promise of another climax, and he dragged his nails across Loch's spine. He was beyond full, barely able to move now, and he moaned, every deliriously blissful thought racing through his head. "Oh, I love you. You're so perfect. You're everything. You're amazing. I love you so much—"

"I love you too. Oh, how I love you." Loch groaned, his tentacock swelling and pulsing as he came.

"I love you," Sloane croaked, blinking away tears as he felt his insides swell from the massive flood of come. The knot was tight and hot, holding the tentacock firmly in place, and his body trembled as he gave up another intense climax. He saw stars dancing in front of his eyes, and all of his muscles were utterly exhausted from the cascading symphonies of bliss.

He forgot how to breathe for a few moments, his hips weakly jerking forward as his cock spilled its very last drop. He wheezed, desperate for air now, gasping, "Oh *fuck*!"

Loch kissed him passionately, allowing quick pauses for Sloane to catch his breath, and he snuggled close. "Mmm, my beloved husband, you were fantastic."

"Thanks," Sloane grunted, laughing a little. "You were pretty freakin' fantastic too."

"Thank you." Loch beamed. "Do you feel better now?"

"Oh, definitely. Much better."

"See, mating is always the answer." Loch snuggled against Sloane's side, burying his head into Sloane's shoulder.

"No, it's not." Sloane laughed quietly. "Although maybe it helps a little." He groaned as Loch's tentacock shifted inside of him. "Ah, mmm, fuck. Okay, fine. Helps more than a little."

"That's what I thought." Loch grinned and hugged Sloane's middle, gently pulling his tentacock free as the knot wilted.

"Mmm…." Sloane closed his eyes and enjoyed the weird, empty feeling. He wrinkled his nose at the rush of leaking fluids, and he was grateful for Loch's magic to clean it up with a thought. "Thank you. I really did need that."

"Happy to help!" Loch said cheerfully. "And I am still going to clean all the things I promised."

"You really are amazing." Sloane smiled, coaxing Loch close enough for a kiss. "Mmm, and now I am really, really tired."

"Sleep, my beautiful husband. I have wrecked your mortal body beyond your understanding. Rest now, and I will take care of everything." Loch bumped their noses together. "I love you."

"Love you too." Sloane smiled as he drifted off into a deep sleep. He didn't stir again until the next morning when he woke up to the sound of Pandora's giggles and Loch's stern voice drifting in from the kitchen.

"And then we command the bacon not to burn by using a very firm tone," Loch was saying. "But because we are not cheating, we must turn it now so that the burning stops."

"Burnnnn!" Pandora growled with surprising malice.

"No, no. No burning, little one. No burning the bacon."

Sloane got out of bed and headed to the bathroom, hoping the smoke alarm wouldn't go off anytime soon. After washing up, he checked his phone. He had at least a dozen missed calls from numbers he didn't know, but no voicemails. While it was a little strange, he decided not to worry about it and went to the kitchen to find his husband and child.

Pandora was perched on Loch's shoulder like a parrot as he cooked on the stove.

"Good morning," Sloane said, reaching up to playfully tug on Pandora's foot. "Hi there!"

"Dad!" Pandora squealed and launched herself into Sloane's arms. "Da-da-dad!"

"Oof, hey, baby girl." Sloane hugged her, leaning up to kiss Loch's cheek. "Mm, morning."

"Good morning, my gorgeous husband." Loch beamed. "Did you sleep well?"

"Very well." Sloane rubbed Pandora's back as he shifted her to his other arm. She was definitely bigger today. "How long have you two been up?"

"Not long," Loch replied. "We were going to surprise you with breakfast in bed. So, if you please, go back to bed right now and pretend you never saw anything."

Sloane laughed. "What's on the menu this morning, chef?"

"Ah, eggs poached in seasoned water on feta and avocado toast with bacon."

"Mm, that sounds amazing."

"May-zinggg," Pandora echoed. "Bayyy-con. Bayyy-con. Mayyyy-zing." She snuggled into Sloane's shoulder, happily babbling away.

Sloane heard his phone ringing, and he carried Pandora with him to answer it where he'd forgotten it in the bedroom. "Hello, Beaumont Investigations?"

"Morning," Chase grumbled. He sounded exhausted.

"Hey, Chase! You okay?"

"Oh, uh-huh, yeah. Fuckin' peachy."

Pandora's eyes widened when she saw the phone, and she tried to grab it.

"Ah-ah, don't touch," Sloane warned.

"Huh?" Chase grunted.

"Not you. Panda." Sloane tried switching the phone to his other ear to keep it from her. "What's up?"

"Long night. Safe drops for the swirly shit aren't fillin' as fast as we'd like. Seventeen more dead, so now we're up to twenty drowning victims."

"Shit." Sloane walked back to the kitchen, still fighting to keep Pandora's eager fingers away from the phone.

"Yeah." Chase sighed. "Needless to say, I did not fuckin' sleep much. This has been absolute hell. Any cool Sage tricks for gettin' rid of fuckin' nightmares?"

"Put jasmine under your pillow. That's what my mom always did for me."

"Huh. Cool. I'll ask Merry when he gets back."

"Where's he at?"

"Tryin' to explain to the captain why we ain't bringin' you in for questioning. Jig is up, Smoane. Someone figured out who you are."

"Shit." Sloane put the phone on speaker. "Seriously?"

"Yup. It's all over the morning news."

"What is?" Loch asked, not even looking up from his plating. He was using all of his tentacles and a slotted spoon to carefully deposit the poached eggs on top of the toast.

"Wait until you see the headlines. Sloane Beaumont, Sagittarian savior or savage Sage?" Chase snorted.

"Great." Sloane sighed, holding out the phone to keep it out of Pandora's reach.

Fussing stubbornly, Pandora stretched her hand toward it. "May… mayyyzing! May!"

"I wouldn't go by your office if I was you," Chase warned. "Press is there. I also would not answer your door. Only a matter of time before these scumbags figure—"

Pandora's hand morphed into a tentacle, swiping at the phone and pushing the End Call button. "Mayzing!"

"Panda!" Sloane scolded. "That was important."

"Mayzingggg!" Pandora cheered and waved her tentacle, laughing excitedly.

"Come here, little one." Loch swept Pandora away with his tentacles and set her back on his shoulder. "Bad spawn, bad!"

"At least she didn't set it on fire," Sloane mumbled, calling Chase back.

"Sloane?" Chase sounded confused. "Sorry, I must have pushed somethin'. Fuckin' phones—"

"No, it wasn't you," Sloane cut in. "It was Pandora. She's decided she likes phones."

"Ha, cute." Chase cleared his throat. "Look, all I'm sayin' is try to keep your head down. Me and Merry are gonna handle our end here, take a statement from you, and that should be the end of it."

Sloane frowned. "I'm not in any trouble, am I?"

"Eh. It's the sword."

"What about it?"

"You were technically brandishing a deadly magical weapon on a public street."

"Seriously?" Sloane scoffed.

"It's a blade of pure starlight that was given to him by Great Azaethoth himself." Loch huffed. "I do not see how mortal laws apply to such a divine gift."

"Well, they do, and it's dumb." Chase sighed.

"Does it matter that I was brandishing said magical weapon at a god?" Sloane demanded.

"Yeah, no, because now the official AVPD stance is that those were summoned abominations. You know, the good ol' Lucian stance. But hey, Merry is on it. If anyone can slide through all that bureaucratic bullshit and come out clean, it's him."

"Gordoth the Slut will be victorious," Loch declared as he carried the breakfast plates and Pandora over to the table. "I know it."

"Thanks for the warning, Chase." Sloane followed Loch and sat down. "Anything else going on?"

"City's gone to fuckin' hell, everybody is losin' their fuckin' minds, and we ain't got no clue where Jeffy boy is hidin' out," Chase replied dutifully. "Same shit, different day."

"I guess Ollie hasn't had any luck with the scroll?"

"Haven't heard anything yet, but it's a little early for him to be up." Chase chuckled. "He was workin' late tryin' to help Alexander and Rota look for Jeff. We'll probably hear somethin' when the time hits double digits."

"Fair."

Even though she was buckled in her high chair, Pandora made a valiant effort to reach the phone again. Her arms stretched out into tentacles, and she nearly got a hold of it before Sloane moved out of the way.

"You guys take care," Chase said. "Later."

"Bye, Chase." Sloane hung up and then stuck the phone in his lap to hopefully remove the temptation. "Shit, shit, shit."

"Shit, shit, shit," Pandora repeated flawlessly.

Loch burst out laughing.

"Don't say that, Panda. That's a bad word." Sloane tried not to laugh, and he ducked his head.

"Shit?" Pandora blinked.

"Listen to Dad. It's a terrible word." Loch cackled. "Oh, is that not the most precious thing?"

"Don't laugh!" Sloane protested. "If she thinks it's funny, she'll keep doing it."

"Oh, but it *is* funny, and I cannot stop."

With a firm handful of avocado, Pandora swung her legs and sang, "Shitttt! Shit, shit, shit!"

Sloane shook his head, still doing his best not to react, and he quickly smothered the urge with a mouthful of toast. He was surprised by how flavorful the combination of feta and avocado worked with the egg, and he moaned loudly. "Mmmm, that's good."

Loch jerked to attention, having to raise his voice to be heard over Pandora. "I'm sorry, what was that? Did you just… was that the Moan?"

"It probably was." Sloane grinned and went in for another big bite. "This is great. I love it."

"But I can't hear you over our child's cursing."

"Serves you right for encouraging her."

"Hmmph." Loch stood from the table with his nose in the air and marched off toward the living room.

"Hey, what are you doing?" Sloane chuckled. "Come back. I'll moan again, I promise."

"I'm going to see what the television has to say about you," Loch said as he parked himself on the couch. "Maybe there will be a tip line I can call in and tell them how cruel you are."

"Your daddy is very silly," Sloane told Pandora.

"Shit," she agreed, munching away on a blob of egg. "Shit, shit, shit."

"Really stuck on that word, huh?" Sloane snorted. "Guess it could be worse." His phone rang, and it was a number he didn't know. That wasn't so unusual given his line of work, and he answered it. "Hello, Beaumont Investigations?"

"Hello!" an oddly familiar male voice greeted him. "My name is William Zabel. I'm a journalist, and I write for the Archersville Star. I was hoping I could interview you for—"

"No. Sorry." Sloane made a face. "You have a great day now!" He hung up.

"Who was that?" Loch asked.

"William Zabel. That tabloid reporter from the press conference? He wanted to interview me."

"Ah. Did he ask about me?"

"No." Before Sloane could say anything else, his phone rang again. It was the same number Zabel had called from, so he ignored it. His phone rang yet again with a different number, and he hesitated before picking up. "Hello, Beaumont Investigations, how may I help you?"

"Hey," a female voice said excitedly. "Is this really the guy on TV? You are so hot—"

"Thanks, uh, that's very nice of you. Goodbye!" Sloane groaned as he ended the call.

"Now who was that?" Loch frowned.

"Some woman telling me I'm hot because she saw me on TV."

"Well, it's obvious her vision is flawless," Loch said cheerfully as he pointed at the television. "Even though I am angry with you, you are so very handsome on television. Hmm, I don't see a number for a tip line. They really should be showing more of me."

"Daaaa! Daddd!" Pandora squealed.

"That's right, sweet one. That's Dad! Your mean, thoughtless Dad."

The news was playing the clip of Sloane jumping on top of the car again, and then the feed cut to a reporter interviewing Olivia Harker from Sagely Wisdom out on the sidewalk somewhere in the city.

"Smoane or Sloane or whatever his name is, is a hero," Olivia was insisting. "I know what I saw, and he totally saved me. I believe the old gods sent him to protect me."

"And you're sure that the man who extinguished the flames at your former employer is in fact Sloane Beaumont, local private investigator?" the reporter prompted.

"Oh, no doubt. He might have been wearing a glamour, but it was totally him. Did you see that jacket?"

Sloane rolled his eyes. His phone was ringing, another unknown caller, and he ignored it.

Pandora was entranced by the television, so at least she had stopped cursing. But when Sloane's phone happened to ring next, she cried and reached out for it as if it was the most important thing in the entire universe.

"Ah-ah," Sloane scolded. "No phone for you, young lady. Eat your eggs. Cuss some more." He cringed as her cries reached a particularly ear-piercing pitch, saying loudly, "Hello! Beaumont Investigations?"

"Hey! Sloane! It's Robert!"

"Hey, Robert!" Sloane smiled. "How are you doing?"

Robert Edwards was Lochlain's husband, and he owned a jewelry store that served as a front for trafficking illegal and rare magical items—usually stolen by Lochlain himself.

"That woman on the news," Robert said urgently. "I know her."

"Olivia Harker, right!" Sloane tried to distract Pandora with a piece of toast, but she only screamed more frantically. "From Sagely Wisdom!"

"No, no. I mean, yes, but no, that's not how I know her." Robert sighed in frustration. "Gods, sorry, I'm just trying to get this out—"

"What's wrong?"

"She's with Jeff Martin. She's one of the cultists."

CHAPTER 9.

"WHAT?" SLOANE almost laughed, because there was no way Robert had said what he thought he'd just said.

"What's wrong?" Loch frowned. "Is this because of the television? Are you getting rabid phone calls from admirers already?"

"One sec!" Sloane waved Loch over to help calm Pandora.

"You let them know that you're happily married!" Loch said firmly as he traded places with Sloane at the table.

"I know her!" Robert insisted. "Well, not personally, but listen. Demand for Sagittarian artifacts has been insane over the last few months, right?"

"Yeah, I remember you and Lochlain telling us about that," Sloane said.

Loch presented Pandora with one of his tentacles for her to play with, and it quieted her crying long enough for Sloane to switch the phone call over to speaker so Loch could hear Robert as well.

"I had gotten tons of Salgumel enthusiasts, no surprise there, and she was one of them," Robert went on. "I'd know that voice anywhere. She called me nonstop, wanting anything and everything she could get her hands on that was related to Salgumel. She had the funding, so we did some business.

"Nothing dangerous, of course, just trinkets and a few minor spells. But the last time we talked on the phone, I heard her talking to a man in the background, and she called him Jeff. Not even thinking, I blurted out, 'Jeff Martin?' She laughed, played it off, and well, that was it. I never heard from her again."

"You're sure?"

"Yes." Robert sighed. "Look, I know it's probably a big stretch, but I talked to Lochlain, and he agreed that I should call you guys and tell you about it anyway."

"What else can you tell me? Address, phone number?"

"No, nothing. I never knew her name, and she always used a burner phone. We only ever dealt in cash, and we arranged drop points to complete transactions."

"That's… less than helpful." Sloane grimaced.

"Sorry. Typical for, ahem, this kind of business deal."

"Stoker did business with Jeff before," Sloane mused out loud. "Do you think he's ever worked with her?"

"Possible," Robert answered. "Like I said, she seemed pretty eager to get a hold of everything she could. I wouldn't be surprised if she went to him too. Money was not an issue."

Pandora grew tired of amusing herself with Loch's tentacle, and her big eyes again found the phone. She reached out for it longingly and started to fuss again.

"No, sweet girl. Not right now." Sloane made sure to stay out of her tentacle grabbing range.

"Aw, is that Pandora?" Robert laughed. "I can hear her babbling about something."

"She wants my phone." Sloane snorted. "And she's not getting it."

"Poor thing." Robert chuckled. "Look, I'm sorry I couldn't be of more help."

"No, hey, it's a lead. I'll take it. I'll talk to Chase and Merrick, see if they can dig anything up on her."

"Tell Lochlain I expect to steal something valuable with him soon," Loch announced. "We have yet to commit a respectable heist since he was resurrected, and I am starting to take it personally."

There was a thump, the sound of something possibly breaking, and an excited string of muffled words—presumably Lochlain.

Robert laughed. "I'll let him know, Azaethoth. Don't worry. He's looking forward to it."

"Hmmph. Thank you."

"Thanks, Robert!" Sloane waited for Robert to say goodbye before ending the call so he could call Chase. He got his voicemail and opted to send a text instead, detailing what Robert had told them.

Pandora gave up eating in favor of trying to escape her high chair. Seeing that she clearly wasn't going to eat any more, Loch got her cleaned up and carried her over to the living room to play.

Sloane got down on the floor with her to stack blocks while Loch cleaned the kitchen. Although he never used magic to cook, he certainly did to tidy up. Loch joined them in the living room after a quick snap took care of the mess, and Sloane dealt with several more phone calls. It was more of the same, reporters and busybodies, and he did his best to politely decline comment and hang up. Pandora had just finished her second round of block demolition when Sloane's phone rang again.

Squealing excitedly, Pandora lunged for it as soon as she saw it come out of Sloane's pocket.

"No, little spawn." Loch plucked her off the rug to distract her with smooches and raspberries on her neck. "You leave that alone, hmm? Let Dad answer the awful little phone."

"Really am starting to dread that ringing sound," Sloane grumbled. He cleared his throat before answering, "Beaumont Investigations, how may I help you?"

"Hey!" Chase said grimly. "It's me. We got some real treats for you. You ready?"

"That good?" Sloane frowned and pushed the speaker button.

"Olivia Harker's real name is Olivia Hutchison. She got busted for shoplifting a few years ago, so we had her prints in the system. Trust fund brat, filthy rich, some other little drug charges Daddy and Mommy made go away… hmm. She's got a place near the mall."

"Okay."

"So here's the deal. Merrick has his fingers in his ears so he doesn't hear me tell you this, but we can't exactly go by there and look around. We have zero probable cause, and I already got the stank eye checking up on her because, oh, you're gonna love this. Guess who her uncle is?"

"Who?"

"Mayor Penche."

"Really?" Sloane made a face.

"Yup." Chase popped his tongue. "Our hands are tied for anything official."

"Oh, but we are not official," Loch said gleefully. "Our hands are free to do many unofficial things."

"That's why Merrick has plugged his ears right now and is humming. Loudly."

"Got it," Sloane said. "You can't go snoop around, but we can."

"Yeah, plus we're still drowning in paperwork—" Chase grunted. "Ah shit. Sorry. Real poor choice of words. You know what I mean."

"It's okay." Sloane grimaced. "Just give us a little bit to get Galgareth over here to watch Pandora."

"Hey! Why don't you let me and Merry come babysit?"

"Seriously?"

"I am super good with kids, and we could totally use a break. We've been goin' nonstop at this shit, and it's not like you're gonna be gone super long, right? Merry can just tell 'em it's a family emergency."

"Uh…." Sloane looked to Loch.

"I'm sure my uncle and Chase are more than capable of watching our little spawn." Loch smiled and bounced Pandora in his lap. "It will be nice for them all to bond together."

"Chase, did Merrick actually agree to this?" Sloane pressed.

"His ears are still plugged," Chase replied, "but I'm sure it's fine. Don't worry about it. We'll be right over, okay? I promise he won't care."

Merrick did care.

Merrick, in fact, cared a lot, and he brought along two banker's boxes full of files.

"Oh, hey! What's all this?" Sloane asked as he held the door open for them when they arrived a short while later.

"Remember the paperwork I told you about that we were, uh, up to our eyeballs in? You know, because my godly partner won't use his magic to just poof it all away?" Chase grunted as he hefted the box he was carrying to the kitchen counter. "This is it."

"It is but a small fraction of what we actually have to complete," Merrick said firmly, following after Chase and setting down the box he had next to Chase's. "I was being kind."

"Kind, he says." Chase tipped his hat to Merrick. "Oh wow, thank you. Your benevolence is fuckin' overwhelming."

Merrick narrowed his eyes. "I should have brought more boxes."

"Uncle!" Loch eagerly greeted Merrick, and he gave him a big hug. "Thank you so much for coming!"

Merrick's grumpy expression softened, and he hugged Loch back. "Of course, Azzath. We appreciate your assistance as well."

"Now!" Chase clapped. "Where is the little lady at?"

Pandora had pulled herself up on the couch, and she was peering curiously at Chase and Merrick.

"Right there." Sloane smiled. "Checking you guys out."

"Wow, she's already standing up on her own too?" Chase headed right over and crouched down to talk to her, smiling as he said, "Hi there, little lady. You've grown a whole freakin' bunch since we saw you! How ya' doin'?"

Pandora's eyes widened, and she was oddly silent, though she did reach for Chase's hat.

He let her take it, smoothing his long hair back. "There you go, little lady. It's all yours. Wanna try it on? I bet you'd look real cute."

Pandora threw it on the floor.

"There, okay. It looks good there too."

"Be careful," Merrick said sternly, speaking to Sloane and Loch. "If Olivia Hutchinson truly is involved with the cultists, she may be more dangerous than we first anticipated. I have already deduced that she must have been using the magical underwear from the store to deflect our truth spells, and there is no telling what else she may have at her disposal."

"We'll be careful, Uncle," Loch promised.

"And you're sure you guys will be okay with Pandora?" Sloane glanced back to see Pandora in Chase's lap now, thoroughly examining his beard.

"Oh yeah," Chase said, grinning even as Pandora gave his beard a firm tug. "We'll be just peachy keen, won't we, little jelly bean?"

Pandora pulled on Chase's beard, frowned when it didn't detach, and muttered an oddly exasperated sounding, "Shit."

Sloane rubbed his forehead and tried not to laugh.

"Ah, already teaching her the finer points of human expression, huh?" Chase grinned.

"Something like that."

"Don't worry. I won't add any more new fancy words to her vocabulary."

"I'm a lot more worried about her setting you on fire."

Chase laughed. Then he frowned. "Wait, are you serious?"

"Oh. Very."

After fretting only a bit more and showing Chase and Merrick where the bottles, formula, snacks, and fire extinguisher were all located, Sloane and Loch finally headed over to Olivia's home. It was a big townhouse near the university, and Loch skillfully blinked them over around the corner from it where no one would see them.

The garage in the rear was empty, but Sloane knew that didn't mean the house was. Olivia or whoever else could still be there, so when they came to the front door, he knocked.

Sloane had put a new glamour on, an older man with a beard, and he had opted to leave his usual black jacket at home. He didn't want to risk being recognized after all that mess on the news.

The incessant phone calls were bad enough.

When no one answered the door, Sloane examined it with a perception spell. "Warded up to the hilt. They're old, and there's a lot of them."

Loch grinned. "Ah, good! I do love a challenge." He turned his back to the sidewalk and held out his hand, a tentacle slipping out from his sleeve to probe the sides of the doorframe.

Sloane stood beside him to help shield anyone passing by from getting a glimpse of an old god breaking and entering.

The lock clicked, and Loch opened the door with a flourish. "Ah! I have achieved a small crime. Today is a good day."

"Let's try to keep it to just the one?" Sloane smirked.

"I cannot make that promise." Loch took the lead inside, strolling into a very posh living room full of Sagittarian artifacts.

There was a giant painting of Salgumel over the fireplace, his thick tentacle beard writhing across the canvas and his wings spread out above his head. There was a mammoth sculpture of him flanking the stairs and dozens upon dozens of various reliefs and icons. Exhibits at museums didn't have a fraction of what Olivia did.

"Well." Sloane clicked his tongue as he closed the door behind them. "I think it's safe to say that Olivia is a big fan of Salgumel."

Loch wrinkled his nose.

"Let's look around. Make sure we're alone?"

"Happily." Loch turned and skipped up the stairs, pausing only to stick out his tongue at the sculpture.

Cautiously, Sloane walked through the living room into the kitchen with a hand raised for a perception spell. The kitchen opened into a small dining room that looped back around to the front door. Other than a few more Sagittarian artifacts and their magical residue, he didn't see anything of note.

He headed upstairs, calling, "Loch?"

"Yes, my beloved mate?" Loch called back. "In here. Bedroom at the end of the hallway."

Sloane followed Loch's voice and the directions, and he found Loch digging through a large chest at the foot of the bed. He leaned against the doorframe, smirking. "Anything good?"

"Hardly." Loch held out a ratty teddy bear with a mournful sigh. "This is pitiful. Four complex magical seals broken and for what? I was expecting something tremendously valuable. Instead, my amazing thieving skills are being insulted with this."

"A teddy bear?"

"It is disappointment. In the form of a teddy bear."

"Ah." Sloane moved over to a desk where a small calendar was propped up against a lamp. He ignored the calendar for now, his focus drawn to a notebook with tentacles doodled all over the cover.

There were pieces of paper crammed between pages, and Sloane was startled to see that they were various stages of the swirling design. "Shit."

"What is it, my sweet Starkiller?" Loch came to his side. "Did you find a clue?"

"Yeah. A big one." Sloane showed him the pages. "If I'm reading these right, Olivia may have been the one who helped turn the death song of the Kindress into a hip cool design to plaster on T-shirts for Jeff and Daisy." He kept turning pages. "Look, she did all of them."

Loch grimaced. "Well, then I would say we can confirm she is definitely in the cahoots with the cultists."

"Yeah." Sloane flipped back to an earlier page. "This is the death song, but it looks… longer. There's a whole other section here by the bottom."

"Is that also a clue?"

"Maybe." Sloane took out his phone to snap pictures, though he had to ignore a few unknown numbers first so he could access the camera. "We can have Ollie take a look, see what it says." He sighed. "I guess you haven't heard anything from Asta yet, huh?"

"Not a peep. Best not to rely on the filthy cat creature for help. They are not to be trusted."

"I was actually hoping for a chance to talk to Professor Kunst if he's still serving as Royal Occult Advisor or whatever."

Loch tilted his head. "To apologize for unaliving him?"

"That." Sloane grimaced at the unpleasant memory. "And he was also an expert on Sagittarian lore and Salgumel in particular. Maybe he'd know something that could help us."

"If only we could rely on filthy cat creatures for help. But we cannot."

Sloane's phone rang, and he answered it when he recognized the person calling. "Hey, Fred!"

"Hey," Fred's gravelly voice grunted. "You got a second?"

"Yeah, of course. What's—"

Loch practically tackled Sloane. "Is it about his penis?"

Swatting Loch back, Sloane tried to keep talking. "Uh, is everything okay?"

"Tell Azaethoth it ain't my dick," Fred grumbled. "I'm callin' for help with somethin' else."

"What's wrong?"

"It's Ell. He got a little roughed up goin' to the store with me. He don't like goin' out much anyway, and well…."

Loch tried to sneak a tentacle over to grab the phone.

Sloane ducked and backed away as he put the call on speaker. "Is he okay? Did he get hurt?"

"No, he's okay," Fred replied. "It's all the assholes in this fuckin' city who have lost their fuckin' minds. Some bastard tried to grab a bag of groceries right out of Ell's fuckin' hands in the parking lot because the place was runnin' out of stuff. Had to stomp that guy's ass and get Ell home as fast as I could.

"Everybody is actin' like we're about to have a blizzard or somethin'. Just goin' apeshit. It's fuckin' stupid. They ain't got a clue about nothin' with the old gods. All they wanna do is fuckin' start shit, and…." Fred took a deep breath. "Ell didn't get hurt physically, okay, but he ain't doin' good. Seein' all this shit on the news, all them poor people dyin', and then that asshole at the store? It's eatin' at him."

This was the most Sloane had heard Fred speak in one go, and he hated how upset he sounded. "What can we do?"

"I need somethin' to help him sleep, but he ain't exactly human, you know."

Ell was a descendant of the Eldress, one of the everlasting people who were putrid equine creatures with horns. Unlike the everlasting people that Stoker protected in his Hidden World, Ell lived out on his own with Fred. Being part Eldress had given him special powers that made him a very talented healer, which was quite the perk since his boyfriend, Fred, was a ghoul.

"Tried tea, tried some dream totems and jasmine and all that other shit, but it ain't workin'."

"Right. So you need a sleep aid for someone who is part Eldress."

"Yeah." Fred paused. "Can you guys help?"

"Of course, my child," Loch promised. "Are you at home?"

"Yeah, but—"

Loch vanished.

"Loch?" Sloane blinked. "Fred, is he there with you?"

"Fuck. Yeah, hang on." There was a frantic shout in the distance on Fred's end, and then a loud thump. Fred sighed grumpily. "Well, Ell is asleep."

"What happened?"

"Loch snapped his fingers and knocked him out. Ell was in the middle of foldin' laundry."

"Oh, well… at least he's sleeping now?" Sloane made a face.

Loch reappeared, smiling proudly. "I hope Ell has a very good rest. He should sleep for the rest of the day and wake up tomorrow feeling wonderful. I will speak to my sister about creating a special sleeping potion for him that he can take at bedtime."

"Thank you, Azaethoth." Fred cleared his throat. "Seriously. You guys need us for anything with all this crazy shit going down, just holler. I'm, uh, gonna get Ell into bed."

"Of course, sweet mortal child." Loch beamed. "We are here for you. And if you need any help with your p—"

"Bye." Fred hung up.

Loch scoffed.

"Maybe stop asking him about his penis?" Sloane suggested, sliding his phone back in his pocket. "Just a thought."

"I wasn't going to say penis," Loch said indignantly. "I was going to say pantry."

"Sure you were."

"I took a quick peek while I was there. They need much better snacks." Loch held out a granola bar. "See? Pfft. Generic. This is peasant food."

"Uh-huh." Sloane walked back to the desk so he could check the drawers. He found more papers, some bills, but not much else that seemed like it would be helpful. He finally looked at the calendar. "Huh. Olivia's got a date tomorrow night."

"A date?" Loch took a big bite of the granola bar.

"See all the little hearts? Looks like a date to me."

"J at nine, Flaming Amy's."

Sloane squinted. "Is that a J or a C?"

Loch hummed thoughtfully through a mouthful of pilfered granola. "I believe it's a J. What's a Flaming Amy's?"

"It's a restaurant. They serve a lot of flambé and fancy food they set on fire at your table."

"Ah."

"Think it's J for Jeff, maybe?" Sloane frowned. "But why would she be meeting him out in public at a restaurant like this?"

"Maybe she's stupid."

"Maybe." Sloane glanced around the room once more. He cringed when his phone rang again. A quick glance revealed it was Mr. Zabel calling, so he ignored it. "We should get back home and check on Panda Bear. Make sure she hasn't barbequed Chase or Merrick."

"I'm sure they're fine. Mostly."

"They may want us to stake out this restaurant. It's a long shot, but this could be our first real chance to get the drop on Jeff on our terms."

"Then what are we waiting for? Let us go prepare for the stakeout at once! We will need coffee and fast food in foil wrappers. No granola bars. Oh, and cigarettes."

"Cigarettes?" Sloane laughed.

"People smoke on stakeouts, do they not? We can get some from Alexander or the local gas station—"

"Hey, hey. We need to be careful. Whatever Olivia is up to, she can't know we're on to her. We gotta keep the element of surprise, okay?"

"Are the drawings of the design not enough to throw her in the slammer?"

"How do Chase and Merrick explain how they found them without a search warrant?"

"Ah."

"Plus, her uncle is Mayor Penche, remember?"

"I do not understand."

"If we fuck this up and she goes crying to her uncle about us harassing her, she could make things difficult. Especially for Merrick and Chase."

Loch frowned. "So what do we do?"

"Hope that date on her calendar means something and it leads us to Jeff. He's the mastermind behind all of this. Always has been. We have to stop him."

"And we shall, my beloved."

"That means we have to be subtle."

"Oh, I'm very good at subtle."

Sloane resisted the urge to argue and said, "Let's get going. I think we're done here."

"I agree. Let us leave and find cigarettes."

Sloane and Loch erased any trace of their visit to Olivia's apartment, including repairing the broken wards and returning the teddy bear to its chest, and then returned home. Nothing had been set on fire, amazingly, and they told Merrick and Chase about what they'd found.

"So you think Olivia is the one who made the design that's killin' everybody, and she's meeting Jeff tonight at some fancy restaurant?" Chase said carefully.

"Yes," Sloane confirmed. "I sent copies of everything to Ollie to read over. Olivia is definitely into collecting all kinds of Sagittarian artifacts like Robert said, so maybe that's how she got the original spells."

"Or Jeff provided them to her for the augmentation," Merrick mused, glancing up from the paperwork he was still filling out.

"Could be." Chase expertly avoided Pandora's swatting hand when she tried to grab his hair. "Okay. Fudge it, we're in."

"A date on a calendar is not much." Merrick frowned. "I am troubled that this is all we have to go on."

"Better than friggin' nothin." Chase and Pandora were on the floor, and he was helping her turn the pages of a baby book with various textured pictures to touch.

Sloane was struck both by Chase's natural ease with her and his obvious efforts not to curse. He sat on the couch beside them, raking his hands through his hair. "If it really is Jeff, we should let Alexander and Rota know too. And Sto—"

"And absolutely no one else," Loch said quickly. "Ah *yes*, good. Perfect plan."

"No. We need to tell Stoker too."

Loch groaned.

"Any and all additional assistance will be needed," Merrick agreed. "It is not just Jeff that we should be concerned with."

"Cleus." Sloane grimaced.

"Yes."

Pandora was no longer interested in the book, and she crawled away from Chase in search of Sloane. When she reached up for him, he scooped her into his lap.

"Maybe have you and Loch be our guys on the inside?" Chase suggested. "I mean, I ain't tryin' to sell myself short or nothin', but if Jeffy boy calls up Cleus for backup—"

"We would be happy to attend dinner at the fancy restaurant!" Loch exclaimed. "I am excited about the potential for fire."

"Fire?" Pandora perked up.

"No, sweetie," Sloane soothed. "No fire—"

"Fiiiiirrrrre!" Pandora roared, clapping and causing the book she'd been reading with Chase to spontaneously combust.

"Fuck!" Chase blurted out as he scrambled away from the flames.

Merrick hurried over to Chase's side, snatching him back with his tentacles.

"Bad spawn! Bad!" Loch scolded. "No more fire in the house."

Pandora laughed.

"That was very naughty," Sloane said firmly. "No fire, young lady. No!"

Pandora stopped clapping and cried, trying to squirm away from Sloane. Tears ran down her face as she kicked her legs angrily.

"Are you all right?" Merrick asked as he hugged Chase close.

"Oh yeah, uh, just peachy." Chase blinked over at Loch and Sloane. "You guys weren't kiddin' about the fire, huh?"

"No." Loch beamed. "Our little spawn is wonderfully talented."

Pandora clenched her hands into fists suddenly, and she growled, "Fuck!"

"And well spoken."

Sloane sighed, doing his best to hold on to her. "And very, very angry."

"Sorry." Chase grinned sheepishly. "That one's on me. So, uh." He stood with Merrick's assistance and then brushed himself off. "Is she all right?"

"Did she nap while we were gone?" Sloane asked, having to raise his voice to be heard over Pandora's growing screams.

"No! We just played a whole bunch, gave her a bottle and—"

"Hey! It's fine." Sloane stood just as his phone rang for the millionth time that day. He groaned and carried Pandora toward her room. "I think it's nap time! We're gonna go take a little nap! Loch, bottle?"

"On it!" Loch zoomed over to the kitchen.

"Here, baby girl," Sloane soothed as he laid Pandora in her crib. He turned off the lights and waved his hand over the little star mobile that hung over her. It glowed brightly, and all the stars began to magically turn in a slow circle.

Pandora kicked furiously, and her hands morphed into tentacles, swinging up at the mobile.

"Shush now," Sloane said softly, petting her hair and smiling. "You're very cranky, huh? Playing with Chase wore you out, I think."

Pandora screamed, and it definitely sounded like a very bad word.

Loch appeared with a bottle, and he offered it to her. "Here, my little angry spawn. Feast on magical formula and rest now."

Though she initially swiped the bottle away, Pandora eventually curled her tentacles around it and dragged it to her mouth.

"There you go," Sloane said. "Good girl. You just take a little nap, okay?"

Loch leaned in to kiss her brow. "Dad and Daddy will be out here if you need us."

Pandora furrowed her brows as if she understood what they were saying and was immediately skeptical, but she started to relax. Her lids closed as she drank her bottle, her tentacles turning back into hands to hold on to it.

Sloane waited until he was certain that Pandora was truly settling down and then headed back out to the living room with Loch. "Whew."

Loch curled a tentacle around Sloane's waist, and he kissed his brow. "We have triumphed."

"Everything okay?" Chased asked. He was on the couch now, and Merrick had returned to the kitchen to tend to the paperwork he had laid out on the counter.

"Yeah, she's okay," Sloane assured him as he shut the door. He checked his phone, swiping away all the missed calls from mystery phone numbers. "No more fires, at least. She just needs to take a nap."

"Kids, huh?" Chase grinned, and it was a fond one. "I remember when Ollie was that age. Happiest lil' guy ever—"

Pandora let out a shrill cry.

Sloane cringed. "Dammit."

"Patience, my sweet husband," Loch said. "Just wait. She will quiet herself. I promise you."

"Perhaps we should discuss who is going to watch her tomorrow evening?" Merrick suggested. "I was thinking we could awaken Urilith."

"Yeah?" Sloane frowned. "What about Galgareth?"

"My honest hope was for Galgareth to accompany us." Merrick set his papers down. "As we have no idea what the true meaning behind Olivia's date is, I want to be prepared for absolutely anything."

Pandora suddenly stopped crying.

Sloane froze.

Something was wrong.

"Including but not limited to the return of Cleus," Merrick went on. He kept talking, but Sloane didn't hear him.

He turned back to the nursery door, terror seizing him right down to the marrow of his bones and cementing his feet to the floor.

Pandora's cries hadn't just trailed off.

The sound had cut off completely.

Cutting through the fear that had locked him in place, Sloane turned to shove the door open so he could propel himself over to Pandora's crib. He grabbed the side of it, the room spinning, and he gasped, staring down at…

Nothing.

Pandora was gone.

CHAPTER 10.

"How? How the fuck did they get in here?"

"Where is she?"

"What happened? How is this possible?"

Everyone's voices were a wild tornado swirling around Sloane's ears, and he hadn't been able to move himself away from the empty crib. He was stuck there, staring down at a forgotten bottle and rumpled blankets. The watchman spell he and Loch had placed on Pandora was broken, so he knew this was not an accidental portal.

His daughter, his baby, was gone because someone had taken her.

"Someone portaled in here," Merrick said. "The trail is faint, but—"

"Let's go! Now!" Sloane tore himself away, and he held out his hands to track the portal.

Loch was faster, and he grabbed Sloane's arm. "Hold on!"

The room vanished in a quick snap, and they were standing in the garage of a body shop. It was empty, closed, and Sloane could smell something burning.

"Pandora!" he screamed, hurrying toward the office. All the bay doors were shut, he didn't sense any portals in here, and there was nowhere else to go.

Again, Loch was quicker, and he pushed the office door open with a wave of tentacles. He was practically feral, tearing into the room with a roar and looking all around. "Where is she?"

"I don't know!" Sloane threw up his hands in a desperate search for another portal they could follow. The longer it took to find, the more difficult it would be to locate. He could see papers on top of the desk were scorched, and he could smell burned plastic wafting from a chair that was still smoldering. He felt certain the damage was from Pandora, but he didn't hear or see any sign of her.

Or any damn portal.

"Loch." Sloane's voice cracked. "I can't...."

"Here!" Loch looped his arm with Sloane's. "Hold on, my love!"

Again the world around them shifted, over and over, as Loch frantically tried to follow the series of portals to find Pandora. They went through a grocery store bathroom, a deli walk-in freezer, parking lots and back alleys, but soon there was nothing to track.

Out of breath and wheezing, Sloane stumbled against the wall of the parking deck they'd ended up in. "No... this can't be...."

Loch stalked back and forth, his tentacles out and flailing angrily. "I can't find another portal. I can't...."

Sloane put up his hands for the most powerful perception spell he could muster, but he didn't see anything either. "Shit! Shit, shit, shit."

Loch was trembling, and he let out an inhuman roar that made the entire parking deck shudder and the cement beneath his feet crack.

It was all Sloane could do not to fall into despair, and he put his hand on Loch's shoulder. "We'll find her. She's our daughter, and we can find her anywhere, right? You've always found me when I needed you."

Loch took a deep breath and nodded. "Yes. And so we shall."

"Let's go back home." Sloane's chest was tight. "I want to know who it was and how the fuck they got into our damn house."

Loch held Sloane tight, smothering a soft, pained growl into his hair. "Whoever they are, they will suffer for this. I will weave their intestines into their own hair. I will do such terrible things to their lungs. I will...." His voice cracked. "I will make them pay."

Sloane hugged Loch close, his body shaking from the leftover adrenaline with nowhere to put it. He didn't want to cry, and it was taking everything he had to keep himself together. Hearing Loch so broken hurt his very soul, and he sniffed back frustrated tears as he whispered, "I know. But first we gotta figure out who they are so we can find her. Okay?"

Loch nodded, his eyes black and glimmering with a mix of starry ink and tears. "Yes. Yes, we will." He embraced Sloane and then blinked them back to the apartment.

Chase and Merrick were in the nursery, combing over every inch together. They both stopped what they were doing to greet Loch and Sloane when they reappeared.

"Hey!" Chase's face fell when he saw it was only the two of them. "You guys didn't find her?"

"No." Sloane grimaced. "We went through at least a dozen portals. We just... we weren't fast enough."

"We are going to keep looking," Loch said sternly. He appeared more confident now, although that may have just been for show in front of Chase and Merrick. "I've found Sloane before in worse situations than this. I will find our spawn."

"We will do whatever we can to help to ensure her safe return," Merrick promised, patting Loch's shoulder. "I swear to you. I have summoned Galgareth and Urilith to help us as well."

Loch wilted for a moment, his despair written all over his face. He nodded and puffed out his chest again, visibly struggling to compose himself. "Yes. Thank you."

"None of the protection wards were broken," Merrick said. "I am at a loss as to how they were able to get inside."

"We also got somethin' here on the crib." Chase walked over to show them. "Weird and rotten, and definitely Jeff Martin."

Sloane's simmering anguish morphed into rage, and he snarled. "Jeff? Why? Why the hell would he take our baby?"

"We do not know," Merrick said quietly.

Sloane confirmed Chase's finding with a perception spell, looking over the eerily decomposed residue on the side of the crib. It was on Pandora's blankets as well, and he didn't know why that just pissed him off more.

"I took the liberty of alerting everyone to the current situation." Merrick paused. "Including Sullivan Stoker."

"Why did you call him?" Loch snapped with surprising venom.

Unflinchingly, Merrick replied, "Because he has dealt with Jeff Martin, and we need all the assistance available to rescue Pandora." He looked to Sloane. "I also asked Ollie to try to divine her location with his starsight. Alexander and Rota are retracing the portals to see if they can find one we missed. Milo is checking very unofficial things to find out more about Olivia and her family. We are doing everything we can."

"Thank you." Sloane hadn't let go of Pandora's blanket. "I... I just can't believe...." He inhaled sharply and tried to focus. "And we have no idea how they got in?"

"No. I have not been able to find anything yet. They could have possibly used a magical beacon that would have bypassed the wards—"

"Beacons are just points of transfer, though. Someone still would have had to get inside to place one."

"Someone or something." Chase's brow furrowed. "Do you or Loch remember Jeff or Daisy touchin' on you at all? They could have planted one on you guys without you knowin'."

"No, they didn't, but…." Sloane suddenly looked down at his arm, and he gasped. He bolted out of the nursery to the bedroom. "Shit!"

"What is it, sweet husband?" Loch called as he chased after him. "What's wrong?"

"It wasn't Jeff or Daisy!" Sloane grabbed his black jacket, scanning over it with a scowl. There on the sleeve was a small sigil.

A beacon.

"It was Olivia." Sloane groaned. "She grabbed my arm at the store after we saved her. It's so small I never noticed it. Fuck!" He hurled the jacket on the floor, crushing the sigil with a wave of starlight that singed the surrounding carpet. "How could I have been so stupid?"

"My beloved." Loch tried to reach out for him.

Sloane held up his hand to keep Loch at bay. "Was all of this some sort of crazy setup to plant the beacon on us? Jeff made sure to put Olivia in danger because he knew we'd try to help her. He just knew it!"

"It was still quite a risk," Loch said quietly. "There was never a guarantee that we'd go to the store."

"Maybe this is why Cleus was screaming my name." Sloane glared at the jacket. "He could have been trying to plant the beacon on me then."

"But why you?"

"You would have noticed." Sloane grimaced. "You're a god. I'm a stupid mortal with a stupid jacket that let that son of a bitch stroll right in here and take our baby."

"This is not your fault. We are going to find her," Loch swore passionately. "I am still searching, even now."

Sloane turned to hug Loch, burying his face against his chest. Dread was knotting up his guts, and he was sick at the very thought of what Jeff and the others might be doing to Pandora. "I'm scared, Loch."

"So am I." Loch hugged Sloane.

"I don't understand. Why her? Why? To hurt us? To make her part of some horrible ritual?"

Chase poked his head in, waving his phone. "Uh, so, about that? I didn't wanna interrupt you guys havin' this moment, but—"

"What is it?" Sloane demanded.

"Ollie just called. We got good news, and we got some bad news."

"Just tell us."

"Ollie can't find Pandora. He tried writin' out sentences and stuff like he used to, but it ain't really workin'. The only thing he's sure of is that she's safe, okay?"

"Okay, is that supposed to be the good news?"

"Yeah." Chase grimaced.

"What's the bad news?" Sloane gritted his teeth.

"Ollie translated the rest of that design thing you sent. They need someone who is half-god, half-mortal to get that stream of tears or whatever to work."

"Huh?" Sloane scoffed. "Why?"

"The tears were traditionally a blend from both mortal and godly sources," Merrick said, stepping around from behind Chase. "Our working assumption is that a being who is both mortal and god must be the one to restart the stream, as it has not flowed for hundreds of years."

"So does that mean they won't hurt her?" Sloane asked, hating how pained his voice sounded.

"They need her alive," Merrick confirmed in what was probably meant to be a comforting tone.

"Fuck." Sloane hung his head and hugged Loch tighter. "How did they even know?"

"Know what, my dear husband?" Loch asked.

"If this was all a setup to take Pandora, how the hell did they find out about her in the first damn place? We haven't exactly been advertising our half-god daughter all around the city."

"It is no small secret in Zebulon that we've spawned. Great Azaethoth himself visited us, remember? Word of our little one spread just as our marriage did. If I had to guess, Cousin Cleus heard and then told the cultists about her."

"*Fuck.*"

Both Merrick and Loch lifted their heads at the same time, listening to something no one else could hear.

"Gal is trying to awaken Urilith," Loch said. "It may take some time."

"Not a morning goddess," Sloane mumbled in a weak attempt to make himself laugh.

It didn't work.

"Once they are here, we can begin searching," Merrick said.

"Officially or unofficially?" Chase snorted. "Because I'm suddenly feelin' really fuckin' unofficial."

"Very unofficially," Merrick assured him.

"I'm not waiting." Sloane pushed away from Loch and headed back to Pandora's nursery. With a perception spell to guide him, he pulled at the rotten essence that Jeff had left behind. It wasn't very much, but it might be enough to divine his current location.

Such spells were notoriously inaccurate. Instead of providing the precise location of the person in question, the spell might instead pick up on an errant crumb and give the location for the source of the burrito they ate last.

Still, Sloane had to try.

"My beloved mate." Loch walked in behind him. "What are you doing?"

"I am trying to gather up enough Jeff gunk for a location spell." Sloane focused his starlight to gather every glittering speck and then combine it into a small glowing orb.

"Sweet Starkiller, please let—"

"Yes, I know it's probably not going to work, but I can't just sit here while our baby is out there!" Sloane snapped. "I have to do something!"

"Sloane," Loch said seriously. "I was going to say, please let me help." He offered a tentacle to join Sloane's hand, giving his power over to gather the fragments of essence that Sloane had missed.

The orb grew, and Sloane prayed it was enough.

He took the orb into the kitchen to lay it out on the counter. He rubbed his hands together and closed his eyes, preparing himself to perform the spell.

It had to work. It just had to.

Loch put his hands on Sloane's shoulders, and Loch's divine power flowed through him to help strengthen the spell.

Chase and Merrick joined them, laying their hands and Merrick his tentacles on Sloane to add their power too.

Sloane concentrated, and he used his starlight to focus the rush of magic coursing through his body. Nothing seemed to be happening at first, but then there was a flash of color. He could see a building of some kind now, a parking lot, and... red shopping carts.

"Food Way," he said. "The grocery store. It's showing me the grocery store. Jeff is or was at that grocery store."

Loch squeezed Sloane's shoulders. "Excellent work, my beautiful husband."

"Yeah, well." Sloane sighed and laid a hand over one of Loch's. "You can tell me that after our daughter is back home."

"I will accompany you to the grocery store." Merrick turned to Chase. "Please stay here in case Urilith and Galgareth arrive. Inform them of the situation. We may need their assistance."

"Will do. You be safe, Merry." Chase kissed him boldly. "Come back in one piece."

"Y-yes, I will." Merrick ducked his head and then cleared his throat. He looked to Sloane and Loch. "Shall we?"

"We shall." Loch hugged Sloane close. "Hold on, my sweet husband."

Sloane braced himself for the rush of teleportation, closing his eyes and clinging to Loch. When it was over, they were standing next to a cart return in the Food Way parking lot.

Merrick was a blink behind them. "Where shall we look?"

"Everywhere." Sloane put up his hands for a perception spell, hoping to find some trace of Jeff or Pandora. "The spell brought us here for a reason. Maybe Jeff shops here? I mean, he's a nutjob cultist, but he still has to eat."

"I can check inside the store," Merrick said. "They may let me search the back under the guise of police business."

"You're going to lie." Loch gasped. "Good for you, Uncle!"

"I am going to do everything I can to find my niece." Merrick offered a small smile. "But this is an isolated incident, so please do not get any ideas about me joining you for any of your crimes."

"Maybe just one or two."

Sloane surged forward through the lines of cars, searching for anything that might help.

It was like trying to find a grain of sand in a pile of rice. The parking lot was full of residue from the many customers and employees, and it was an absolute mess. He saw flashes of glamour magic, an old watchman spell, hints of fire and air and everything imaginable. He was getting overwhelmed and frantic, and he kept racing through the cars.

So focused on his search, he didn't even see the truck coming around the corner right at him.

"Ah shit!" Sloane gasped, cringing at the truck's horn sounding as it swerved to avoid running him down.

"My love!" Loch had caught up and grabbed Sloane around his middle, pulling him back. "What are you doing?"

"I was looking! I was, I was trying to find something! Anything!" Sloane tried to push away, but there was no escaping Loch's tight hold. He was angry and frustrated, and he kept fighting to get away.

"My sweet, sweet husband," Loch soothed. "You cannot search for our daughter if you are squished."

"I just…." Sloane blinked away hot tears, and he bowed his head against Loch's chest as he sagged in defeat. It was hard to breathe, and he was on the verge of sobbing. "I can't sit back and do *nothing*."

"I know, my beloved mate." Loch rubbed Sloane's back and rocked him gently. "I know." He kissed Sloane's hair. "Let us continue searching, yes? The location spell brought us here for a reason."

"Yeah." Sloane wiped at his cheeks, sniffing back his tears. He took a deep breath. "There has to be something. Maybe Merrick is having better luck inside than we are out here."

"I would join you inside, but I am not allowed inside this particular grocery store."

Sloane sighed. "Is this the one you stole the palm tree from?"

"Yes."

"Let's keep looking out here then, okay?" Sloane took Loch's hand. "I love you."

"I love you too." Loch squeezed Sloane's hand. "Fear not, my love. I will tear all the stars down from the sky and open up the streets of this fair city to the planet's molten core to get our sweet spawn home safe."

"Hopefully it won't come to that."

They continued searching together, checking every car and every row. They checked around the rear in the dumpsters and empty pallets, and even in the trees of the lot next door. There was nothing.

No trace of Jeff, no trace of Pandora, nothing at all that would help them.

Sloane wanted to scream.

Merrick came out to join them, and he was equally empty-handed. "I am sorry to report that there was nothing amiss inside the store." He paused. "Well, one of the employees is stealing expired sodas, but nothing pertinent to our needs."

"I don't get it." Sloane stared out into the parking lot. "Why would the spell bring us here?"

"I can alert dispatch and request for a patrol to keep an eye out for any suspicious activity. We have not been here very long. Perhaps Mr. Martin frequents this store, and he is simply not shopping right now. The location could still be correct, and our timing is wrong."

"Maybe." Frustrated, Sloane grumbled, "Let's just go home and wait for Urilith and Gal."

Back at the apartment, Sloane wandered into the kitchen. He was doing his best to stay calm, but his stomach was still clenching with the most horrible dread. He had no idea where Pandora was or what Jeff might be doing to her, and he had never felt so helpless.

What was the point of having Great Azaethoth's blessing if he couldn't use it to save his child?

He barely heard Merrick and Loch updating Chase with their whopping discovery of absolutely zilch, and he leaned against the counter to steady his shaking hands.

"Please," he whispered. "Great Azaethoth, the First of Gods, the Father of All, please help me. Please, send me a sign. Something, anything." He squeezed his eyes closed. "I need to find her. Please hear me, please—"

The energy in the room shifted, and a violent vortex opened up in the ceiling right above Sloane.

"A portal!" Merrick shouted, his tentacles unfurling in a violent blur as he pushed Chase protectively behind him.

"Shit!" Sloane shouted, scrambling back into the living room and out of the way of the swirling winds.

Loch snarled, and his eyes turned black, his tentacles whipping around him as he prepared for whatever was about to come through.

Sloane stood between Loch and Merrick, and he summoned a sword of starlight. He took a deep breath as the pommel formed in his hand. The power was always overwhelming, and he had to focus through the intense waves and pain to keep a hold of it. The blade grew and sparked, sending cascades of prismatic light that flashed against the dark swirling shadows of the portal.

Sloane was ready.

Ready for anything.

Anything at all.

A glowing blue orb popped out first, floating wildly in the air, and a shrill and weirdly familiar voice was shrieking, "You put me between your legs! Your very naked legs—!"

"For the love of utter fuck!" Another voice joined the first, and it sneered, "Shut up! You wanted to come with me!"

The orb glowed brighter, and Sloane swore it was shaking as it screamed, "Your unadulterated bare *bits* were on top of me!"

A very slender and very naked young man with dark hair dropped onto the kitchen counter, smoothly propping himself on his elbow as he adjusted his chic round sunglasses. "Bitch, bitch, *bitchhh*. Fuck, I knew I should have left you behind."

"I wanted to be of service—!"

"Oh, hey!" The young man peered at the others over his sunglasses with a fanged grin. "Are all those tentacles for me? I mean, I'm not entirely opposed, but I usually want some dinner before getting probed."

"It's Asta!" Sloane gasped, instantly recognizing the prince of the Asra.

"And still as vile as ever." Loch groaned loudly. "Ugh."

"Don't kink shame me." Asta's bright eyes settled on Loch. "We both know what you do with those things, okay?"

"I can't believe you're here!" Sloane exclaimed.

"Hey, of course I'm here." Asta scoffed dramatically. "I mean, it would be rude to ignore a totally insulting letter written by a child shoved into a bottle of ketchup, right?"

"It was not insulting," Loch argued. "It was honest!"

"Does he have two dicks?" Chase blurted out, clearly trying not to stare but unable to help himself.

"Yes, he does, grandpa ginger," Asta confirmed with a sly smile. "Wanna try 'em out? I like garlic bread, moonlight serenades, and really big—"

"Your Highness!" the orb wheezed. "Please!"

"Okay, and who's that in the floating hamster-ball thing?" Chase blinked.

"That's Kunst," Asta drawled. "He is very dead and apparently very hurt that I carried him over here between my thighs and might have soiled him with my naughty bits or whatever." He perked up. "You guys got any cheese?"

"None for you, you foul vermin," Loch warned.

"Kunst," Chase repeated. "Wait, the same Kunst who got murdered to death or whatever and I got my memory fuckin' erased when I figured it out?"

"Ah yes! I did that to you." Loch smiled. "Good times."

"I am Professor Emil Kunst," Kunst announced haughtily. "Royal Occult Advisor to His Majesty, King Thiazi Grell of the Asra and the Kingdom of Xenon, Royal Historian, and Official Record Keeper."

"He gave himself those jobs." Asta snorted. "I think he just made them up."

"Professor," Sloane said quietly, wishing he could read the expression of a glowing blue ball—especially one currently possessed by the soul of a man whose chest he'd personally driven a dagger into to sacrifice him as part of a ritual to save the world last year.

"Hello, Sloane," Kunst greeted with what sounded like a smile in his voice. "It is very good to see you."

"It's good to see you too. I, uh… you've… lost weight?"

"Hi there, uh, Professor. Your Royal Highness person." Chase waved. "I'm Detective Elwood Q. Chase, and this is Detective Benjamin Merrick."

"Hello," Merrick said stiffly.

"Merrick, huh?" Asta sniffed the air. "Well, the tentacles are kinda giving me old-god vibes, ahem, so I'm gonna guess you're actually Gordoth the Untouched."

Before Merrick could reply, Loch chimed in, "He's going by Gordoth the Slut now."

Merrick glared and smacked Loch with a tentacle. "No. He is not."

"Okay, great, everyone knows everybody now," Sloane cut in quickly. "Asta, Kunst. What are you guys doing here?"

"Answering that bullshit message in a bottle?" Asta snorted. "My dad and the cat kicker are busy planning their wedding, so I thought it would be cool if we came by to help you out." He winked. "Consider your IOU cashed in."

"We could really use your help," Sloane said urgently. "Our daughter is missing. She was taken by the leader of this horrible cult. They're working with an old god, Cleus, and he attacked the city. They're trying to wake up Salgumel again, and, and, and—"

"Hey, hey, relax your rack, Starkiller. We got this shit." Asta sat up with a bounce and flashed his pointy teeth in a big grin. "Let's save the world again, bitches."

CHAPTER 11.

"IT'S NOT just the world that needs saving," Sloane said. "We need to find our daughter."

"Mm. I'm not really a big fan of kids." Asta looked thoughtful, and he popped his tongue. "That's gonna cost extra."

"Your Highness!" Kunst scolded.

"Fine, fine!" Asta groaned as he slid off the counter. "I'll help you find your crib critter."

"Do you know who took her?" Kunst asked gently.

"Jeff Martin," Sloane replied. "He's the leader of a cult that's been trying pretty much everything to wake Salgumel up. We think...." His voice caught. "We're pretty sure that's why he took her. For a ritual involving the death song of the Kindress."

"The Kindress?" Kunst managed to look worried. "Oh dear."

"They're trying to restart the flow of tears in this stream that's in Umbriech's—"

"Umbriech's Glen!" Kunst gasped. "Of course! They'll use the tears to create that magical fruit in Babbeth's Orchard in order to entice the Kindress to do their bidding! Namely, awakening Salgumel himself!"

"How did you know?" Sloane was honestly stunned.

"I have always been an accomplished scholar, thank you." Kunst huffed. "And now I have full access to the Royal Asran libraries. I have not squandered a single second of such a rare and wonderful opportunity."

"He's dead," Asta whispered loudly. "Limited choices for hobbies."

"Ahem." Kunst ignored Asta. "Ever since we had that little tiff with Gronoch over the Asran bones, I have been researching all the various ways that someone might attempt to wake Salgumel or the Kindress. This actually makes perfect sense. What I have discovered about the Kindress in particular is quite fascinating—"

"And I wanna hear all about it, but can we have the dissertation later?" Sloane cut in. "We need to find our daughter."

"Oh! Oh yes, of course." Kunst's light flickered, and he seemed to pout. "My apologies."

"He has a mute button, just FYI." Asta rolled his eyes. "Where was the kitten when she was taken?"

Sloane pointed. "Her room, the nursery. We already tried tracking the portals and using a location spell—"

"How long ago?"

"It's probably been... I don't know. An hour?" Sloane rubbed his forehead. "They snuck in a beacon and portaled in through our wards." He narrowed his eyes. "How did you guys get in here anyway?"

"Uh, hello." Asta grinned. "I'm an Asra. I'm the prince. That makes me, like, *the* Asra. There's not much I can't portal through, Starkiller. I think being naked helps. No resistance, you know?"

"What are you going to do?" Loch demanded.

"Hopefully put some clothes on," Merrick mumbled, having found the ceiling very fascinating throughout the entirety of the discussion.

Chase had opted to turn around.

"I'm gonna sniff out where they took her." Asta blinked as if it was obvious. "Hello. Meow. Asra. I can track down a portal in my sleep. I got this. We used to have to find asshole gods when they went off on crazy asshole god benders."

Loch snarled loudly, and he went to take a step toward Asta.

Sloane cut Loch off by pressing his hand to Loch's chest, and he tried to avoid the tone he typically used to chastise Pandora as he said, "Asta! Are you serious? Please. You cannot joke around about this."

Asta looked offended, and he immediately argued, "What? No! I would never joke about something this serious. Come on." He slinked by Sloane, wagging his hips as he walked into the nursery. "Gods really used to go on crazy asshole benders."

"Oh, you little—" Loch barked, growling as he gave chase.

"Loch!" Sloane shouted and tried to drag him back.

There was the pop of a portal, and by the time Loch and Sloane stumbled into the nursery, Asta was gone.

"Where has that nasty little creature gone now?" Loch snapped.

"Hopefully wherever Pandora is," Sloane said quietly, his grip on Loch turning loose now that the threat of regicide had passed for the moment. His phone rang with a new onslaught of unknown numbers, and he put it on silent. He was not in the mood.

"Is that Asta guy always like that?" Chase wondered out loud to no one in particular.

"Always," Kunst grumbled sourly. "He's been extra sassy since he had a little romantic adventure that did not end well. The result of his poor behavior and having to deal with the consequences of his actions makes him cranky."

Chase and Merrick exchanged a suspicious look, and Chase asked, "That little adventure wouldn't happen to have been one with a guy named Jay, would it?"

"It is!" Kunst gasped. "That's such—"

The swirling wind and telltale pop of another portal interrupted Kunst, and Asta stood before them with wide eyes. His sunglasses were askew, and the scent of singed hair filled the air.

"Did you find her?" Sloane asked urgently.

"Is she a small ginger who is surprisingly spicy for her size?" Asta replied. "Because then yeah, I found her."

"Where is she?" Loch practically howled.

"Chill out, Azaethoth!" Asta barked back. "For fuck's sake. She's here." He nodded, and a new portal opened up. "Some big fancy house with a whole bunch of stupid wards. This will get you guys through."

"Why did you not just grab her?"

"She tried to set me on fire, and then—"

"Thank you, Asta! Come on!" Sloane grabbed Loch's arm. "Let's go!"

"Wait! The fire—"

Sloane didn't hear what Asta was trying to tell them as he and Loch raced into the portal. He didn't care. They had to get to Pandora as fast as they could. That was the only thing that mattered.

The ride in the portal was much wilder than in Loch's portals, and Sloane was quite dizzy by the time his feet touched solid ground again.

They were standing in a posh bedroom that was easily bigger than Sloane's entire apartment, but he didn't have long to take in the surroundings because he immediately realized what Asta had been trying to tell them.

The room was on fire.

The source of the blaze was Pandora, standing up in a crib by the foot of the bed, screaming and slapping at the bars with her tentacles, and the flames grew higher.

"Our spawn!" Loch cried, swinging out his tentacles and clearing a path through the fire as he ran to her.

"Daddd! Da-Daddy!" Pandora wailed as tears ran down her face. "Daddy! Daddy!"

"Panda! We're coming, sweetie!" Sloane tried to follow, but something hit him.

It was a wave of magic, solid like a slab of earth, and it sent him flying into a burning wall. So focused on getting to Pandora, he hadn't seen the figure standing behind them through the smoke before it was too late.

He tried to shield himself as he went right through the scorched wall, crashing into the floor of the next room with embers and chunks of smoldering drywall flying around him.

He sat up, scrambling away from the flames now climbing out from the hole he'd made. He was in a hallway, and the fire in the room Pandora and Loch were in was spreading fast. The smoke was thick, and he coughed through it, trying to catch his breath. He kept his shield up to fend off the flames, calling out, "Loch!"

"I've got her!" Loch shouted. "She is indeed very spicy right now!"

Relief flooded Sloane's entire body, and he grinned from ear to ear, despite having just been attacked. "Thank the gods. Now hey, listen! Someone just blasted me, and—"

"Sloane!" Daisy emerged from the smoke billowing out of the bedroom doorway. She was dressed all in black, and she didn't look like she'd slept in days. Her hands were raised, poised for another spell.

"Oh shit!" Sloane brought his shield around to deflect it, but it was another giant wave of earth. It slammed into him, knocking him back several yards. An additional wave forced him to tumble down the stairs.

At the bottom of the stairway, he planted his feet against the railings and pushed away, trying to get out of Daisy's line of sight. His head was ringing, but at least the fire hadn't spread down here yet, so it was easier to breathe.

The home was enormous, with marble floors and fancy furniture, and there was an elaborate fountain beside the bottom of the staircase. Sloane kept moving until his back hit the base of the fountain, and he crawled around behind it for cover.

"What have you done?" Daisy screamed, stomping down the stairs. "What are you doing here?"

Sloane glared, rising into a crouched position and holding his shield in front of him. He used the precious time he had to pour more of his magic into the shield until it was crackling with energy. Wanting to bait Daisy over to him, he shouted in reply, "Taking my daughter back!"

"No!" she snarled. "You won't! You're not messing this up! Not this time!" Her voice became frantic and shrill. "Everything is perfect. Everything is ready! Your daughter is going to help usher in a new era for this world. Salgumel will finally rise, and then we—"

As soon as Daisy's foot hit the last step and she started to come around the railing in the direction of the fountain, Sloane hurled his shield forward and busted her in the head with it.

Daisy collapsed.

Sloane tried not to enjoy it too much, but it was very satisfying to watch her fall over in a big heap. He stepped over her to head back upstairs. There was a light tap on his shoulder, and he whirled around to find himself face-to-face with Jeff Martin. "Shit."

"Hey, Starkiller." Jeff smiled, and the worn bandage on his face crinkled, revealing a flash of teeth through his rotten cheek. "You've got quite the kid there."

"You bastard!" Sloane snapped. "You! All of this is because of you!" He brought his shield back up, and he threw a spear of starlight right at Jeff's chest.

Jeff teleported out of the way, and the spear hit the wall behind him. He reappeared a few feet away. "Nice try."

"Oh, you son of a bitch!" Sloane threw his shield at Jeff, but he was left groaning in frustration when Jeff simply ported out of the way again.

The fire had made its way down the stairs, and its flames were crawling around the railings and across the ceiling above them. There was a loud groan from the wall Sloane had struck with his starlight, and then it collapsed in on itself.

Sloane swore he felt the whole house shift beneath his feet, and he had to duck when Jeff threw a fiery missile right at him. Another one came zooming through the air, and Sloane managed to get a shield up and deflect it, shouting, "Loch! Hey! Come on! Could use some help here!"

"On my way, my most beautiful mate!" Loch replied.

"Faster, please!" Sloane pleaded, whirling around to block another fiery projectile that came from behind as Jeff teleported there. It was almost impossible to tell where Jeff would attack from next, and Sloane expanded his shield to fend off a new barrage of fierce fiery blasts.

Everything suddenly froze.

The flickering flames, the smoke, the magical missiles in the air, even Jeff—time itself had actually stopped.

Loch came marching down the stairs, Pandora strapped to his chest with a sheet from the crib, and his tentacles whipping around him like a wild tornado. His eyes were sparkling black pools, and when he spoke, it was a roar. "Jeff Martin! How dare you take my spawn from my home! My home! Mine! I am Azaethoth the Lesser, brother of Tollmathan, Gronoch, Xhorlas, and Galgareth. I am the son of Salgumel, he who was spawned by Baub, the child of Zunnerath and Halandrach, they who were born of Etheril and Xarapharos, descended from Great Azaethoth himself, and *I am not to be fucked with*!"

"Rawrrrr!" Pandora growled, waving her tentacles in an imitation of her father's. "Rawrrrr, rawr!"

Sloane's heart swelled, and he did his best not to get too distracted by how extremely hot it was when Loch went full-out old god. He rushed to Loch's side, petting Pandora and kissing her hair. "Oh, sweet girl! Our little Panda! You're okay!"

Pandora's face was blotchy from crying, but she was grinning wide. "Da! Daddy!"

"Oh, my baby! I'm so glad you're okay!"

"Rawrrrr!"

"Touching, really. Good for you. I have no idea how the fuck you got in here, but I don't really care." Jeff was speaking. "Ugh."

Wait, how was Jeff speaking?

Sloane turned around to see that Jeff wasn't frozen despite time still being stopped around them. "How the fuck—"

"Salgumel will rise," Jeff promised. "I don't care what it takes."

"It'll be very hard to wake anyone up when your insides are twisted into french braids!" Loch threatened, several of his tentacles whipping through the air at Jeff.

Jeff teleported, just barely dodging Loch's tentacles.

Sloane surged forward to intercept Jeff when he reappeared, and he swung a new shield of starlight at him. "No! We are going to stop you!"

Jeff brought up his forearm to block the shield, and magical sparks erupted as they collided, flying like fireworks between them. He struggled to brace himself against Sloane's shield, and he gritted his awful teeth, snarling, "No. Never. I will never stop! I will never ever fucking stop!"

Sloane cringed as Jeff teleported him into a grand ballroom with a piano, still locked together with him in battle. He growled and pushed Jeff away as hard as he could to avoid being taken in another jump. "Loch!" he shouted, hoping Loch would hear him. "Ballroom! Ballroom! Now!"

Jeff was right back on top of him in a blink, slamming his forearm against the shield of starlight with a low hiss. "Oh, your precious god isn't going to save you! Not this time!"

Sloane didn't understand how Jeff could possibly be blocking his shield—much less do anything else he'd just done—and he focused more of his starlight into it. He reached deep within himself to summon power he rarely tapped into, and he let out a roar as the force made his entire body shake. He put in more and more until the magic ignited in a fantastic explosion, propelling Jeff across the room.

Jeff went through the piano, crumbling behind the destroyed instrument with a wounded cry.

Sloane went right after him, prismatic light buzzing all over him and bursting from his palms. He'd never tried to take on this much magic, but he was determined to beat Jeff this time.

Jeff had to pay—for everything he had done and everything he'd do if they didn't stop him right now.

"I am Sloane Beaumont," he yelled, "son of Pandora and Daniel Beaumont, and I will—"

"Will what? Wake up another god?" Jeff spat.

"What?" Sloane sputtered, some of his spark fading. "I didn't mean—"

"It was your prayer that first woke Tollmathan," Jeff accused. "Or did you already forget that, huh?" He pulled himself up into a sitting position. "Personally, I'm thankful to you, Mr. Beaumont. When the world is remade in Salgumel's hands? It will be because you made it possible."

"No." Sloane raised his hand, a pommel of a starlight sword forming there. "Whatever I did, I am going to fix it. And I will do whatever it takes to make things right." He pointed the fully formed sword at Jeff. "Starting with you!"

"Gotta catch me first." Jeff flashed a foul grin.

"Oh no you don't!" Sloane swung the sword, but it hit nothing but an empty floor.

Jeff was gone.

Again.

"Fuck!" Sloane sliced the sword into the trashed piano, reducing it to tiny splinters, and bits of keys and wood scattered everywhere.

"My beloved!" Loch called, his voice getting louder as he rushed into the ballroom. "What happened? Where is Jeff?"

"He's gone!" Sloane growled. "I can try to track his portal. It's fresh enough. I can find him." He tried to sense its path, but it seemed to lead right back upstairs and then vanish. "Shit. Okay. He couldn't have gone far. We could—"

"Sweet husband." Loch pulled Sloane close, though he was mindful of the starlight sword. "I cannot keep time at bay for very long, this imitation Tudor style house is on fire, and we just got our daughter back. Forgive me, but it also seems as if Jeff just colleged us, so we should seek out playtime with his internal organs at a later time."

"Schooled," Sloane corrected with a halfhearted smile. He let go of the sword so it would vanish, and he nodded. "He has to be using some powerful totems. He shouldn't have been able to defend against my starlight or your powers so—"

"Sloane Beaumont," Loch said firmly, "hold our spawn."

Sloane flinched as Loch pushed Pandora into his arms, but he melted when she hugged his neck.

Loch was right.

This was what mattered right now.

"Panda." Sloane held Pandora against his chest, and he cried into her hair. "Oh, my baby. My sweet, sweet baby. You're okay. You're safe. Daddy's got you. I got you, and I'm never, ever letting you go again."

Loch curled his tentacles around the two of them, kissing Pandora's brow and then Sloane's. "That might make changing her difficult, but being a god, I think we can manage."

Sloane laughed, leaning his head on Loch's shoulder. "Let's get the fuck out of here." He smiled at Pandora. "You ready to go, baby girl? Ready to go home?"

"Fuck," Pandora cooed without hesitation.

Sloane sighed.

"You really need to stop teaching our sweet daughter such nasty things," Loch scolded playfully.

Pandora clapped and giggled, snuggling into Sloane's chest. "Fuckkkk, fu-fu-fuck!"

They checked upstairs for Daisy before they left, but she was nowhere to be found. The portal Jeff had used must have been to get her, and they could find no other magical evidence to indicate where they had gone.

If Jeff had used a portal to escape the burning house, they could not find it. More likely, he had a perfectly normal route of escape, like a door, and the fire had erased the trail.

Back at the apartment, they found everyone fighting and screaming at the top of their lungs—Asta seemed to be winning in terms of volume— and Galgareth and Urilith had joined them.

Apparently Asta had refused to open another portal to let anyone follow Loch and Sloane, and the others had taken serious offense to that. Urilith, here in a new vessel of an elderly Spanish man, was doing her best to keep the peace, but she was the first one to jump on Sloane and Loch when they returned.

"Oh! My darlings! My children! My little baby!" Urilith tackled them in a giant group hug, nearly crushing them with her bright yellow tentacles.

"Hi, Urilith," Sloane managed to grunt as he patted her back. "It's great to see you!"

"Hello, Mother!" Loch cheerfully kissed her cheek. "Nice of you to join us!"

"Yes! Hello!" Urilith gushed. "I'm so sorry I took so long to wake up!" She cooed at Pandora, and she offered a tentacle for her to play with. "Our little darling is safe! Oh, look at her! She's so beautiful! And she's all right? She is unharmed?"

"She's doing wonderfully." Loch beamed. "She set a very expensive house on fire."

"Fire, rawrrrr!" Pandora declared, shaking Urilith's tentacle. "Rawrrrr!"

"Ah, how delightful!" Urilith swept Pandora away from them. "Come with Grandma Uri and tell me about it, my darling little one!"

Sloane wanted to protest since they'd literally just gotten Pandora back a few minutes ago, but he was exhausted. He'd never felt so drained, and he flopped onto the couch with a loud groan.

"So?" Asta was still naked, now lounging on the living room rug. "Everything's cool now?"

"It's not over yet." Sloane scrubbed his hands over his face. "Jeff got away again."

"What happened?" Merrick demanded.

"He can apparently defend against starlight and break out of time spells. Even Loch's. Cleus must be helping him. Jeff is just getting more powerful, and we're back at square one."

"We still got that date for tomorrow on Olivia's calendar, right?" Chase perked up. "That could be somethin' big."

"You really think so?"

"We can get all hands on deck for a possible epic god-fightin' brawl-type situation," Chase declared. "We can let the AVPD know we got a tip about some possible illegal shenanigans goin' down, maybe have some units on standby just in case. They ain't gonna be much in a fight against Jeff if he's as souped-up as you say, but they can help get people outta the way so they don't get hurt."

"An excellent idea." Merrick beamed.

"Thank you." Chase winked his way.

"We should also be prepared to glamour ourselves. Jeff and Olivia know our faces."

"What's the plan, then?" Sloane asked. "We just hang out at the restaurant and wait for her or Jeff to show? Glamoured or not, a whole group of people standing around is gonna look suspicious."

"Restaurant?" Asta lifted his head. "As in food?"

"You're not invited to our stakeout." Loch scowled.

"We can coordinate with the AVPD to pose as guests or employees of the restaurant," Merrick said. "We will keep civilian presence to an absolute minimum, and I will personally install anti-teleportation wards. When Mr. Martin arrives, he will be surrounded, and we will arrest him."

"What can I do to help?" Urilith asked. She was still cuddling Pandora, feeding her a new bottle. "I've never been on a stakeout before. I have heard there will be cigarettes."

"I would like you to please take Pandora," Loch said. "I do not believe that Aeon will be safe for her until Jeff is apprehended."

"What about me?" Galgareth piped up. "Do you want me to go with Mother or come with you?"

"Come with us, dear Sister. I would be honored to fight another one of our relatives with you by my side."

"So, who we got comin', then?" Chase scratched his beard. "Merry, me, Sloane, Loch, Gal, and I already know Alexander and Rota will be down. Anybody else?"

"We could ask Lochlain and Robert to come. Maybe Fred?" Sloane suggested. "They're powerful witches."

"And rogues. And one of 'em is a ghoul."

"With the increased presence of the AVPD, we will have enough trouble concealing multiple gods," Merrick said gently. "It may be best not to involve anyone who could be arrested."

"What about you, Asta?" Sloane looked over in the kitchen where Asta had snuck off to and was rooting through the fridge. "Do you think you could put on some pants and help save the world?"

"I'm all about saving the world, but pants? Meh. Forecast cloudy with a chance of fuck no." Asta ripped open a package of sliced cheese. "You have no idea how uncomfortable it is to portal with clothes on."

Chase had a strangely smug smile, saying, "If you cover up, I'll put in a good word for you with Jay."

Asta narrowed his eyes. "You know Jay?"

"Sure do. He works with me and Merry at the AVPD."

"How good of a word, exactly?"

"Look, kiddo, I could sell life insurance to a dead man."

Asta nibbled on the piece of cheese. "All right. *Fine*. I'll do it." With a wave of his hand, he was wearing skintight leopard print leggings in the same shade of red as his sunglasses. The leggings left little of his unique anatomy to the imagination. "There, happy?"

"Overjoyed."

"Can you do something about this area?" Loch gestured to his face. "That's still quite offensive."

Asta rolled his eyes. "Azaethoth, you can go right on and suck both of my—"

"I'm very proud of you, Your Highness," Kunst cut in. "You've made a very mature choice, and I urge you to—"

"Kunst? I'm trying to get dicked down. The only urge I'm worried about is the urge to orgasm."

Kunst sighed loudly.

"All right, so!" Sloane took a deep breath. "We get everybody in disguise and wait for Jeff or Olivia to show up. We stop them once and for all."

"Cleus is still out there as well," Merrick reminded him. "Apprehending Mr. Martin is essential, but it still leaves an old god out there who is willing to openly attack the city. There are also still many items with the lethal design unaccounted for. The danger is hardly over."

"You're so cheerful," Asta said dryly. "I bet you're a real hit at funerals."

Merrick stared at him, and he replied in his most serious tone, "I put the fun in funeral."

Asta blinked. "Did… did you just make a joke? Holy shit. I didn't realize you knew what a joke was." He laughed.

The tension immediately evaporated, and Sloane was treated to watching his friends and family chatting amongst themselves as the latest adventures were retold. Urilith was soon making food with Pandora while Kunst hovered nearby to ask her a barrage of questions.

Chase jumped in to help Urilith cook while Merrick observed closely, and Loch fussed about how much better he could have done everything because of what he'd seen on television. Asta was trying to steal a bite from every dish, and Galgareth bribed him to stay away with more cheese.

Whether by marriage or blood or IOUs sent in ketchup bottles, everyone here was bonded together—if nothing else, by the mutual desire to stop the end of the world.

Despite the newfound sense of camaraderie, Sloane's heart was heavy. Even the relief of having his daughter back was not enough to ease the weight on his shoulders as he heard Jeff's words ringing in his ears over and over again.

All of this was his fault….

Sloane glanced at his silenced phone, and the urge to smash it was strong. He had dozens of missed calls, voicemails, and text messages. He was about to shove it back in his pocket, but there was a new call was coming in.

It was Stoker.

Sloane still wanted to throw it but chose instead to pick up. "Hello, Stoker. I have had a very, very bad day, so please don't be an asshole right now."

"How's your daughter?" Stoker asked with surprising concern. "Merrick's last text was not very clear—"

"No, no, no, she's good. Seriously, she's fine. She's home now. We're all okay. Thank you. Sleeping. Being kidnapped and burning down houses is apparently exhausting."

"I'm very glad to hear it. I hope you have a chance to rest as well."

Sloane frowned. "What do you want? You're being nice."

"You wound me, Mr. Beaumont."

"What's going on?"

"Well, I wanted to check in on you and yours...."

"And?"

"And I thought you would be interested to know that Jeff Martin just called me and has asked me to see him in person tomorrow."

Sloane's pulse quickened. "Where?"

"At Flaming Amy's. Nine o'clock."

"That's the same date Olivia had on her calendar." Sloane scowled. "What is the meeting about?"

"An acquisition. Mr. Martin is offering me a piece of something touched by the Kindress in exchange for my assistance creating a spell to find your daughter. You understand—"

"Take the damn deal," Sloane snapped.

"Mr. Beaumont?"

"I need to know he's gonna be there. Tell him whatever you want. Spin whatever lies it takes. Just make sure he's there." Sloane took a deep breath. "Tomorrow. We end this."

CHAPTER 12.

"So, JEFF wants to meet Stoker out in public?" Chase asked, immediately skeptical when Sloane shared the news. "And it just so happens to be the same place and time as the date we think he was already gonna have with Olivia?"

Urilith's brow furrowed. "It does seem a bit concerning."

"Stoker told me once that he would never bait Jeff into a meeting because it might somehow hurt his precious criminal reputation," Sloane said. "But this was Jeff asking him, so I guess he's willing to risk it. I want to believe he's doing this with the best intentions...."

"I do not trust him as far as I can heave his limp, intestine-less body," Loch snarled.

"Wait, why is it intestine-less?" Chase asked.

"Ah, because I've already theoretically removed his intestines and braided them into a little basket."

"Oh."

"There is an additional danger to consider." Kunst floated over to address Sloane. "Jeff is offering him something touched by the Kindress, yes?"

Sloane frowned. "Yeah?"

"Doesn't it seem odd that he would be able to procure an item touched by one of the most elusive figures in our entire religion? A figure he has claimed is responsible for the hole in his face?" Kunst glowed brighter. "The Kindress must, in fact, be here on Aeon."

"What?"

"Impossible." Merrick crossed his arms. "That simply cannot be."

"Please." Kunst flickered. "After speaking with all of you tonight and my own very in-depth research, it is the only logical conclusion."

"Explain yourself, Royal Advisor," Merrick demanded.

"There is a distinct pattern to the Kindress's cycle of rebirth and death, usually in conjunction with unique celestial events. King Grell of the Asra has witnessed the phenomenon many times over his long life, and yet it seems as if the Kindress is overdue for a death. King Grell and the people of Xenon are actually able to see the Kindress's death because its soul blacks out the bridge when it passes over into Zebulon."

"So, you're sayin' that because nobody's turned off the lights or whatever in a while, that means the Kindress star-baby thing ain't dead?" Chase said carefully.

"Yes, but there's more," Kunst said. "The Fountain where Great Azaethoth must perform the drowning? It remains full of tears as long as the Kindress is dead because Great Azaethoth continues to weep for his loss."

"But the Fountain is empty right now." Sloane recalled what Alexander had told them. "So what does that mean?"

"If the Fountain is empty, it is because Great Azaethoth is not weeping for a dead child. Ergo, his child is not dead."

Sloane's heart thumped with dread. "Well, that's… that's probably not good."

"The Kindress is clearly not in Xenon, and Jeff's reports of interacting with it place it here on Aeon. It would also explain why he's using the Kindress's death song. Instead of tracking down specific totems or people with stars in their blood for complex rituals to wake up Salgumel, he's decided to go after the Kindress directly."

"And if the Kindress is indeed here on Aeon, there is no dreaming or veil to obscure contact like there is with Salgumel, who is still sleeping in Zebulon." Merrick frowned. "This… this is not good."

"Sure don't fuckin' sound like it," Chase quipped before biting into a slice of the cake Urilith had baked. "So, what do we do?"

"The plan remains the same," Sloane said firmly. "We stake out the restaurant, wait for Jeff and Olivia, and we stop them. Jeff won't be able to contact the Kindress or anybody else if he's locked up."

"Mother will take Pandora away to keep her safe," Galgareth promised, "and I'm coming with you. If there's any chance of the Kindress showing up, you'll need some serious backup."

"Thank you, dear Sister," Loch said. "Battle is always more fun with you!"

"Aww, thanks!"

Pandora, who had been snoozing in Urilith's tentacles, woke up and fussed, kicking her legs. "Rawrrr! Dad, Dadddyyy!"

"Here, little spawn," Loch said as he hurried over to take her. He bundled her up in his tentacles against his chest and rocked her. "Aww, what do you need, little one?"

Pandora pushed at Loch, and tears welled up in her eyes. "No! No! Daddy! Not Daddy! I want Daddy!"

"Ah, other Daddy." Loch carried her to Sloane with an apologetic smile. "It seems I am not who she seeks."

"Hey, that's fine." Sloane was happy to take Pandora, smothering her cheeks with kisses and bouncing her in his lap. "Hey, baby girl. Hey, what's the matter? Mm? Are you hungry?"

Pandora's cries quieted, and she pushed herself against Sloane's chest. She buried her head under his chin, her hands twisting into his shirt as she whined.

Sloane closed his eyes and rubbed her back, his chest fluttering with a whirlwind of emotions. He'd been so worried about her, and he didn't think he'd ever felt so scared or helpless. It was the worst feeling in the world, like a rusty dagger in his heart that kept on twisting, and his eyes got hot with tears as he hugged her close.

Loch sat beside them, offering his tentacles to wrap around them both. "Perhaps she just wanted you, my sweet mate."

Sloane leaned into Loch's embrace, smiling at a tentacle brushing against his cheek. He kept rubbing Pandora's back, and he laughed when he heard a soft snore. She was asleep again. "I guess so."

Urilith fluttered over and then kissed their heads one by one. "Oh, my little darlings. I love you all so much."

"And we love you, Mother," Loch said. "Thank you for everything."

"Hey!" Galgareth plopped on the arm of the sofa next to Sloane, sliding a tentacle around them. "What about me?"

"And we love you, dear Sister," Loch crooned. "Very much."

Merrick stood beside Urilith, a bit more awkward with affection than the rest of his family, but he smiled as he said, "I love you all. We are going to be victorious."

"Or get our asses kicked tryin'!" Chase chimed in, wrapping his arms around Merrick's waist.

"Together," Kunst affirmed, "we will triumph."

Sloane was overwhelmed by all the love he felt in that moment, beaming wordlessly at his family and friends and....

Asta was back in the fridge, chugging orange juice from the container.

Sloane couldn't help but smile.

No matter what happened tomorrow, they would certainly be an awesome force to be reckoned with.

Merrick and Chase bid farewell after a while, Merrick citing that they still had to finish the boxes of paperwork before preparing for tomorrow's stakeout. He promised to keep in touch, and Chase would coordinate with Alexander and Rota. Asta left with Kunst and a promise to return tomorrow.

Asta also took a tub of ricotta cheese.

Loch cleaned the kitchen and complained how his mother and Chase hadn't put anything back where it was supposed to go, and Urilith and Galgareth offered to stay over to help watch Pandora. Sloane was grateful for the additional protection, but after today he didn't want to let her out of his sight. Loch was in agreement, and although he moved Pandora's crib into their bedroom, he had her in bed between them when it was time to go to sleep.

Pandora woke back up, needing to be changed and hungry. Loch cleaned her, summoned a fresh bottle of magical milk, and wrapped her up in his tentacles with a baby blanket.

Sloane was propped up on his elbow, petting her hair while she drank from her bottle. No matter how relieved he was to have Pandora home safe, there was a lingering ache weighing down his bones.

"What is wrong, my beautiful husband?" Loch asked. "Your luscious thick brows are furrowed in a most troubling way."

"Just something stupid that Jeff said," Sloane replied quietly. "It's nothing."

"Nothing is nothing. What is it, beloved?"

"It's what he said about all of this being my fault." Sloane adjusted the baby blanket around Pandora. "He knew about my prayer waking up Tollmathan when I was little, and—"

"My dearest love," Loch cut in, one of his tentacles touching Sloane's cheek. "Please forgive the abrupt interruption, but this is not your fault. None of it is. We have talked about this before. If you hadn't been the one to wake the old gods up, they would have risen some other way. The hatred in their hearts that they carry for this world? The resentment they feel for being denied a kingdom to rule? You did not put that there."

"I know." Sloane sighed. "I know, I *know*. But it doesn't make me feel any less like shit, thinking about all those poor people who have died the last few days."

"You blame yourself." Loch shook his head. "Blame Jeff Martin and the gods who are helping him. They are the ones who need to pay for these crimes. Not you, my beloved mate."

Sloane nodded, still thumbing the hem of the blanket. "I'm trying. I want to fix this. I want to make it right."

"Oh, sweet husband. You already are. You were gifted a sword of starlight from Great Azaethoth himself, and you've used it to save the world and vanquish evil many times."

"An evil that's only here because of what I did," Sloane grumbled.

"The evil was always going to come," Loch argued stubbornly. "You just... hmm." He paused to think. "You put in a doggy door for them to sneak through."

Sloane made a face.

"Trust me. The doggy door matters not." Loch leaned over Pandora to kiss Sloane's brow. "All will be well. I am here. Our spawn is here. Our family and friends are with us. Jeff can have all the magical totems and corrupted gods in the world, but he will never win."

"How can you possibly know that?"

"Your memory must be going, my gorgeous mate." Loch smiled, and his eyes sparkled with stars. "I'm the favorite, remember?"

Sloane actually laughed. "Oh, how could I possibly forget."

"Don't worry. I'll remind you more often from now on." Loch took Sloane's hand, and his smile brightened. "I love you, Sloane Beaumont. You are the breath in my lungs. The blood in my veins. The butter in my hollandaise sauce."

"By all the gods, you're so cheesy." Sloane laughed again, delighted.

"Mmm, well, you know the addition of cheese would disqualify a sauce from being classified as a true hollandaise." Loch winked. "But it would be delicious."

"I love you so much." Sloane grinned. "Thank you. For everything. For always making me feel better no matter what. And for being a great husband, a great father, and a great friend."

"I will always be here, my beautiful husband," Loch declared. "No matter what. I will love you through all disease and misery, the sad times and the glad, and even when you don't wish to mate...."

"But in that scenario, you'll check first to make sure my body wasn't possessed, right?"

"Naturally." Loch beamed. "What other reason could there be for refusing my sexual advances?"

Sloane snorted. "I love you."

"And I love you." Loch kissed Sloane's cheek. "Fear not, my love. We shall be triumphant."

Sloane really hoped so.

IT WAS time.

After a long nerve-wracking day, Sloane and Loch were on their way to Flaming Amy's.

Per Chase and Merrick, most of the waitstaff would be undercover AVPD officers, themselves included. Alexander refused to play the part of an employee, so he opted to be another guest inside the restaurant. Sloane and Loch would also attend as guests, and everyone would be wearing their most powerful glamours.

Even with a perception spell, it would be difficult to see their true faces. *Though not impossible*, Sloane worried to himself as he and Loch walked up to the hostess stand.

There was so much that could go wrong.

Pandora was at least safe, far away in a world between worlds with Urilith watching over her. No matter what happened, Jeff Martin was not going to take her again.

It had been agreed that Asta wasn't likely to blend in even if he glamoured himself, so he would be waiting close by with Kunst—who would hopefully be keeping Asta on his best behavior and fully dressed.

Stoker and Galgareth were already inside, though Sloane couldn't see them from where he and Loch were standing.

The hostess stand was currently empty.

"The service here is terrible!" Loch loudly announced. He was glamoured as an older man with a long mustache, and he'd gotten a cane from gods knew where that he smacked against the side of the stand. "Hello! Some of us want to eat!"

Sloane, who was disguised as an older woman, elbowed Loch's side. "Will you quit it?"

"I'm just getting into character," Loch protested.

"Yo! I'm comin'!" The hostess emerged, a petite young woman with long dark hair. "Hang on a fuckin' second," she griped, fumbling with the menus. "Two of you? Okay, cool. I got this."

Sloane couldn't be sure, but he thought the hostess might be Chase.

The hostess smiled. "Right this way, please."

As the hostess led them to a table on the edge of the outdoor patio, Sloane surveyed the restaurant.

It was spacious, lush, with plenty of room for the waitstaff to perform their fancy fire tricks tableside. Galgareth was seated at table near the door, already enjoying her meal. Sloane still didn't see Stoker, and he wondered if he too was wearing a glamour.

"Here you go." The hostess slapped the menus down on their table. "You guys enjoy, and, uh, I'd recommend ordering dessert first." She fixed Sloane with a knowing stare. "You feel me?"

"Got it." Sloane dropped his voice. "Chase."

The hostess beamed, and she whispered, "I am so pleased you thought so."

"Huh?"

Without another word, she left.

"Was that… your uncle pretending to be Chase pretending to be a hostess?" Sloane blinked.

"It appears that way." Loch looked thoughtful. "He doesn't have the walk down right. Chase's hips have a much more defined strut than that."

"Mm, I'll be sure to let him know."

"Hello!" A young man wearing a restaurant uniform with waist-length black hair came to their table. He appeared a bit nervous, his hands fumbling as he spoke. "Welcome to Flaming Amy's! My name is Thiago, and I'll be your server this evening. May I get you something to drink?"

"I would like a mojito," Loch replied immediately. "With extra mo."

"Uh, okay. I'll check on that. And you, ma'am?" Thiago asked.

It took Sloane a moment to remember how he was glamoured. "Oh! Yes!" He tried to raise his pitch. "Just a water, please."

"We would like to go ahead and place an order for sustenance," Loch said. "We require two Baked Alaska Saint Pierres. Very quickly."

"Uh, yes, sir." Thiago nodded. "Coming right up, sir! I'll go put your order in and be back with those drinks." He smiled and turned to leave, nearly crashing into an adjacent table on his way out.

Sloane felt a pang of sympathy for him, and he wondered if he was an actual member of the waitstaff. He eyed Loch, trying to hide a little smile. "Dessert? Really?"

"We have fourteen minutes," Loch replied. "I want to enjoy this. It's our first date in a very long time."

"It's not a date, though. It's a really important evening, ahem."

"Well, I'm going to enjoy the remaining thirteen minutes of it that we can." Loch took Sloane's hand over the table and then squeezed it. "You look radiant."

"I look like an old lady."

"Well, you're my old lady, and I find you radiant."

Sloane smiled. "Thank you. I really like your cane."

"Isn't it neat?" Loch paused. "Did you mean my cane, or my *cane*?" He wagged his brows.

Sloane rolled his eyes affectionately. "This is actually nice. Maybe we should try to go out to eat more. Not that I don't enjoy eating at home, of course."

"Of course." Loch smirked. "It's good for you to try other chefs' food, you know."

"Oh?"

"Yes. So then you can see how vastly superior mine is."

They lightly chatted and tried to appear nonchalant as the minutes ticked by, and Sloane threw quick glances at the front door. He could see it through the tall patio windows, and the hostess stayed busy seating more customers.

One of the new patrons was a woman wearing a long black dress that reminded Sloane of a certain someone's trench coat.

There was also a clean-shaven busboy who kept scratching at a beard that wasn't there.

Galgareth was still eating away and looked to be ordering seconds.

Everyone seemed to be here that was supposed to be except the one person they were waiting for.

"Kinda weird we haven't seen our, uh, *friend* yet," Sloane noted.

"He is not our friend," Loch said.

"I'm trying to be subtle?"

"Ah yes. I am very good at that." Loch nodded. "Our friend who I intend to eviscerate so that I may braid his intestines into festive patterns."

Sloane looked back to the window, and he tensed immediately when he saw Olivia there waiting for service. "Hey. She's here."

"She who?" Loch followed Sloane's gaze. "Oh yes. Her. Olivia. She's on my list as well."

"List?"

"Of people whose intestines I intend to braid in festive patterns."

"Try not to stare," Sloane warned. "Remember, this is a stakeout. We need to be covert."

Right then, Thiago came up to them with a tray packed with two huge desserts. "Here we go, guys!" He set the tray down on the table between Sloane and Loch, mumbling a fire spell under his breath.

Loch was delighted. "Yes! Fire! Brown that sweet meringue!"

Thiago's arm went up in flames instead of the cakes, and he screamed.

"Shit! Are you okay?" Sloane jumped to his feet, trying to smack out the fire.

"That's a most unusual way to flambé," Loch noted, still seated and pouting at the cakes. "Not to be a critic, but it was not very good. Disappointing, in fact."

"Little help here, please!" Sloane hissed. He was still trying to smother the fire out from Thiago's flailing arm.

"Oh yes. Right." Loch put out the flames with a mere thought, and he ignited the cakes as well. "Ah! There! Much better."

"I'm so very, very sorry!" Thiago panted. "Please! I didn't mean for that to happen! One second, I was looking at the cakes, but then I looked at my arm—"

"It's all right," Sloane insisted. "Really. Are you okay? Are you hurt?"

"I'm okay." Thiago groaned. "Man, I am so gonna get fired for this!"

"Seriously, it's okay!" Sloane checked the patio window, hoping they hadn't drawn too much attention. He didn't see anyone looking, though he did spot Olivia sitting at a table by herself reading something on her phone.

She was smiling.

Then Sloane felt the ground shake beneath his feet.

"What the fuck was that?" Thiago gasped.

Loch, who had a mouthful of Baked Alaska and was staring off into the street, mumbled, "So, uh, that *J* might have been a *C* after all."

Sloane turned around quickly. "Oh no."

It was Cleus, fully restored and lumbering down the middle of the street right toward the restaurant. His swinging tentacles were clobbering cars and taking down telephone poles, and he let out a roar that made the glass in the windows rattle.

People were trying to flee, screaming as they ran, and Sloane could see…

A giant ball of crackling magic was headed right for them.

It was the size of a bus, absolutely massive, and moving at supernatural speed.

Sloane summoned his most powerful shield, trying to cover himself, Loch, and Thiago as the ball hurtled toward them. "Loch, watch—!"

The force of the blast blew Sloane right off the ground. He didn't know which way was up, scrambling to right himself and maintain his shield. His ears were ringing, his stomach lurched, and he grunted in pain as he went through the window.

Before he could hit the restaurant floor, strong tentacles snatched him up and held him.

Loch!

"My beloved!" Loch cried. "You're bleeding."

Sloane could barely hear him, but he shook his head. "I'm okay! I'm fine!" He touched his head, finding it wet with blood. He must have lost his shield at some point during the blast. He looked around to see Thiago cowering under a table. "Hey! Are you okay?"

"Uh, uh, no?" Thiago whimpered. He was trembling in fear, but he seemed unharmed, other than a few scrapes and bruises. "What-what is that thing?"

"A very angry god. Stay put, all right?" Sloane dropped the glamour, glancing around the restaurant to survey the damage.

The patio was smoking, the windows were shattered, and Cleus was still coming at them. There was no sign of Olivia or Jeff. Galgareth was helping customers and civilian staff members flee, and Chase and Merrick ran to join Loch and Sloane. Chase and Merrick had dropped their glamours now as well, and Stoker emerged from a back corner booth.

Alexander had his trusty trench coat back on, and he was scowling. "What the fuck is Cleus doing here? Where's Jeff?"

"I don't know." Sloane wished the ringing in his ears would stop already. "I know Olivia was here, we were waiting, and then boom!"

Merrick was speaking into a radio, commanding, "All available AVPD units report to Flaming Amy's restaurant. Please assist civilians in avoiding harm from a rampaging class-five entity. I repeat, a class-five entity."

"Hey!" Galgareth hurried over. "Everybody is out of the restaurant except us and the undercover staff, but there's still a ton of people on the street! They're just standing there, watching Cleus and filming him with their phones!"

"Go! Go!" Chase urged the undercover waiters. "You guys are AVPD! Get your butts moving and get those people outta there!"

"Somewhere in that wreckage were two perfectly delicious Baked Alaska Saint Pierres," Loch lamented. "What a terrible waste."

"Loch? Perhaps you should, you know." Sloane waved his hands to imitate wings. "Get into something more comfortable? Ahem."

"Oh! Yes, of course." Loch grinned. "Hold my cane."

Sloane took the cane, watched Loch's lifeless body drop to the floor, and sighed.

"I will also go become more comfortable." Merrick headed toward the restrooms.

"On my way!" Galgareth closed her eyes, stumbled forward a step, and shook her head. "Whew. That's weird."

"Toby?" Sloane confirmed.

"Yeah! Hey." Toby waved.

"Is that guy okay?" Thiago asked worriedly, still crouched under a table as he gawked at Loch.

"Uh, low blood sugar. He's fine," Sloane assured him.

"Oh, shoot." Toby frowned at Thiago. "Thought we got everybody out. Sorry. Didn't see you there."

"Uh, no, that's okay. I'm cool right here." Thiago stared at Sloane. "Wait. You. You're the guy. The guy from the news! The sword guy!"

"Yup, that's me. Sword guy." Sloane turned to the others. "Asta should be on the way any second now. Alexander, can you—"

"Alexander is staying here to wait for Jeff," Alexander snapped.

Easy, sweet boy, Rota soothed.

"Fine," Sloane said. "Alexander and Chase, you two stay here with Stoker and keep an eye out for Jeff. He might still show up."

"And where are you going, Mr. Beaumont?" Stoker asked.

Another blast hit the restaurant, imploding the patio wall and causing the awning outside to collapse with a loud groan.

"I'm going to deal with Cleus." Sloane marched to the busted wall, summoning a sword of starlight and a new shield. He hurried outside and grimaced at the chaos unfolding before him.

Loch was in his dragon body, flying overhead and raining down prismatic flames on Cleus. He stayed out of reach of Cleus's long tentacles, and he let out a ferocious roar as he launched another fierce attack. Merrick slithered around Cleus in wide circles, trying to contain his carnage and block flying projectiles from the retreating crowd. Galgareth's godly form was a smaller version of her father, Salgumel, though her tentacle beard was much thicker. She was using her wings to herd people away and also help shield them, roaring furiously to encourage them to a flee a bit faster.

Sloane dodged a mailbox that Cleus had tried to throw at Loch, and he lifted his shield as he charged forward.

Loch! Sloane shouted as loudly as he could inside his head. *Can you hear me?*

Yes, my beloved! Loch's voice replied.

We've gotta get Cleus out of the city! He's gonna hurt someone! If I distract him, can you and Merrick open up a portal and get him out of here?

Yes! Be careful, my sweet husband!

Sloane ran to Cleus, being careful to avoid his tentacles, and he hurled his sword at Cleus's fleshy side to get his attention. "Hey!"

"Ohhh, Starkiller!" Cleus roared, hissing as a few of his tentacles clawed at the new wound. "You will pay for that! Sooooon!" He turned away from Sloane and continued his advance to the restaurant.

Having cleared most of the crowd off the streets, Galgareth joined the attack on Cleus. She lit up an abandoned bus with godlyfire and swung it at him like a baseball bat. Merrick and Loch continued their assault alongside her, but even the might of three gods was not enough to pull Cleus off course.

The first swipe of Cleus's tentacles nearly took the front side of the restaurant off. Another strike dented the roof.

Sloane's heart dropped.

The others were still inside with Stoker!

"Okay! New plan!" Sloane shouted, sprinting to the restaurant. "Try to get him away while I get everybody out!" He ran as hard as he could, hurrying through the busted wall. As soon as he was inside, he aimed his shield at the ceiling.

He made it bigger and bigger, his hands burning from the strain as he yelled, "Everyone has to get out! Right now!" The roof collapsed with a horrible groan, and Sloane grunted as he fought to keep his shield up to stop the ceiling from caving in on them. He could see the support beams cracking, and there wasn't a second to lose. "Everybody… out! Now!"

A hand dropped on Sloane's shoulder and the shield suddenly brightened, spreading over the fractured ceiling like glowing paint.

It was Stoker.

"Having trouble out there, Mr. Beaumont?" Stoker asked.

"I don't understand!" Sloane snarled in frustration. "We can't get Cleus to leave the damn restaurant!"

"He's not going to stop until he gets his half god," Stoker drawled. "Obviously."

"What are you talking about? Pandora isn't here!"

"Not her." Stoker's eyes turned black, shining now as endless pools full of swirling stars. "I was referring to me."

CHAPTER 13.

"YOU?" SLOANE WANTED to argue, but there was no denying the galaxies swirling in Stoker's eyes. "You're half god?"

"Yes." Stoker continued to fuel his magic into Sloane's shield, and it soon consumed the entire ceiling to keep it from falling. It went on to encompass the walls and windows, effectively creating a giant bubble around them.

You're Jake the Gladsome! Rota gasped. *You're the son of the first Starkiller! The book that led us to the Fountain, it was yours?*

"Yes, and while I'm sure that's very fascinating to you all, perhaps we can discuss it later, hmm?"

"Who?" Chase asked helplessly. "What the fuck is going on?"

"Okay, so this one time there was a woman named Abigail," Toby began, "and she wanted the god Zunnerath for herself, so she very romantically murdered his mate—"

"All you need to know is that Jeff and his friends have figured out who I am," Stoker replied, "and now they want me for their ritual. This was clearly a trap."

"Whatever." Alexander was unimpressed. He scowled when the building violently shook again. "You're still a dickweed."

"Thank you, Alexander. You always say the sweetest things."

Loch suddenly sat up, prompting Thiago to scream.

"Hey! Loch!" Sloane called. "What are you doing here?"

"Well, none of you were coming out, so I decided to investigate. We tried to open a portal, but Cleus very strongly declined. My uncle and sister are still attempting to persuade him." Loch's eyes narrowed, zooming in on Stoker's hand. "Stoker, you know you shouldn't touch something that doesn't belong to you."

"I'm helping Mr. Beaumont power the shield that's keeping all of us alive, since you and your lovely family have been unable to deter Cleus." Stoker rolled his eyes. "Please focus. I know it's difficult when your brain is the size of—"

"Stoker is who they're after now," Sloane hurriedly interrupted. "That's why Cleus won't leave. We're gonna have to portal him right where he is." The restaurant trembled. "And soon."

"Why do they want Stoker?" Loch asked.

"He's a half god. He's the son of Zunnerath and Abigail the Starkiller."

"Ew." Loch wrinkled his nose. "That means we're related."

"While I do so enjoy these stunning displays of maturity," Stoker drawled, "we need to escape this little trap immediately."

"But hey, wait. This date thing was set up for tonight before he said he wanted to see you," Sloane argued, his mind reeling. "We saw the date on Olivia's calendar days ago. Why are you so sure it's a trap?"

"I imagine they were always planning for Cleus to make an appearance to inspire more fear and panic. It is no coincidence Mr. Martin asked me to meet him here at the same place and time. Once they lost your daughter, they decided to kill two birds with one stone."

"Inspire fear and panic, and grab you for the ritual?"

"Precisely."

"Don't worry," Sloane said firmly. "We're not gonna let Cleus take you."

"How sweet of you," Stoker crooned. "It's nice to know you care. But don't worry, Mr. Beaumont. I have a plan."

"You do?" Sloane grimaced as the building trembled. The shield was holding, but he was getting tired from the intense magical strain.

"Alexander, Rota," Stoker called. "Would you be so kind as to assist me with opening a portal? A very large one, if you please."

"What are you doing?" Sloane demanded.

"You think I didn't realize what Mr. Martin might have been doing when he asked to meet with me?" Stoker winked.

"You knew?" Sloane fumed. "Seriously? That would have been nice to share with the rest of us!"

"You fuckin' slimy skeet stain!" Chase shouted angrily. "Ohhh, you…. You…! Half god, full motherfucker!"

"I strongly concur!" Merrick's voice joined in as he marched out from the bathroom in his vessel again. "You are a full *motherfucker*! My nephew has been telling me everything!"

Loch smirked smugly.

Sloane sighed.

Well, that explained why Loch had been so quiet.

"You have put us and this entire city at risk by keeping sensitive information to yourself," Merrick raged on. "I will find a way to ensure that you are prosecuted for this to the fullest extent of the law!" He huffed. "Motherfucker!"

"I'm sorry to use such strong language, but I have to agree. Stoker, you're acting like one big, giant motherfucker!" Toby's tone had changed, indicating Galgareth was back now. She paused as if listening to something. "Ah, thanks, Toby. Stoker? You're also a moldy butt-nugget-smuggling cockwaffle."

"I can draw Cleus into a world of my choosing." Stoker ignored the cursing. "Using the magic from the Xenon tree in my possession, I can prevent anyone or anything from teleporting out without facing dire consequences. Even gods. My intention had been to take Mr. Martin there to deal with him personally—"

"That's what this was about? You trying to get back at Jeff?" Alexander accused. "Because, oops, you sold him that fuckin' book and got a bunch of everlasting people killed?"

"Yes," Stoker replied without hesitation. "It was my own arrogance that cost those people their lives, and I intend to serve justice—"

"Fuck you!" Alexander scowled. "You were gonna kill him, weren't you? Were you even gonna tell me and Rota? You know we've been wanting to talk to Jeff in our own very special violent way—"

"Very strongly worded way," Rota corrected out loud.

"—about what he knows about Gronoch and Rota's body!"

"This serves our current needs," Stoker insisted. "We can gather our forces and take care of the threat right outside. The one that's actually here. The old god."

"Stoker is right." Sloane gritted his teeth. "We'll figure out what to do about Jeff later. Right now we need to deal with Cleus. Loch, Galgareth, Merrick, Alexander, and Rota, you'll come with me and Stoker to this other world to fight Cleus. Toby and Chase, you'll stay here with Thiago—"

"Who?" Chase blinked.

"Uh… me?" Thiago poked his head out from under the table.

"Who the fuck are you?" Chase asked.

"I'm… the waiter?"

"He is one of the civilian employees of the restaurant. Keep him safe, and we shall deal with the details after we are victorious." Merrick grabbed a fistful of Chase's hair and kissed him hard.

Chase's hat nearly fell off.

"Stay safe," Merrick said firmly.

"You too." Chase licked his lips and adjusted his hat. "I'm gonna need a lot more of that when you get back."

Outside, Cleus roared and tore a massive hole in the roof. He was hovering over them, his goopy skin trying to squeeze through while his tentacles slapped against the shield—the only thing separating them from his blows.

Sloane hissed as the shield flickered. Even with Stoker's assistance, it was a lot to maintain. "Jeff and the others could still be close by, so I wouldn't be surprised if they follow us. But we need to go! Now! Open the portal!"

"Did someone say portal?" Asta appeared with Kunst tucked under his arm, lounging on top of the table Thiago was hiding beneath.

Thiago screamed again.

"Nice shield, by the way," Asta chirped. "I think I may need a massage later. Might have pulled something getting through it. Any volunteers?"

"Asta!" Sloane was glad to see them both, and he was actually proud to see Asta was wearing clothes.

Okay, yes, it was a pair of lime green short-shorts, but it was clothing nonetheless.

"Greetings, all!" Kunst said. "I hope we have arrived in time! His Highness wanted to, and I quote, make an entrance."

"I would say your timing is perfect!" Galgareth beamed, as it was certainly from her serendipitous influence.

"This place looks like shit." Asta glanced around through his coordinating green shades. "What's going on?"

"Did you not see the very large god outside?" Sloane asked.

"Oh yeah." Asta looked up at the hole in the roof where Cleus was trying to get in. "The really angry one?"

"Yes. We need to get that very angry god out there somewhere else!" Sloane said quickly. "Can you help with a portal?"

"Uh, duh." Asta shrugged. "Portals are my jam, jelly, and my preserves."

"We don't need help from some stupid cat boy." Alexander glared. "Me and Rota got it, okay?"

"Oh, because you totally look like you do, Count Suckula." Asta grinned. "Anybody tell you goth is so fuckin' out this season?"

"So are filthy cat creatures." Loch made a face. "And yet, here you are."

A crack appeared in the shield, and Cleus continued to hammer in the newly weakened spot.

"Portal! Sloane demanded. "Stoker! Now!"

"On it!" Stoker created a small portal in the floor.

"That's our cue, kiddo!" Chase helped pull Thiago out from under the table. He grabbed his arm and then bolted to the back of the restaurant to take cover.

"Go kick some godly ass!" Toby shouted as he ran after them.

Alexander raised his hands, channeling Rota's power to expand the portal. The resulting winds were wild, creating a vortex of flying napkins and menus, and it kept growing.

Sloane's feet slid across the floor, but Stoker held him in place. Loch was on his other side now, holding on to him as well and offering his magic to keep the shield going while the portal grew.

"Shit!" Sloane hissed. "If we drop the shield to get Cleus into the portal, we might get crushed when the rest of the roof comes down!"

"Look, I love all sizes equally," Asta teased, "but when it comes to portals? Bigger is always better." He moved effortlessly through the swirling winds to the edge of the portal and threw Kunst in. "Heads up!"

"Your Highnesss!" Kunst shrieked as he got sucked in and promptly vanished.

"Hey, guys." Asta winked slyly. "Better hold on to your butts." He blew a kiss and then gracefully dove in after Kunst.

The moment Asta disappeared from this side, the portal turned into a massive void. The winds picked up, and Sloane could see it was dragging in furniture and parts of the wall and—oh shit!

The portal exploded, and everything went black.

Sloane had the distinct sensation of falling, and Loch's tentacles coiled around him, drawing him close. He clung as tightly as he could, grunting as they landed on….

Wait, they were back in the restaurant, but it was tilted, as if the building was being lifted up on one end.

No, wait, cancel that.

Yes, they were inside the restaurant, but only because Asta had managed to portal an entire section of the city block. The front section of the restaurant was here, plus part of the sidewalk and street.

Sloane stared at their new surroundings, and he blushed when he realized where they were.

It was Urilith's fertility temple, a massive step-style pyramid full of columns, wide open spaces, and lots of graphic murals painted on the walls within.

He and Loch had been here once or twice.

The city block section had landed on the side of the pyramid, and Sloane could see a familiar level full of lush beds through the broken windows of the restaurant. Since the back half of the restaurant wasn't here, that hopefully meant that Chase and Thiago were still safe on Aeon. There wasn't any immediate sign of Cleus, but Sloane could hear him roaring not far away.

Merrick had righted himself and was busy dusting off his suit. "Well, we are here."

"You're welcome," Stoker said from where he was sprawled across a pile of tables that had collected as a result of the severely uneven floor.

Alexander appeared to be floating thanks to Rota's ghostly tentacles and didn't seem ruffled in the slightest. With a wave of his hand, Rota set him down, and he lit a cigarette. "Whatever."

"Wow!" Galgareth was in her godly form, her massive body perched on the broken ledge of the restaurant. "That was a pretty impressive portal, Your Highness." She looked around. "Your Highness?"

"Huh. Where the hell did Asta go?" Sloane frowned.

"Hmmph. Probably cowering somewhere, licking himself." Loch huffed impatiently. "Just like an Asra to flee when—"

The restaurant suddenly moved, sliding several yards down the side of the temple. The unexpected movement unbalanced them all, sending them tumbling about, except for Stoker, who hadn't gotten up yet.

Orange tentacles slithered through the broken windows and over the tops of the wall where the roof once was.

It was Cleus!

He went immediately for Stoker.

Galgareth snarled and grabbed part of the broken restaurant wall to heave over at Cleus, trying to drive him back. Merrick dropped from his vessel, his true body now filling the cramped restaurant space as he lunged forward to snap at Cleus's intruding tentacles as Galgareth went for a chunk of the sidewalk.

"My love." Loch kissed Sloane passionately before letting go of him to join Merrick and Galgareth. His empty body slid across the floor as he took on his dragon form to fly up into the air. He immediately attacked, breathing out blasts of fire at Cleus.

Sloane took a deep breath as surges of adrenaline ran through his body. He hurried around Merrick's side, calling on his magic to summon the sword of starlight. He squeezed the handle tight and swung it over his head to slice through Cleus's tentacles.

Merrick and Galgareth had fended off several of them, Merrick using his giant jaws and Galgareth her immense strength to weaponize the building around them to drive Cleus away.

"Go! You got wings, use them!" Alexander shouted, urging Merrick to take off to join Loch's aerial assault. He took Merrick's place, using Rota's tentacles to tear Cleus's into meaty chunks.

Galgareth charged a long section of the sidewalk with her bright fire and leaped into the air after her uncle to clobber Cleus with it. "Cousin! You are not being very nice at all! You should really consider standing down!"

Cleus roared in reply.

"Rude!"

On his feet now, Stoker stretched out his arms and aimed a mammoth wall at the tentacles coming in over their heads.

Cleus howled in pain, and another bodily explosion seemed imminent. Instead, he started to retreat with a miserable wail.

"Yeah!" Alexander shouted triumphantly. "Can't portal outta here, can you, bitch?"

"He's running!" Stoker pointed. "Starkiller, go!"

"Loch!" Sloane looked up, trying to find Loch. "I need a ride!"

For you, my darling husband, always! Loch's thoughts replied. With a big flap of his wings, he turned around and circled back to the restaurant.

Sloane was ready.

They had Cleus on the run, and there was nowhere for him to go. He was severely outmatched in terms of firepower and numbers, and there was no way he was going to escape this time.

All Sloane had to do was figure out how to get to his core to destroy him, and then—shit!

A blast of fire hit Sloane's back and forced him to his knees. He lost the sword, hissing in pain from the awful burn. He turned to see where it had come from, staring in horror at Jeff Martin and Daisy Lopez coming right at them.

"We got company!" Sloane shouted.

"Ding-dong," Jeff taunted. "Honey, I'm home. What's for dinner?" Stoker stepped forward with a snarl.

"Jeff is mine!" Alexander stepped around Stoker and then launched himself at Jeff.

"Wait! Alexander!" Sloane exclaimed. "Just—!"

The entire restaurant jolted again, staggering down the side of the temple and picking up speed rapidly. It was not going to stop this time. It crashed into the ground, cracking down the middle and collapsing most of the remaining walls.

Alexander had managed to brace himself using Rota's tentacles as before, but Jeff went zooming almost comically through the air into the surrounding trees. Daisy slammed into the side of a busted wall with a pained cry before collapsing, and Sloane....

Was wrapped up in iridescent black tentacles that were definitely not Loch's.

It was Stoker!

"Are you all right?" Stoker demanded.

"I'm fine." Sloane pushed Stoker away roughly, amending his seemingly rude actions with a quiet, "Thank you."

"Of course." Stoker bowed his head. "Mr. Beaumont."

My sweet husband! Loch called to Sloane, hovering overhead. He was zipping back and forth, avoiding Cleus's tentacles reaching up for him. *Are you all right?*

"I'm okay!" Sloane shouted back. "Watch out!"

Loch soared higher, narrowly dodging Cleus's next attack. He let loose another barrage of magical fire from his jaws to drive Cleus away from the ruins of the restaurant.

"Oh, that fuckin' asshole!" Alexander snarled in frustration. He was up again, dragging himself over part of a collapsed wall. "Where the fuck did he go? Where's Jeff? Huh?"

Are you all right, my sweet boy? Rota asked worriedly.

"Just great. Peachy! I'll be even better after we choke out Jeff!" Alexander scanned the forest surrounding the temple, and then he broke into a full sprint into the trees.

"Alexander!" Sloane protested.

"Fuck you, Starkiller!" Alexander shouted over his shoulder. "Go kill a fuckin' god already!"

Our sincerest apologies! Rota called out. *We are so very sorry—*

"The fuck we are!"

Sloane hoped that Alexander and Rota would be able to take on Jeff more successfully than their previous encounters. He looked over to see Cleus being driven around the temple into the tree line by Merrick and Loch still blasting him from overhead while Galgareth continued to wale on him with her sidewalk bat, and oh....

Oh no.

There were two of them now.

Two Cleuses.

Cleusi. Clei?

Whatever.

"Shit! Come on!" Sloane groaned. "Can't we ever catch a fucking break?"

"Sloane!" Daisy screeched as she rose up on shaking legs. "You cannot stop this! We will beat you! We're taking Stoker and getting out of here. Salgumel will rise, and he—"

Stoker whipped one of his tentacles across her face, sending her right back to the ground.

She didn't move again.

"Ah." Stoker popped his neck audibly. "There. Is that better, Mr. Beaumont?"

"Yeah, thanks." Sloane crawled through the debris of the restaurant. "Come on! We have to help them!"

One of the Cleuses had been able to get a few tentacles around Loch when he flew too close. He was dragging Loch down into the trees, hitting him with magical blasts and burning him with his searing flesh. Galgareth stopped her assault to help her brother, and the other Cleus choked her with several tentacles the moment her back was turned.

Loch roared in agony, twisting and turning in a desperate attempt to escape. He roasted Cleus with his godly fire, but Cleus refused to let go. Galgareth swung her bat at the tentacles holding her, but more kept coming.

Merrick was circling around to help them, but it didn't look like he was going to get back before Loch got grounded.

"Shit, shit, shit!" Sloane dropped his hand to his side, taking a deep breath and calling on another sword of starlight. "Loch! Baby! I'm coming!"

"Got one of those to spare?" Stoker asked, falling into step beside Sloane as they raced toward the battle.

"What?" Sloane scoffed. "You can't—"

"I can." Stoker held out his hand. "Now, Mr. Beaumont!"

Sloane handed the sword over, and he was surprised to see that it didn't evaporate when Stoker grabbed it. "Okay! Awesome! Now help them!"

Though clearly straining to keep a hold of it, Stoker had a tight grip on the starlit sword. He narrowed his eyes, aiming carefully, and he then hurled the blade with ferocious strength.

It spun through the air, and Sloane watched in awe as it sliced through Cleus's tentacles that were holding Galgareth and kept on spinning to slice through the ones that were holding Loch.

Free now, Loch rapidly flapped his wings to get out of harm's way. Galgareth whirled around the Cleus that had been strangling her and roared, releasing a blast of fire from her mouth.

Sloane summoned a new sword. "Want another one?"

"I won't be able to kill with it," Stoker said quickly, "but I can sure as hell wield one."

After passing it over, Sloane hurried to create another. He cringed at how badly his hands were burning from exerting so much magic, but certainly two swords of starlight would be better than one.

The second Cleus was launching a counterattack against Merrick and Loch while the other Cleus moved up the side of the temple like a slug to get away from Galgareth. From this higher vantage point, he fired huge balls of magic and swung his tentacles out to try to catch the flying gods and keep Galgareth at bay.

Sloane and Loch reached the second Cleus on the ground, and Sloane swung at the barrage of flailing tentacles. He got his shield up, blocking a heavy blow. He gasped when that tentacle suddenly writhed on the ground, cleanly cut.

Stoker was right beside him, helping him battle through the volatile appendages.

Merrick and Loch continued to fiercely battle the Cleus climbing up the temple while Stoker and Sloane closed in on the Cleus on the ground. Two swords of starlight were making it much easier to advance, and Stoker expanded Sloane's shield to help fend off Cleus's attacks.

Sloane struck over and over, his shoulders and arms soon singing of exhaustion. The tentacles never seemed to end, and there wasn't enough time to cast anything else in between dealing or dodging blows.

He and Stoker were in danger of losing all the ground they'd claimed, and Cleus just kept sending more of his tentacles at them.

"This isn't working!" Sloane shouted as he was forced back another step. "I'm never going to get close enough!"

"Damn!" Stoker gritted his teeth. "All right. New plan!" He threw the sword in his hand at Cleus.

It struck one of Cleus's eyes, and he snarled furiously. "Ohhh, you will suffer for that, wretched halflingggg!"

Stoker shot out his thick black tentacles, wincing in obvious pain as he used them to lasso all of Cleus's tentacles that he could reach. He then parted them in half, creating a perfect opening for Sloane to go after Cleus's blobby torso. "Go! Now!"

Cleus screamed and flailed, struggling in Stoker's powerful grasp. When he couldn't break free, he screamed loud enough to make the ground tremble.

Stoker's eyes turned black, and he refused to let go, roaring back defiantly.

Sloane lunged forward, running up between the spread tentacles and swinging his sword at Cleus's side. His hand was searing down to the bone, and his entire body ached from the strain of holding this much magic for so long. He sliced on, over and over, using his shield to deflect as much of Cleus's toxic skin as he could.

When he stabbed Cleus next, he was up to his elbow. He cut again, and then he was up to his shoulder. He had to be close to Cleus's core by now, and he poured all that he had into each swing even as his arm burned from a combination of Cleus's nasty flesh and muscle failure.

There—! The sword hit something solid, and then—!

Cleus exploded.

Sloane ate dirt after flipping through the air, and he groaned through a mouthful of grass. He was covered in fleshy orange gunk, and his hands were stinging and numb like he'd been playing in snow for too long.

Lifting his head, he could still see Loch, Galgareth, and Merrick dueling the other Cleus, and the home team was not doing well. Loch was visibly wounded across his chest and legs, and Galgareth, also hurt, was fighting to shake off some of Cleus's tentacles from her arm. Merrick's wing was injured, and he was breathing fire from the ground.

"That wasn't him?" Sloane groaned as he got back up and flung off some of the orange slime. "We got the copy? This is some bullshit!"

"We have to kill him before he divides again!" Stoker growled.

"No shit!" Sloane took a deep breath. "It's fine, it's fine. There's still just one of—"

Cleus's mammoth body suddenly split, split again, now making three Cleuses on the battlefield instead of one.

"Fuck!" Sloane screamed.

"Hey! So, nobody be mad, but—" Asta came bounding out from the forest, transformed into his sleek Asra body, a giant panther the size of a Clydesdale with a tentacled tail. "—I totally tripped on Kunst and smashed my head on what may have been a rock or Kunst himself."

"Don't blame me!" Kunst seethed, his ball flickering in annoyance. He was right behind Asta, and he sped up to bop the top of Asta's head. "I've warned you about your reckless portaling, Your Highness! If you had just been looking where you were going—"

"I was!" Asta swatted at him. "It's the shorts! I can't function in clothing!"

Kunst gasped, wheezing sharply, "By all the gods!" He took a breath. "Cleus has multiplied!"

"Yeah, we noticed!" Sloane snapped. "Any idea how we find his core or whatever?"

"We have to figure out which one is the original!" Kunst made a sound like he was sucking air through his teeth, which was weird since he didn't have any. "If we destroy him, the others shall fall!"

"Hey!" Sloane said. "Asta! Can you sniff out which Cleus is the real deal?"

"Huh?" Asta stared down the trio of gods and bared his pointy teeth in a sneer. "Ew. Fuckin' gross. Yeah, hang on a sec." He lifted his head, smelling the air. He must have caught a scent because he suddenly flinched, followed by a loud sneeze. "Ugh, okay, got it."

"Which one?"

"See the one with the extra droopy eyeball in the back, like, where his butt would be if he had a butt?"

Sloane searched for what Asta had described. "Yes!"

"That one. The old god stench is super ripe." Asta cocked his head at Stoker. "And you… you smell like a cheap god knockoff."

"Charming," Stoker drawled.

"Like, if gods are Mountain Dew, you're a Mountain Don't."

"Right, so. We need that one." Sloane kept tracking the original Cleus as he and his copies crawled about. "Hey, Stoker. If you and Asta can provide a distraction, maybe I can get close enough."

There was a loud cry of pain, drawing all their attention.

Merrick had fallen, and he was trying to break free and slither away. There were too many tentacles on him, and he was trapped. Galgareth ran to help, but Cleus swarmed her with tentacles and dragged her to the ground. Snarling furiously, Loch dove to snap his jaws at the tentacles holding his family and breathe more of his godly fire, but it only took one quick swipe for Cleus to seize one of Loch's hind legs.

Sloane's chest felt tight, and his eyes were getting hot. His hands were blistered, raw, and he was helpless, watching his husband getting slashed and burned by Cleus's tentacles. "Fuck! Come on! We have to do something! Right now!"

"You will have to penetrate the deep recesses of his fatty layers," Kunst added helpfully. "It may be several yards of flesh before you come across the actual core of his being. It is well known that Cleus can implode himself and—"

"Yes, for the love of the gods, yes. I know. Thank you, Professor. I'm fuckin' all over it," Sloane growled. "I'm just trying to figure out how the fuck am I supposed to do that? Look!" He pointed where Loch, Galgareth, and Merrick were struggling. "We're out of time! Come on! To cut through all that, I'd have to—"

"Mr. Beaumont." Stoker grabbed Sloane by his shoulders and kissed his forehead. "Please forgive me."

"Wait, what? Forgive you for wha—oh! *Shit*!" Sloane shouted as Stoker launched him into the air, right into....

Cleus's gaping jaws.

CHAPTER 14.

SLOANE WAS aware of three things very quickly.

The first was that Stoker had struck Cleus with some sort of hostile spell that made him howl in pain and had caused his mouth to open wide enough to gobble him up.

The second was that being instantly surrounded by Cleus's hot, sticky flesh was disgusting, and he had to swallow back bile and hope the sour taste on his tongue was his own.

The third was that Stoker's kiss had created some sort of barrier around Sloane's entire body. Though he could feel the warmth of Cleus's body, there was no burning from his noxious flesh. As he was swallowed, he didn't get cut on any of the thousands of sharp teeth that lined Cleus's throat.

He couldn't see anything, and struggling only seemed to make Cleus's throat close tighter around him. He was beyond pissed off, a bit terrified, and still on the verge of puking. He was worried about Loch, his heart aching to think that his beloved husband was wounded and there was nothing he could do.

Stoker had thought feeding him to Cleus was such a fantastic idea, that jerk, and Sloane was going to kick his ass from here to Aeon and back.

As soon as he figured out how to get out of here, that is.

It was hard to focus, being trapped in the dark, practically immobile, and not being able to breathe. Sloane found himself about to panic and fought against the rising swell of emotions. He had to get out of here, save Loch, and somehow kill Cleus, whose stupid core was deep inside of his body....

Oh.

That was the moment he realized what Stoker wanted him to do.

Gritting his teeth, Sloane tried to gather the strength to summon one last starlight sword. His hands were throbbing, and he was getting light-headed from holding his breath for so long. He tried to create the sword, but the magic fizzled right out.

No, no, no.

Sloane had to fight. He had to keep going. He had to survive. He closed his eyes against the suffocating darkness he was trapped in and prayed.

Please, hear me, Great Azaethoth. Please. I need you. I need your help. I have to save Loch.

Our daughter. Our family and friends....

Everyone.

The whole world!

I know all of this might sort of maybe be my fault a teeny, tiny bit because of that prayer when I was a kid, and yeah, Loch said it was like I put in a doggy door or something, but please. I need the chance to keep fighting. I need to fix this. Please just let me! I need your help!

Silence.

Nothing.

Then a brilliant spark of magic lit up in Sloane's hand, growing into the shape of a glittering pommel. He was obviously grateful for the sword, but he could have gone without seeing the inside of Cleus's digestive tract illuminated with starlight. Ignoring the repulsive surroundings, he raised the sword up as the blade grew, fighting the cramped space to swing.

It was more of a stunted stabbing, but Sloane tore through Cleus's flesh. The blade of starlight cut the godly skin like a hot knife through butter, and Sloane soon had enough room to swing it properly. He hacked away, not sure what exactly he was looking for, but he couldn't stop. He had to find that damn core, and then—!

The blade hit something. There was resistance. This had to be it!

Lungs burning in dire need of air and head spinning violently, Sloane pointed the tip of the blade in that same direction and thrust as hard as he could.

Sunlight poured into his eyes, blinding him, and he found himself soaring through the air in a wave of orange goop. He landed on his back, wheezing and soaked, and he croaked, "Oh *fuck*."

He had done it. He had killed another god.

Cleus had exploded, along with his duplicates, and the ground and temple were totally covered in his fleshy guts. A few bits were still coming back down like the most revolting rain imaginable, and Sloane hissed in pain as his skin burned.

The spell Stoker had cast to protect him from Cleus's searing flesh was gone, and he frantically tore at his clothes to get it off him.

"My love!" Loch swooped in, limping as he wrapped himself around Sloane. "You're all right! Oh, sweet husband. I was so worried about you!"

"Loch!" Sloane flung off his jacket and his shirt. "Hey! Little help?"

"I really don't think this is an appropriate time for initiating mating, but I suppose I could—"

"Cleus! Burning guts! Help!"

"Yes! Of course!" A flap of Loch's wings removed the fleshy goo from Sloane. "Ah, is that better?"

"Yeah, thank you." Sloane hugged Loch's broad chest, sighing in relief. "Are you all right?"

"Yes, my gorgeous husband." Loch bowed his head to nuzzle Sloane's hair. "Now that you are here, I am well."

Merrick joined them, butting his snout against the side of Loch's head affectionately. "Yes. We are all safe now."

Galgareth pounced Loch and Merrick, swinging an arm around them both and hugging them tight. "We did it!"

"Thanks to me and my brilliant plan," Stoker said with a smirk. He was goop-free and appeared completely refreshed, the bastard. "I'd say it went beautifully, wouldn't you, Mr. Beaumont?"

"You!" Sloane broke away from Loch's embrace to charge Stoker. "You threw me into Cleus's mouth! His freakin' mouth? Really? Are you insane?"

"Did you really want me to waste precious time explaining my plan when my motivation was obvious?" Stoker didn't flinch, though his eyes turned black.

Sloane stuck his finger in Stoker's face. "You're a fuckin' asshole!"

Stoker cast a cursory glance over Sloane's bare torso before replying, "It worked, did it not?"

"Do you know what else works?" Loch piped up. "These little plastic tools for french braiding hair. They're shaped like wiggly serpents, made out of hard plastic, and I am confident I could get Stoker's intestines through the loops if I sliced them thinly enough."

"You can weave your cousin's viscera later," Merrick griped. "We have more important things to worry about."

"Visceral arts and crafts are very important, Uncle."

Even though his eyes were empty sockets, Sloane swore Merrick had just rolled them.

"You guys are so damn weird." Asta was still in his Asran form, delicately picking his way through the slime. "*Sooo* not a surprise that you're all related."

All that remained of Cleus was turning into blips of glowing light before blinking away into nothing, and Asta sneezed when a piece got too close to his nose.

"You are victorious once again, Sloane." Kunst hovered close, and it sounded like he was smiling. "You have truly become a magnificent Starkiller."

"Thank you, Professor." Sloane smiled back, though his heart wasn't in it.

Whether it was a voluntary sacrifice like Kunst had been or slaying any of the numerous old gods that had fallen beneath Sloane's sword of starlight, he didn't take any joy in ending a life. He would do what he had to for the sake of his loved ones and the world, but he wasn't going to like it.

Watching the last of Cleus's orangey flesh evaporate made Sloane's stomach twist, and he secretly hoped this would be the last time he'd ever have to raise his starlight sword.

"Just a thought here?" Asta rubbed his nose. "You know, just thinking out loud, maybe we should go see what Count Suckula is up to?"

"Shit." Sloane jerked his head around to stare at the trees. "Alexander. He must still be fighting Jeff!"

"Let us go!" Merrick dropped to the ground and slithered away, bolting forward at supernatural speed.

"Loch, can you fly?" Sloane asked.

"Yes, my sweet husband." Loch lowered his neck so Sloane could climb up. As soon as Sloane was safely mounted, he took off into the air after Merrick.

"Hey!" Asta shouted. "Wait up! Fuckin' assholes! Some of us can't fly!"

"Run faster, vile cat beast!" Loch yelled back.

"Oh! Come here!" Galgareth reached for Asta. "I'll carry you, Your Highness!"

"Hey, hey!" Asta hissed. "Easy on the fur!"

Loch cackled, flapping his wings and soaring over the trees.

"We've gotta find him," Sloane urged. "I know Alexander is powerful, but—"

"Fear not, dear husband," Loch soothed. "We will save the grumpy one, I promise."

As they flew high above the trees, it was easy to track Alexander and Jeff by the path of destruction their battle had left behind. Entire sections of the forest were nothing but smoldering craters.

Sloane caught a quick glimpse of Rota's big spikes peeking out from the tops of the trees, shifting between translucent and solid form.

"I see them!" Loch dove, circling down to the edge of a large clearing.

The clearing was in fact another wrecked crater, and Alexander had Jeff pinned flat on his back in the middle of it with Rota's tentacles.

"What's the matter, fuck face?" Alexander was sneering down at Jeff. "Can't use your little bullshit spell on my marks, now can you?"

"That's all right," Jeff croaked. He was bloodied and bruised, but he was smiling. "I'll find… another way. There is always… another way."

"Fuck you." Alexander twisted one of Rota's tentacles around Jeff's neck. He smirked when Jeff choked. "I'm sorry, what was that? I can't hear you, Je-*fahfah*."

"By all the gods." Jeff gurgled. "It's… Jeff! My name is… Jeff!"

Sloane hopped off Loch's back as soon as he landed beside them. "Hey! Alexander! Rota!"

Starkiller! Rota greeted cheerfully. *Cleus has been defeated?*

"Yes. He's gone."

Alexander frowned. "Why aren't you wearing a shirt?"

"Toxic flesh. Everywhere." Sloane made a face. "And I do mean everywhere. Are you guys okay?"

"Peachy keen," Alexander replied. "Me and fuck face are just having a little chat." He loosened the tentacle on Jeff's neck, allowing him to catch his breath and cough. "Aren't we, fuck face?"

"It doesn't matter." Jeff inhaled sharply. "There are more like Cleus… more like me. So many more."

Merrick slithered up then, and the others were only a few seconds behind him. Galgareth was cradling Asta like a baby, and he didn't seem to mind being carried now. They had Jeff totally surrounded, and yet he didn't seem the least bit afraid.

"Please, tell me all about how you're going to stop me," Jeff taunted, his teeth flashing through his rotted cheek as he grinned. His usual bandage was hanging on by a thread. "Tell me how you're gonna win when I'm a breath away from—"

"We've already won," Sloane snapped. "Cleus is dead, and so is every other god who has stood against us. We have stopped you over and over again. This is it. You're not waking up Salgumel or the Kindress or anyone else. This is the end for you."

"You cannot escape, Mr. Martin." Stoker walked up to kneel beside Jeff, smiling cruelly. "You know, I think this is a rather good look for you."

"Oh?" Jeff spat. "How's that?"

"Helpless."

Jeff laughed. "Shows what you know, you arrogant prick."

"Hey, focus, fuck face." Alexander slapped Jeff across the face with a tentacle. "Tell me everything you know about Gronoch and his experiments right now. If you do, I'll put you out of your misery before letting Stoker take a poke at you."

Jeff laughed again. "Wow." He looked around at them all. "You idiots really think you've beat me, don't you? Me? Who has been touched by the Kindress himself and survived?"

"You got your ass kicked, you're silenced, and oh yeah, if you try to teleport, you're probably gonna lose more than a leg this time." Alexander smiled sweetly. "I hear the disruption from a Xenon tree can cut you right in half."

"Count Suckula speaks the truth," Asta said. "It's like running through a giant Slap Chop."

"Then again, you know what? Fuck it." Alexander shrugged. "Portal away, Je-fahfah. I think I'd actually like to see that shit."

"If Mr. Martin has truly been incapacitated, then we will place him under arrest," Merrick said firmly. "Ask him what you will, but then we are taking him back to Aeon to answer for his numerous crimes."

"I don't think so." Stoker narrowed his eyes. "I believe he is going to answer for them right here, right now."

Merrick rose up to his full height and fixed his dead stare on Stoker. "Then I will have you arrested for premeditated murder, Stoker."

"You do realize that if Jeff is taken into official custody, any shred of secrecy we have will be destroyed the second he opens his mouth on the record." Stoker snorted. "So, are you arresting me before or after you're revealed as a god?"

"It's certainly after the intestinal braiding, because that has now become my new priority," Loch said haughtily.

"You really need to come up with a new threat, Azaethoth."

"How about I just eat you?"

"Hey, hey!" Sloane raised his hands for calm. "Look, we need to figure this out. As much as I hate to admit it, Stoker has a point. Bringing Jeff to justice also means exposing the truth of who we are—"

"Unless I erase his memory." Loch shrugged. "Just a suggestion."

"No one is erasing shit until he tells me what the fuck I want to know," Alexander warned.

"Gentlemen, gentlemen, please!" Jeff laughed. "There's no need to fight over little ol' me. Look, I'll be honest with you. I am definitely not being arrested, and while I might die, none of you will be getting the pleasure."

"*You.*" Alexander glared down at Jeff. "Stop bullshitting and start talking." He tightened the tentacle around Jeff's neck. "Now!"

Jeff choked, and he began to turn a deepening shade of red.

"Alexander!" Sloane shouted. "Stop! You're going to kill him!"

"That's kind of the fuckin' idea!" Alexander argued.

Even as his face was turning colors, Jeff was smiling. Alexander loosened his grip enough so Jeff could wheeze and cough, and Jeff gasped out a weak laugh. "You can't stop me, you know. What's done is done. Salgumel will rise. This is the end."

"For you, it's about to fuckin' be!" Alexander snarled, his eyes now a bright and glowing red. He squeezed Jeff's throat again, and it didn't seem like he was going to let go. "Fuckin' tell me—"

"Alexander, remove yourself from him," Merrick warned, "or I will remove you."

"Suck it, Gordoth! For fuck's sake!"

"Unless you relish in the flavor of soil, I would suggest you stand down immediately." Merrick lowered his head as if about to charge.

"Hey, hey!" Sloane pleaded. "Everybody calm down!"

"You can suck it too, Starkiller!" Alexander barked back. "I've got this!"

"Alexander," Stoker tried next, "listen to me. We want the same thing, but—"

"Fuck you, Stoker!" Alexander scoffed. "That's pretty incredible. One complaint from Starkiller and you're all half god, full *bitch*."

Jeff appeared to be chewing on something, like there was a big wad of gum in his mouth, and he cleared his throat loudly to be heard over the bickering. "Ahem."

"What?" Alexander roared in frustration.

Jeff smiled, and there was a small stone totem between his front teeth.

"No…." Alexander's eyes widened.

Jeff turned his head and spat the totem out.

"No, no, no!" Alexander screamed furiously, seizing control of every last one of Rota's tentacles to grab the totem and dive back into Jeff's mouth. "You stupid son of a bitch! No! Don't you fuckin' dare!"

Sloane watched in horror as Jeff's face rotted away, his skin turning bright red and purple and then green and black. It was the rot that had infected his cheek, the touch of the Kindress, and without the totem to keep it at bay, it was consuming him.

Alexander couldn't put the totem back because there was nowhere to put it in mere seconds.

Sloane had never seen anything like this, and he took a step back, certain that touching it in any way was a terrible, terrible idea.

Even Alexander was retreating now, withdrawing all of Rota's ghostly tentacles and staring wordlessly at the slick gooey mess of Jeff's rapidly decomposing body.

Jeff was laughing, his smile made all the more horrible by his teeth flashing through the last remnants of his face. "Salgumel… will… rise… I've seen it… in my dreams…."

The awful magic didn't stop, and Jeff melted until there was nothing but a black puddle of goo and a sliver of a white bandage.

Jeff Martin was dead.

Sloane clung to Loch, trying to figure out what to say. They had all witnessed something horrible happen to an equally horrible person, and it was hard to believe Jeff had been willing to go that far to escape facing judgment for his crimes. After so many months of hunting him, it felt weirdly unsatisfying in a way Sloane couldn't explain.

"Well, that was fucking disgusting," Asta blurted out.

Galgareth sighed and dropped Asta.

"Your Highness!" Kunst hissed.

"It was!" Asta shook himself off. "That's what the fuckin' Kindress's shit does? Major ew."

"Death," Merrick said quietly, "to where there is life."

"No…." Alexander said, practically shaking. "It can't end like this. It just fuckin' can't."

Oh, Alexander, Rota soothed.

There was a distant explosion.

"What the fuck was that?" Asta blinked.

"The tree." Stoker turned back toward the temple. "Shit."

Dread curled up inside Sloane's stomach. "Daisy. Has anyone seen Daisy since the restaurant crashed?"

"Fuck."

On foot and by air, they all rushed to the temple. They stopped to check the ruins of the restaurant and found it empty. After Loch and Merrick retrieved their mortal vessels and Galgareth brought Toby over, Stoker led everyone into one of the inner chambers, where the splinters of a once-glowing sapling were all that remained.

"Oh, I like this room." Loch was beaming. "I believe I had at least three of my tentacles inside my beautiful husband right there on that wall—" Sloane elbowed him. "—ow! Violence is never the answer, my sweet love."

"It was definitely Daisy," Sloane confirmed with a perception spell, ignoring Loch. "She must have stayed behind to find the tree."

"Once she destroyed it, she was free to portal right out of here," Galgareth said glumly.

Stoker kneeled to sort through the shattered pieces of the tree and gather them up. Each one that he touched turned black, and he threw them down in frustration.

"Sorry about your twig, demigod guy," Asta offered with a shrug of his big furry shoulders.

"It's all right. This was a sapling I had cultivated from another tree I own." Stoker grimaced. "Though I don't suppose anyone has any ideas how Daisy found this one?"

"There are a variety of spells she could have used to track the unique energy of the Xenon tree." Kunst was somber, and his ball wasn't glowing as brightly as before. "Magical wood from another world tends to stick out a bit, even to a basic witch."

"As much as I am dying to comment on that magical wood thing, how about we get the fuck outta here?" Asta asked. "Bad guys are dead or gone, good guys win, woo, rah. I'm bored."

"Yeah. It's so fuckin' great." Alexander huffed. "Except you forgot about the part where thanks to all you fuckin' assholes playin' with your dicks back there, I've got fuckin' nothin'.'"

"What?" Sloane sputtered. "What are you talking about?"

"I was definitely not playing with my dicks," Asta mumbled. "You would have noticed."

Alexander, be kind, Rota cautioned. *It is not their fault.*

"No, fuck that!" Alexander snapped back before turning his wrath on the others. "You were all so fuckin' worried about what to do with stupid-ass Jeff that I didn't get a chance to ask him shit before he decided to fuckin' off himself! Fuck you. Fuck all of you. Fuck this place. This is bullshit—"

"Hey!" Sloane barked. "I'm sorry, okay? I know how important it is for you to find Rota's body, but we were trying to figure out what was going to be best for everyone—"

"Yeah, everyone else except me and Rota!" Alexander shouted. "I just needed him to answer one fuckin' question!"

"Ooo, on second thought, let's stay," Asta whispered loudly to Kunst. "This is gettin' good."

"Shut the fuck up, you fuckin' idiotic furball." Alexander snarled. "No one was even talking to you!"

Alexander, be nice, Rota urged.

"Aww, do you need a hug, little guy?" Asta batted his eyes. "I mean, I don't really wanna give you one, but maybe somebody else will if you ask nicely."

"You think this is a joke, asshole?" Alexander was now seething. "I will fuckin' skin your ass and make fuckin' mittens—"

"Alexander, no!" Rota interrupted, shouting out loud in a desperate attempt to calm him.

"Oh no, what you mean is Alexander, *yes*. Mittens, big fuckin' mittens so I can strangle him with them—"

"I don't hate this plan," Loch chimed in.

"Brother!" Galgareth scolded.

"Alexander. Please." Rota wrapped his ghostly tentacles around Alexander's chest, briefly becoming visible as he embraced him. "Be calm, my sweet boy. It's all right."

Alexander took a deep breath, clearly struggling to calm down. "Okay, okay. I'm fine. I'm fuckin' fine, okay? I don't wanna hear one more word from that stupid cat or else—"

"Well." Asta scoffed at Alexander. "Now I'm definitely not hugging you."

"That's it!" Alexander yelled as he charged toward Asta. "It's fuckin' mittens time."

"Enough!" Stoker roared, a flicker of his prismatic tentacles creeping out from the collar of his suit.

His voice was enough to stop Alexander in his tracks, and Asta stared warily.

Stoker stood, turning to face Alexander. "You're not the only one who lost the chance to get what they wanted today. But Daisy is still out there, Jeff's partner and confidant."

"You think she knows something?" Alexander demanded.

"I think it's an avenue worth exploring, don't you? If Jeff knew anything, I suspect he would have told her. Which means she also needs to pay for her role in the deaths of my people. Alexander, Rota, our complicated past aside, come work for me. I can promise you that we will go find her ourselves without any interference."

"Fuckin' deal," Alexander said without hesitation.

Alexander, please think about this, Rota pleaded. *Are you sure that this is what you want?*

"Very sure."

Stoker smirked. "Good. It's settled, then."

"Stoker, hey, what the hell?" Sloane protested. "Why would you do this? We should all be working together, not against each other!"

"Should we share a common goal again in the future, I would be happy to offer my assistance," Stoker said firmly, "but I am not going to put myself in a position ever again where I don't get what I want."

"Please reconsider, guys," Sloane urged. "We all want the same thing, don't we?"

"You don't know fucking *anything* about what I want," Alexander replied bitterly. "Even with everything Jeff did, you were trying to save him. Jeff, who's killed gods know how many people, took your fuckin' daughter, and would have continued to do very fucked-up things." He narrowed his eyes at Sloane. "There are times to be the good guy, and then there are times to do whatever the fuck it takes."

"No." Sloane shook his head. "There is always another way."

"Says the guy who's killed how many gods?" Alexander rolled his eyes. "And that Kunst guy? The one who's in a damn bubble right now? Was there another way then?"

"Hey! That's not fair!"

"I'll have you know that I'm quite happy in my bubble, young man!" Kunst added with a dramatic scoff.

"Grumpy one," Loch warned, his eyes turning dark as he stared down Alexander, "you're upsetting my mate. I do not like that."

"It's okay, Loch." Sloane placed a reassuring hand on Loch's arm. "I get it. He's pissed."

"This is a few steps above pissed." Alexander lit up a cigarette and then addressed Stoker. "Hey. You. Just say when. We'll be there."

"Thank you." Stoker offered his hand. "This is the start of a beautiful working relationship."

Alexander eyed Stoker's hand but didn't take it. "Whatever." He took a long drag of his cigarette, and he and Rota vanished.

"Dammit!" Sloane groaned. "We need to get him back! We have to fix this!" He glared at Stoker. "No freakin' thanks to you! We're supposed to be on the same side. You know, us versus all the idiots trying to end the world?"

"The only side I'm on is my own," Stoker said calmly. "I'm sorry you had any other impression."

"Oh, look. The criminal is a selfish fiend." Merrick scowled. "Forgive me if I am not surprised."

"Wow." Sloane scoffed in disgust. "For a second, I really thought…." He didn't even want to finish what he was going to say, and he felt like a fool. "I hope Merrick and Chase arrest the crap out of you when we get back."

"Unfortunately for them, I don't see that happening, as there's absolutely nothing they can charge me with." Stoker smiled. "Always a pleasure, Mr. Beaumont. Until we meet again." He bowed politely, and then he also disappeared.

"Fuck." Sloane threw his hands up. "Great! This is just fuckin' swell!"

"Let him go." Loch leaned against the temple wall. "We do not need him or the grumpy one's help. But especially not his."

"It's going to be all right," Galgareth said confidently. "We have each other. We have our family."

"Technically, he is family."

"Well, he's not invited to any of our family events. Like, ever."

Merrick pinched his brow. "Perhaps it is time for us to return to the city. There will be much to answer for."

Sloane slumped against the wall beside Loch. "Yeah? And what answers are we gonna give, exactly? What do we say? That I killed another old god by stabbing him with my starlight sword after letting him swallow me whole, and oh, by the way, the stupid leader of the Salgumel cult who's the mastermind behind all those innocent people drowning in their own tears managed to kill himself with the Kindress goop because we couldn't stop arguing over what to do with him?"

Loch hummed thoughtfully. "No, sweet mate. I think that's a bit too on the mouth."

"Nose."

"Knows what?"

"Never mind."

"Wow. You're an idiot." Asta laughed.

"I'm suddenly feeling the urge to make mittens," Loch growled. "Big fuzzy black ones."

"Well, huh, the urge to leave is coming back with a quickness." Asta bared his pointy teeth in a big grin. "Consider your IOU cashed in and then some, Starkiller."

"Thank you, Asta." Sloane managed a smile. "Really. For everything."

"No need to thank me." Asta transformed back into his human form, naked as usual save for a pair of round purple shades. "Go home, snuggle that kid of yours, and make sure ol' ginger daddy sends Jay my way, okay?"

"Do you mean Chase?" Merrick blinked slowly. "How exactly is he supposed to do that?"

"Have him tell Jay I'll be hanging out at our usual spot for a little while." Asta winked coyly. "He'll know what it means."

Kunst hovered over to Sloane. "Take care of yourself and your family, Sloane. It was good to see you again."

"You too, Professor." Sloane's smile perked up.

"Your parents would be very proud of you."

Sloane's eyes stung unexpectedly. "Thank you. I, uh, I appreciate that. A lot."

"Hey, hey!" Asta teased. "Enough mushy shit. I'm trying to go get dicked down, okay? You guys are killing my boners."

"Charming," Loch drawled.

Sloane grinned and waved farewell. "Take care, guys."

"You too. Even you, Azaethoth." Asta opened a portal in the floor and then grabbed a hold of Kunst. "See you bitches later!" He shoved Kunst between his thighs, fell back into the portal, and disappeared with a loud pop.

"I guess now it really is time to head back, right?" Sloane sighed.

"Yes," Merrick agreed. "Chase and I will handle the… details."

"You mean, what you're going to say happened?"

"Jeff Martin was a wanted criminal with powerful teleportation abilities who was meeting Stoker for an illegal transaction of black-market magic. Mr. Martin transported the restaurant to another world when his deal with Stoker went south, and he summoned an abomination to kill us all. We were able to dispatch the abomination, and Mr. Martin ended his own life when we attempted to take him into custody. His accomplice, Daisy Lopez, escaped. Olivia Hutchinson is a person of interest, and her whereabouts are also currently unknown."

"That's the truth at least." Galgareth cringed. "You know, more or less."

Sloane frowned. "But hundreds of people have seen Cleus. They're not going to believe he was just an abomination."

"I know." Merrick smiled sadly. "But this is the only version of the truth that we can share. We still have to protect ourselves and those we love."

"Fear not." Loch wrapped a tentacle around Sloane's waist and kissed his cheek. "All is well, my darling husband. We are safe, and we have stopped Jeff."

"Did we, though?" Sloane raised his brows. "I mean, Jeff seemed so cocky right up to the very end. Like he'd already gotten what he wanted. Daisy and Olivia are still out there, you know, and it's not like the cult is going to stop just because Jeff is dead."

"But despite my best efforts, Stoker left unharmed? They needed him or our spawn to complete the ritual, yes?"

"Yeah, I guess." Sloane rubbed Loch's tentacle. "I don't know. I just can't shake this feeling that something isn't right."

"Oh, my beautiful mate." Loch hugged Sloane close with more tentacles. "Even if it is not, there is nothing to worry about. We are here. We are together. And together, I know you and I can do anything."

Sloane smiled warmly. "Yeah?"

"Absolutely. We have saved the world, ended evil experiments, stopped heinous rituals, solved many murders, and we are successfully raising a wonderful spawn with minimal fire damage. I would say that yes, there is nothing we can't do with our awesome forces combined."

"By all the gods, I love you."

"And I love you, my beautiful Starkiller." Loch pressed a sweet kiss to Sloane's lips. "Now. Let us return home and snuggle our spawn, yes?"

"Yes," Sloane agreed. "Let's go home."

"That is unless you'd like to engage in a riveting repeat performance of the last time we visited this temple. The mating that day was so very vigorous—"

"Home, Loch. We're going home."

"As you wish, my darling husband."

CHAPTER 15.

THE WEEKS following the battle with Cleus were hectic. Most of the news stations ran with the fabricated story that it was an illegal deal gone wrong to point the finger at the now deceased Jeff Martin, but the public at large was not buying it. Various footage of Cleus tearing up the city and Flaming Amy's restaurant being teleported away were circulating on social media, and the general consensus was that it was a government coverup.

Mr. Zabel, the outspoken reporter, was very vocal about pushing the narrative that the old gods had, in fact, returned and Lucian authorities were trying to hide the truth. He was quick to point out that no one had seen Sullivan Stoker since the alleged deal, and he also outed Olivia as an alleged member of Jeff Martin's cult and the mayor's niece. He made a promise to his viewers that he was going to stop at nothing to get the truth.

There were no more drowning victims, and the AVPD released a statement that they had successfully recovered all of the items with the tainted design. The abominations were gone, they were still diligently searching for Jeff's accomplices, Daisy and Olivia, but they were confident that the city was safe from any more large-scale magical threats.

Construction began to repair the damage left behind by Cleus, the news found other stories to report on, and it seemed like things were going back to normal.

Well, normal enough for someone married to a god with a demigoddess child who really liked fire.

Sloane had to temporarily close down Beaumont Investigations because of the public attention. He got a new phone number in hopes of avoiding the influx of calls, but soon that one got out as well, and he decided to take an extended vacation until the frenzy died down. Chase and Merrick made the weapon charges go away by claiming Sloane was sanctioned by the AVPD to wield the sword.

Merrick had the paperwork to prove it.

Urilith and Galgareth stayed on for a few more days to help assist with the overload of attention and a group effort to fire-train Pandora. It was quite successful, and they went a whole week without the smoke alarm going off.

Merrick and Chase remained swamped at the AVPD as they tried to work through the sea of paperwork left in the wake of Jeff's chaos. Per Chase, Ollie confirmed that Alexander and Rota were working for Stoker now, though Ollie promised to keep everyone in the loop despite Alexander's objections.

The most pertinent update was that while there was no lead on Daisy's current whereabouts, there had been some strange activity at Umbriech's Glen—namely mysterious evidence of moisture in the once barren streambed.

Sloane and Loch personally visited both the Glen and Babbeth's Orchard, but they could not discern if any fruit had actually been created. It should not have been possible. No stream meant no fruit, and since they'd rescued Pandora and Stoker was never taken, nothing should have happened.

Then again, the wording of the ritual hadn't been very clear about what the half-god person was supposed to do, and Jeff had remained confident to the very end. His horrible death proved that the Kindress was real, that it was here on Aeon, and Sloane half expected it to show up at their front door to ask for a cup of sugar or whatever a god might want when they were preparing to end the world.

He tried to stay positive and enjoy the break with his family, but he still couldn't shake that nagging feeling that something was amiss.

Jeff's death should have felt like justice served for all of his victims, but Sloane's guts rung hollow. It didn't feel particularly just when Jeff himself had chosen his miserable end, and it left Sloane wondering if this wasn't part of some other nefarious plot.

Jeff had always been two steps ahead of them, a dreadful and constant threat, and it was hard to believe that he was truly gone.

And the danger was far from over.

Daisy was still out there, and she was sure to continue Jeff's mission with equal fervor.

To help ease Sloane's troubled mind, Loch had offered to cook anything Sloane desired that night for dinner. He was a bit offended when Sloane requested pizza, because apparently that was an insult to his immense culinary skills, but he still agreed to make one.

He didn't say anything about not complaining, however.

"You could have asked me for anything," Loch was fussing as he sliced the freshly baked pizza. "Filet mignon, duck pate, cheese soufflé, but *no*. You wanted pizza. This is peasant food."

"Delicious peasant food," Sloane said with a grin. "Besides, you made your own sauce. And you made the dough from scratch. I'd say this is a pretty fancy pizza."

Loch scoffed. "As if I'd make it any other way."

"Daddy!" Pandora waddled into the kitchen, raising her arms over her head. She was walking and running everywhere now.

"Hey, baby girl!" Sloane scooped her up. "Are you getting hungry? We're gonna have pizza."

"Pizza! Pizza!" Pandora clapped her hands.

"See?" Sloane grinned. "She likes pizza too."

"She gets her peasant taste from you." Loch wrinkled his nose playfully as he brought their plates over to the table.

Sloane's phone dinged.

"Damn phone," Pandora said, imitating Sloane's usual response to any time his phone made a peep now.

"Shhh, don't say that, sweetie." Sloane regretted ever cursing in front of Pandora, and he got her settled into her high chair before checking to see what it was.

"Is everything all right?" Loch asked.

"It's Milo." Sloane read over the text. "Him and Lynnette may end up having a Dhankes baby. She had some contractions earlier, but she's not dilated. The midwife is gonna stay the night just in case. Said she's ready to pop any day."

"Have they chosen a name for their spawn yet?"

"The girl name is Mara Organa. Can't remember the boy name. Din or Luke or something."

"I don't understand."

"They don't know what they're having yet because they wanted it to be a surprise. So they picked a girl name and a boy name." Sloane sat beside Pandora to break up her pizza into bite-sized pieces, but she took it away from him to gnaw on it whole. He laughed. "Okay, big girl. Go for it."

"We may need a new prison chair for her," Loch observed. "She's grown quite a bit."

"It's called a high chair, and yeah, probably." Sloane had also noticed that the chair seemed a bit small for her.

And her clothes.

And her crib.

And, well, everything.

At four months old now, she was quickly approaching toddler size. It was all happening so fast, but Sloane was glad for every thrilling moment.

Dhankes was right around the corner, Pandora's first, and Sloane could not wait to share the special day with her. In addition to being a Sagittarian holiday, it was an anniversary of sorts for him and Loch, not to mention the anniversary of his parents' death was just a few days after. It would always be bittersweet, but for the very first time, Sloane was actually looking forward to it.

After all, he'd finally gotten justice for his parents, and he could enjoy the holiday like all Sages did—honoring those who were gone and remembering to love those who were still here.

Plus, seeing Pandora probably set some pumpkins on fire was guaranteed to be a real hoot.

Sloane took a bite of pizza, and then he *moaned*.

A deep, guttural moan of pleasure.

It was positively delicious.

"Oh, Loch," Sloane gushed. "This is amazing."

Loch's eyes were wide, and he gasped. "That sound. That rich, resonating cry of pure pleasure. Truly I have achieved the Moan with pizza?"

"Most definitely," Sloane mumbled through a mouthful. "Mmm, it's so good. The fresh mozzarella is awesome, the crust has the perfect amount of crunch. Yeah, it's the best pizza I've ever had."

"All this time I have been climbing the mountains of culinary perfection to inspire your sinful cries of satisfaction, and the answer was down in the rocky underbelly all along."

"Pizza is always the answer."

Pandora seemed to agree, judging by how fast she'd gobbled up her slice. She was reaching for another piece from Sloane's plate, but he noticed she hadn't finished the crust.

"Hey," Sloane said, urging the crust closer to her on her tray. "Eat this too, baby girl."

"No!" Pandora pushed it back. "I don't want pizza bone!"

Snorting out a laugh, Sloane tried to make sense of what she'd just said. "Pizza bone?"

"No pizza bone!"

"Perhaps she is thinking of the crust as an inedible vessel that delivers the soft flesh of the pizza, like how we devour chicken meat from the bone, but not the bone itself?" Loch mused.

"Maybe?" Sloane nudged Pandora. "Or maybe somebody is just being picky."

"No pizza bones," Pandora insisted, pushing the crust to the edge of her tray. When her arm wasn't quite long enough, she turned her hand into a tentacle to tip the crust over the edge and onto the floor.

Sloane sighed.

It was at least better than her setting it on fire.

After finishing dinner and cleaning up the kitchen, it was time to get Pandora ready for bed. They tucked her in together, and Sloane made a mental note to also look for a bigger bed when they went shopping for a new high chair.

Pandora was fussy, so Loch sent a tentacle over to the bookshelf to grab a worn storybook.

It was *Starlight Bright*, a wedding present from Ell and Fred. Sloane had mentioned having the book as a child once months ago, and Ell, sweet guy that he was, had remembered. He'd wanted to give it to Loch and Sloane for their future spawn, and it had easily become Pandora's favorite book.

Sloane leaned against the doorway, watching Loch read to Pandora in a soothing tone. A few of Loch's tentacles crept into the crib to hold Pandora's hands, and her eyes were slowly starting to close.

A surge of warmth filled Sloane's chest watching them, and he couldn't help but smile.

Loch was many things—a stubborn thief, an insatiable goofball— but most importantly he was an adoring husband and father, and Sloane's heart overflowed with the love he felt for this man.

Ah no, for this *god*.

A god who had come crashing into Sloane's life and changed it forever for the better. He couldn't imagine a single moment without Loch and the family they had together now. Sloane had never been this happy, and wow, there was something about Loch being so very fatherly that was making his pulse flutter in more ways than one.

"And in our hearts, we carry that spark, of the gods and goddesses above," Loch's voice dropped to a whisper. "We sleep, we dream their dream, and we will always feel their love. Oh starlight bright, beautiful starlight bright, to all the stars, we say good night."

Pandora was out.

Loch kissed her brow before tiptoeing over to Sloane with a triumphant smirk. "The spawn has been lulled to slumber."

"Uh-huh." Sloane slid his hands up Loch's chest.

Loch watched his hands curiously. "You are pleased, yes?"

"Very pleased." Sloane kissed along Loch's neck and pressed close.

"Why, my beautiful husband," Loch purred, "it feels as if you are trying to initiate mating with me."

"Mmm, a gold star for you." Sloane wrapped his arms around Loch's shoulders, purposefully nuzzling against his jaw. "I am very much trying to initiate mating."

"It was the pizza, wasn't it? My impressive culinary skills have raked the coals of your lust for me?"

"No." Sloane laughed. "It was actually watching you read to Pandora."

"Truly?"

"Yeah. Something about it was just so sweet, and it made me think about how much I love you. How much you mean to me, how happy I am being with you." Sloane smiled playfully. "Then I couldn't stop thinking about how hot it is when you're being a good daddy, and yeah, well, that did it. Now I pretty much just want you to tear all my clothes off and see if we can break our bed while I try to take three tentacles at the same time again."

"All that from reading to our spawn?"

"Yup."

"I shall steal her an entire library, then," Loch declared as he scooped Sloane into his arms to carry him off to the bedroom. "I will read to her until the sun vanishes from the sky to hear you speak of such bountiful desire for me, my sweetest mate. You are my everything, the center of my universe, the pulse of starlight that illuminates the very heavens." He laid Sloane across their bed and then kissed him. "I love you, Sloane Beaumont."

"And I love you, Azaethoth the Lesser." Sloane grinned. "Always."

"And forever," Loch promised with another kiss.

Clothes vanished away until there was nothing left between them, and Sloane kissed Loch with all he had, breathless and hungry. He loved the soft touch of Loch's lips, the minty taste of his tongue, and he was so turned on that he was nearly trembling in want of stimulation.

Loch's hands and tentacles traced each and every line of Sloane's body, greedily mapping them out from Sloane's collarbones to the crease in his groin.

Being caressed like that was making Sloane squirm, and his skin was hot and tingling from so much attention. He lost track of what was where, unsure if it was a tentacle teasing his nipple or Loch's fingers, but then there were more tentacles sliding over his cock and maybe fingers again between his cheeks and on and on until he felt like he was being completely enveloped by touch.

"Loch," he mewled, his voice strained with need. "Please, baby, mm, come on."

"Yes, my love." Loch kissed Sloane's cheek, and he smiled. "I am here. I will give you what you need. I will give you everything."

One of Loch's tentacles pushed inside of Sloane's hole, magically wet and stretching him easily as it sank deeper and deeper.

Sloane went limp against the bed, moaning his pleasure at being filled. It only alleviated the ache for a moment, and he was soon grinding down on the tentacle for more friction. "Mmm, yeah, please. Give it to me. Fuck me, please."

"Oh, my delicious mate, I am reading so very often," Loch mumbled against Sloane's throat. "Every night. Forever." His smaller tentacles spread Sloane's legs, and he thrusted the tentacle in his ass hard and fast, grunting with each powerful slam.

"Loch!" Sloane gasped, his entire body jerking from the force of Loch's pounding. The intensity was nearly blinding, and he gave himself over to it with a happy moan. It was so rare that Loch used his full strength, much less this soon into their lovemaking, and Sloane was falling apart.

Being fucked by a god was incredible.

Loch curled more tentacles around Sloane's wrists to pin them against the headboard, and he continued to ravage him. He was relentless, never tiring for a second, and his tentacle thrusted away into Sloane's asshole like a machine.

All Sloane could do was moan and whine and beg for more, his toes curling in the air as Loch plunged inside of him without reprieve. It was overwhelmingly hot, and Sloane's eyes were watering, his mouth dry, and his cock was throbbing harder with every bounce.

Sloane was sure he was floating away, and the only thing keeping him grounded was the ferocious pressure of Loch's tentacle fucking him into oblivion. Despite the frantic pace, time actually seemed to slow down, and his pulse was running like thunder up through his ears, the roar punctuated by the smack of their colliding bodies.

Just when he was sure he was reaching the peak of mortal experience, Loch pushed his other slitted tentacle in alongside the other.

"Loch! Yes! Fuck! Fuck me!" Sloane wailed, trying to spread his legs and open himself up impossibly wider.

Loch's response was a growl, an inhuman sound of desire that made Sloane's scorched skin prickle with goose bumps. Both tentacles were pumping away as one giant appendage, and Sloane's thighs started to twitch and quake in anticipation of climax.

"Make me come," he demanded between clenched teeth. "Fuck, come on, make me fuckin' come!"

"My love." Loch's voice sounded broken, and he grabbed on to Sloane to fuck him faster. All of his tentacles were trembling as they moved over Sloane's body, and he dragged his teeth across Sloane's throat. "Come for me... come for me, right now!"

"I'm almost, ah, there, there, ah, *there*!" Sloane sobbed, his tensed muscles melting as his orgasm took over, his entire body submerged in a warm rush of bliss that started back behind his balls and zoomed through the head of his pulsing cock before spreading over every inch of his skin.

Now he truly was in danger of floating off, lost in the heavy waves of pleasure as Loch's tentacles flooded his body with thick loads of come. It was gushing out as they continued to thrust, and Sloane moaned low, savoring the slick sensation.

"More, my love?"

"More. Gods, yes. More!" Sloane cried.

Loch moved onto his back, and he used his tentacles to bring Sloane on top of him. He stroked Sloane's thighs as he gazed up at him, licking his lips. "Then more you shall have, my gorgeous mate."

Sloane groaned as the two tentacles inside of him spread his hole wide and Loch's come dribbled down his thigh. The other tentacles were holding him tight, so he didn't even have to worry about keeping his head up. He let himself relax, and he didn't struggle as Loch posed his arms over his head.

"You're so radiant like this," Loch murmured. "Full of my seed and ravenous for another helping...." He moved his tentacock between

Sloane's legs, the head teasing around Sloane's spread hole. "Breathe for me, sweet husband. Breathe, relax, and open up for me."

"Yes. Gods, yes." Sloane let out a deep moan when the tentacock pressed in. Just that monster on its own was a challenge, and having it plus the other tentacles was probably insanity.

But Sloane wanted it. Craved it. Needed it.

And he wasn't going to stop.

Not until it was all inside of him.

The first thrust of the tentacock in Sloane's stuffed hole brought forth a sharp sensation that was almost like pain, and it made tears well up in his eyes. It was a very good thing Loch was holding him so securely because there was no way Sloane could have moved. He was frozen in place because the slightest twitch exploded his nerves with a burst of immense feeling.

Oh, but how he wanted to. He longed to grind and rock and do anything to ease the maddening fullness. He had to have friction, something, anything, and he moaned appreciatively when Loch thrusted again.

"My love, oh, my sweet love," Loch whispered adoringly. "My perfect mate, my everything, my heart, my soul." He raised Sloane's body to grind up inside of him, all three of his tentacles gliding in and out of Sloane's slick hole. Loch's eyes were black and glittering with stars, and he never looked away from Sloane's face, lost in the sweet moment as his tentacles writhed deep within Sloane's hole.

Helpless to do anything but wail in pleasure, Sloane surrendered to Loch completely. He could see his stomach bulging from the girth of Loch's tentacock, and the press of the knot against his hole was a promise of more ecstasy. It felt like his orgasm was still happening in little floods of searing warmth that made his breath catch, and then he was definitely coming again from another incredible slam, spilling over the tentacles holding him so tenderly.

The knot finally popped inside, and Sloane thought he might have screamed. He couldn't be entirely sure because his vision went fuzzy, and he thought he was going to pass out right at the start of a new mind-shattering orgasm. He came so hard that the roots of his hair tingled, and his nose and lips were numb.

"Azaethoth!" Sloane wept, his entire existence reduced to the hot throb down in his cock and the ache deep inside his hole as he was filled by Loch's cocks again. He leaned forward, desperate for touch to deepen their connection.

Loch brought Sloane down against his chest, his tentacles winding them together as he pressed a loving kiss to his lips. "Mmm, Sloane. My beautiful, beautiful Sloane."

Sloane could barely keep their kiss going for need of air, gasping and moaning from the rush of adrenaline zooming through him. He was shaking, his hair was soaked with sweat, and he could not stop smiling. "Oh, *Azaethoth*."

"My love." Loch laid Sloane out in bed next to him, sweetly petting his hair and face. He gently withdrew his tentacles from Sloane's body, asking, "Mmm, and how was that? Has your carnal lust for me been satisfied, or should I go read some more books?"

"Wow." Sloane laughed breathlessly. He flopped onto his back, stretching his arms and legs across the bed like he was going to make a snow angel in the rumpled sheets.

"I take it that means you are pleased, my sweet husband?" Loch grinned.

"Very, very pleased."

"Mmm, good. Then I am pleased as well." Loch took Sloane's hand so he could kiss it, magically tidying the mess between them. "You were amazing, my beautiful mate."

"You too," Sloane gushed. "So amazing."

"Awe-inspiring? Mind melting? The very pinnacle of primal pounding passion?"

"Oh, definitely." Sloane smiled. "Azaethothian, in fact."

"Now that's one I haven't heard before," a deep and unfamiliar voice said. "Azaethothian, huh?"

Sloane jerked up to see who had spoken.

Two men were standing at the bedroom door. They had to have used a powerful portal to get in, but it was so clean and quick that it was as if the pair had appeared right out of thin air.

The first was the biggest man Sloane had ever seen, like "professional wrestler, had to duck to get through the doorway" big. He was dressed casually in jeans and a T-shirt, scruffy and handsome. The second man was of average height, perhaps a bit shorter than that, and stocky. He was wearing a purple brocade suit with matching purple shades, and he looked like a singer from a band that Alexander would have liked.

When the second man smiled, Sloane saw a mouthful of pointy teeth.

Considering that and the very smooth portal, Sloane quickly surmised that this man was an Asra like Asta. Even so, he didn't trust that these men were friendly.

He wrapped the sheets around his waist, up on his knees as he summoned a sword of starlight. Beside him, Loch's tentacles unfurled from his skin as he rose from the bed, still quite naked, and he snarled.

"Whoa, that's fuckin, cool," the big man said. "That's the sword. The starlight sword! And holy fuck, look, tentacles!"

"I'm aware, love," the shorter man drawled in a deep, rumbling voice. He was the one who had first spoken and gotten Sloane's attention. "Not my first time seeing a god."

"Sorry, uh, if we were interrupting." The big man grinned. "I fuckin' hate when that shit happens."

"What is with everybody barging in here after we've had sex?" Sloane mumbled to himself.

"Better than while you're in the middle of it, right? That's the fuckin' worst. There's this one dude named Mozzie who is always—"

"Can we help you?" Loch demanded, narrowing his dark starry eyes at the intruding guests.

"Right. Hey!" The big man waved. "What's up? I'm Ted Sturm, and this is Grell."

"*King* Grell," the second man corrected with a dramatic roll of his eyes.

"Yeah, King Grell." The big man grinned. "My fiancé."

"Oh. Hello!" Sloane dropped the sword, and he stared. He had no idea how to react to royalty, especially royalty that was magical and ancient. Clumsily, he dropped his head and bowed. "It's nice to meet you, Your Highness."

"A pleasure," Grell said. "You're the famous Starkiller we've heard so much about. You look fabulous on television, by the way. Very dashing."

"Thank you, I think?" Sloane laughed.

"And this magnificent specimen must be Azaethoth the Lesser," Grell went on, his bright eyes now on Loch.

"Magnificent? Yes, well, of course I am." Loch seemed to relax, though he did not put his tentacles away. "You are very intelligent for a filthy cat creature."

"So I've been told. I'm also aces at Hungry Hungry Hippos."

"All right." Loch pursed his lips. "You may continue. State your business, please."

"Look, we won't keep you too long," Ted said. "Asta says you guys got a new baby and all that shit, but here." He offered an envelope. "Wanted to give you guys this in person."

"What is it?" Loch sniffed the air suspiciously.

Sloane accepted the envelope, opened it, and pulled out a gilded card. "It's… a wedding invitation?"

"You're hereby invited to our official fancy wedding at the Angus Barn." Ted was beaming. "We gotta do the whole royal bullshit back in Xenon, so we'll do that shit first, but this one is actually gonna be fun. Plus, you know, gods can come."

"Wow. We're honored." Sloane smiled. "Thank you so much."

"Asta's idea." Grell winked. "He's quite fond of you two."

"Make sure you invite Starkiller and that bozo Azaethoth so I have somebody to talk to," Ted recited, obviously quoting Asta. "I think he's gonna be bringin' Jay as his plus one. I heard one of your friends maybe put in a good word?"

"Yeah, Detective Chase." Sloane smiled. "He works with Jay at the AVPD. And he was your roommate, right?"

"Yeah. You're the one he went to after, you know, I got sort of sucked into a portal into another world."

"Yeah!" Sloane laughed. "I'm really glad it worked out for you."

"Oh, it worked out beautifully," Grell purred, his bright eyes feasting on Ted in a way that reminded Sloane at once of how Loch looked at him.

"Yeah, yeah." Ted grinned shyly. "I guess it worked out okay. You know. All things considered."

"Just okay?" Grell eyed him, a playful glare that betrayed the obvious love he felt for this man. "Oh sure, my voluptuously thick minx. You have everything your heart could ever desire, I worship your body for hours at a time, but it's just okay."

"Maybe a bit more than okay." Ted winked.

It was weirdly surreal meeting Ted after all this time, not to mention the honor and delight of Asta's father, King Grell.

Sloane could practically taste the power coming off Grell, and his unassuming mortal body was hiding a deep wealth of magic. Grell's fanged smile was a mirror of Asta's, full of mischief and humor, and yes, a hint of danger as well.

"Is Ell coming?" Sloane asked politely.

He knew that Ell and Ted hadn't had the best relationship, and according to Ell, they hadn't spoken in a long time.

"Yeah. We just came from his place. Met his boyfriend, Fred." Ted's expression softened. "Thank you for being so good to him. I haven't exactly been the best brother to him, but I'm real glad to hear he's got his own family now to watch out for him."

"Family," Sloane repeated, unable to resist another smile. It felt good to know Ell thought so highly of him. "Thank you. That's sweet of him. He's a great guy."

"Excellent taste in personal lubricant." Loch nodded in agreement.

Ted laughed. "You know, he said you might say something like that."

"Then he is also very wise."

"As lovely as this is, we have a few more invitations to deliver, and we're late for an erotic charcuterie class," Grell said smoothly. "We have registries at Target, Build A Bear, and Bad Dragon, and please remember to RSVP as soon as possible."

"We're not registered for anything he just fuckin' said, but yeah, definitely RSVP," Ted said. "It was really nice to finally meet you guys."

"Yeah! You too!" Sloane waved. "Congratulations!"

"Thanks!"

"Thank you." Grell bowed graciously. "Be well, Starkiller and Azaethoth the Lesser. We'll see you at the bachelor party." With a toothy grin and a wink, Grell took Ted's arm and vanished away with him.

"Bachelor party?" Sloane glanced at the invitation, and there was indeed a note for a bachelor party at the Velvet Plank preceding the wedding. "Ha. It's at Stoker's club."

"Hard pass," Loch muttered, rolling his eyes as he got into bed. He snuggled up against Sloane, forcing him to lay back down so he could hold him. "Mmm. I do not think we shall be attending that part of the festivities."

"Ditto." Sloane smiled and hugged Loch back. "We can just go to the wedding, yeah?"

"While it cannot possibly surpass our perfect wedding, I have hopes that it will be an improvement over Robert and Lochlain's lackluster nuptials. It's being held in a barn, so there is a lot of potential."

"The Angus Barn is a restaurant."

"Damn. Oh well."

Sloane chuckled. "So, we finally got to meet Ted and King Grell. That was pretty cool."

"Yes, and we're going to their disappointing wedding."

"How do you know it's going to be disappointing?" Sloane quirked his brows. "It could be really awesome."

"It's being held at a restaurant. Which means little to no chances of a fire, orgy, or fire."

"You said fire twice." Sloane smirked.

"Fire is very important."

"Mm, is that why our wedding was so perfect?"

"Of course." Loch smiled warmly. "And because I had the honor of marrying the perfect man that day."

"Oh?" Sloane grinned, and he leaned in for a kiss. "Did you now?"

"I most certainly did," Loch replied. "My perfect, beautiful, wonderful Starkiller. The love of my life. The tantalizing tempter who fuels the fires of my primal passions, my flawless mate who drives me to the brink of erotic madness and causes my loins to swell—"

Pandora cried loudly.

"Ah, the man who will go see what our daughter needs?" Sloane chuckled.

"No need, sweet husband." Loch playfully bumped their noses together. "I'll go see to her. And when I come back, we will discuss the swelling of my loins in more detail."

"Mm, can't wait." Sloane smiled, watching Loch get out of bed and head to the door.

No matter what the future held—weddings with or without fires, unknown dangers of raising a tiny demigoddess, mysterious attempts to end the world—Sloane knew he could take on anything as long as he had the love of this wonderful god.

"You really are perfect too, you know," Sloane said.

"Oh." Loch grinned. "I know."

"I love you."

"And I love you, always."

Keep reading for an excerpt from
Inkredible Love
by K.L. Hiers.

CHAPTER 1.

ONE YEAR AGO...

FRED WILDER decided the most frustrating thing about being a ghoul was not being able to eat.

Despite the lack of appetite or need for any sustenance, he still often found himself hovering in front of his empty fridge. He didn't keep anything there for guests because he never had any over, and whatever he bought would have been wasted since he couldn't eat it.

He missed cake, chocolate in particular, and the mere memory made his mouth want to water. But he could not eat food now any more than he could drool over it.

Fred was a ghoul, a member of the only slightly undead. He'd suffered severe burns in a fire five years ago, and the doctors said he would not survive his injuries.

His best friend's sister, Lynnette Fields, refused to accept that prognosis and broke out the family grimoire. After some very rough translating, she was able to bind Fred's soul to a wooden spoon before he died and then later created a copy of his body to complete the ritual. His soul now bound to the ghoul vessel, Fred had cheated death. Like all forms of the forbidden art of necromancy, it came with a heavy cost.

High up on the list was the frustration of not being able to eat any damn chocolate cake.

Fred also couldn't feel much of anything, emotional or otherwise, except pain. Being a ghoul meant constant and unavoidable anguish as his body continually tried to rot. All of his prayers to the old gods went unheard, and there was nothing he could do except rely on magic.

Magic could be a bitch. It was heavily regulated in modern times, including the necessity of rigorous testing to determine specific disciplines and an annual state license to use it legally.

Being a Sage and a rogue witch, Fred's death certificate said unregistered.

Sages were followers of the Sagittarian faith, witches who worshipped a monstrous pantheon of gods who roamed the earth long ago. Gone into the dreaming, an eternal state of sleep, the gods had left their mortal followers and allowed a new monotheistic religion to take root in the form of the Lord of Light.

Most people considered the ancient ways to be nothing more than a joke and gave into the Lucian system willingly.

But not Sages.

They had their children at home, resisted testing that they thought was unnecessary, and though few in number, some lived proudly as rogue witches. They could be fined, arrested, or even jailed, but at least these witches were free of what they saw as an oppressive system.

If Fred had allowed himself to be registered, his discipline would have been fire. Lucians were fine with that, but that made no sense to Sages. Fire wasn't just fire. It could be warm and comforting like Shartorath's hearth, or it could be simmering and hot like Merikath's embers.

Or like Fred, who had Baub's rage, it could be wildly destructive and lethal.

The Sages believed that the gods would return one day. Then they would no longer have to fight, and they would be able to practice their religion and culture freely. Fred was pretty sure of it too.

After all, Fred knew the gods were alive and well because it was one such being who had solved his best friend's murder. It was also a god who had done the murdering.

Lochlain Fields had been killed almost a month ago by Tollmathan, the god of poetry and plagues, over a piece of a mystical totem that had the power to wake up Salgumel, the god of dreams and sleep. Salgumel was said to have gone mad in his dreaming, and waking him would end the world.

That was Tollmathan's plan anyway, but Lochlain happened to be the favorite of Azaethoth the Lesser. The patron god of thieves himself took over Lochlain's body and found a private investigator named Sloane Beaumont to avenge Lochlain's death.

They solved the crime, destroyed the totem, and during a fierce battle, Sloane was gifted a sword of pure starlight by Great Azaethoth himself to kill Tollmathan and become a Starkiller, a slayer of gods.

As if that wasn't spectacular enough, Great Azaethoth gave them another miracle: Lochlain came back from the dead, completely restored.

Lynnette made a ghoul copy of Lochlain's body for Azaethoth the Lesser to inhabit to continue his romance with Sloane, and they didn't have to worry about the usual pitfalls as Azaethoth's godly essence kept the body from decomposing. Their mutual friend Robert Dorsey finally confessed his secret love to Lochlain, and Lynnette was getting ready to move in with her boyfriend, a geeky forensic guy named Milo.

It was a happy ending for everyone all around.

Except Fred.

Each day for him was more of the same, and it sucked.

As a ghoul, he wasn't supposed to have any emotions. He was supposed to be disconnected from them and feel nothing except constant physical pain. But Fred was becoming aware that he felt something else, a sense of being hollow that had transformed into an ache that often rivaled his physical agony.

He was lonely.

Since Lochlain had begun his new relationship with Robert, Fred rarely saw him. They hadn't gone out on a job all month, leaving Fred to work on his own. He still had rent to pay and ghoul doctors were expensive, and like Lochlain, Fred was also a thief.

He'd just returned from a heist, breaking into a warehouse to jack some old ugly paintings for some very enthusiastic collectors. The job was easy enough, security was light, and he would make the drop tomorrow night.

That left Fred with all of this evening and most of tomorrow to amuse himself, and standing in front of his empty fridge had lost its charm.

He didn't bother calling Lochlain because no doubt he was busy fawning over Robert. Lynnette was either waitressing or packing up to move in with Milo. He briefly considered calling Sloane or Azaethoth, but he didn't think it wise to disturb a god and his mate, no matter how chummy they were.

Everyone had someone now and while he wanted to be happy for them, he was resentful. He wanted someone of his own to spend time with, to watch television with or to cook for even if he couldn't eat it, someone he could read to, a person to laugh with.

He wanted a friend who had time for him, maybe more than a friend.

Romance wasn't unheard of between ghouls and the living, but they had to be pretty fresh for anything to be palatable. Fred had been rotting for years and outside of his own decomposition, he couldn't feel much. A hug was distant pressure and shaking someone's hand was a cold tease of sensation.

He couldn't imagine trying to physically be with anyone now, but he still longed for company. Even if he couldn't feel it, the mere idea of holding someone eased his discomfort and made his anger vanish.

Fat chance of that ever fuckin' happening.

Fred slammed the fridge door closed harder than he should have, and he felt a new stab of pain on his arm. He looked down and saw a giant rotten sore that had been festering was starting to leak.

"Shit."

Quickly bandaging it up, he stalked across his apartment to find his phone. He scrolled through his contacts, finding the entry titled "Doc" and hit Send.

It rang a few times before a sleepy woman's voice answered, "Hello...?"

"Hey, Doc," Fred grunted. "It's me."

"I know who it is," Doctor York replied with a grumpy yawn. "What's wrong?"

"That spot you fixed ain't fixed no more. Need help."

"On your arm?" Doc sounded concerned. "Fred, I've tried to heal you three times now."

"So, do it four times."

"It doesn't work that way. I've told you. Ghouls are not forever. You're gonna keep rotting."

"Four times. Let's go." Fred refused to accept this dismal prognosis. "Come on, I'm good for it. I'm getting paid tomorrow."

"It's not about the money. It's just... I don't think I can help you. Your rot is getting worse."

"What about a new body?"

"No, your rate of decomposition will only increase if you try that. I've seen it before with other ghouls."

There was the sound of a door opening and shutting noisily through the phone, and Fred could hear the jingle of the fancy wind chime Doc kept on her front porch. A lighter clicked and then she inhaled, coughing on the smoke from her cigarette.

"Hmmph, if you try to jump ship and transfer your soul," she continued, "your new body will rot even faster."

Fred sat down and tried not to get angry. Anger was always so easy. "So, what the fuck do I do?"

"I know another ghoul doctor who might be able to help," Doc soothed. "He only takes patients by direct referral, and I don't know what he charges these days."

"Already said, money don't matter."

"He's local," Doc said. "I'll get in touch and find out how soon he can see you."

"How soon?"

Doc sighed. "I'll call him right now, okay? I'll tell him it's an emergency."

"Thanks, Doc."

"Be good, Fred. I'll let you know as soon as I can."

"Okay. Bye."

Fred hung up and set his phone down on the coffee table. He didn't need to sleep, so the only option left to him was to wait.

He had given up trying to pass the time with television. Even commercials made him angry because of the sheer volume of smiling faces. Oh sure, they might be frowning over a drain being clogged or excess belly fat, but once the miracle product was introduced, they were happy again.

There was no magical switch for Fred, so screw that.

Reading was equally irritating, and he could only get through a few paragraphs before he'd lose focus. He wasn't sure whether that was a side effect of being a ghoul, but it was maddening. He could read out loud without much bother, but it seemed pointless to read to himself without anyone to hear him.

Screw that too.

The only thing that ever seemed to pacify his sour temperament was popping in an old VHS tape with some episodes of his favorite television show, *Legends of Darkness*. It was a fantasy about a young man named Trip who went off to a magical land full of goblins and unicorns and had the most incredible adventures. Although it was easily over thirty years old, the special effects atrocious, and the quality of the footage was abysmal since he'd recorded it off his TV, nothing else brought him any level of comfort.

It reminded him of a simpler time, being a kid with Lochlain when they'd watch it together for hours on end. They'd act out their favorite scenes, make up new stories, and play until they passed out.

That was ages ago now, but watching the show still eased that bothersome ache inside of Fred. In thirty-minute increments, he could submerge himself in the magical world of the show and escape the cruel reality of his constant suffering.

At least until the end of the episode anyway.

He'd just made it to the second episode when his phone rang.

"Hey, Doc," he answered. "Gimme some good news, please."

"Hey," Doc said, sounding more awake than before. "Good news. He's agreed to meet you, but he's got some conditions."

"Which are?"

"You don't ever give out his name, where he lives, or what he does for you."

"Sure." All typical rules for ghoul doctors.

"Also. You don't question his age, his scar, or anything else about him."

"Okay." A little more unusual, but fine.

"Try not to be weird if he gets really handsy. It's just how his magic works, so don't be freaked out. Good? Good."

"Okay. How much?"

"He doesn't actually want a cash payment. You'll have to go shopping for him," Doc said, and it sounded like she was smiling. "I'm going to text you his address and a list of things he needs."

"Things? Like what?"

"Just get whatever is on the list if you want him to help you. Look, he doesn't get out much. Do it and be there tomorrow before noon."

"Fine." Fred tried not to sound agitated and failed. He took a deep breath, trying again when he said, "Thank you, Doc."

"Take care of yourself, Fred."

Fred ended the call and waited for the list to come through. He preferred dealing in cash, but if a simple shopping trip would settle the debt, that was fine too.

When the text popped up, Fred quickly realized there was nothing simple about it.

"A fuckin' faucet?" He blinked, continuing to read out loud. "Bread, but not white, the brown kind with crumbled oats on top. A trash can, small enough for a bathroom and any color except green, but blue would be really good. Body lotion, cucumber melon if you can find it, but the pinkie orange kind is okay too. Can't remember what it's called, but the bottle is pink with orange stripes. Donuts with sprinkles, but if there are no donuts with sprinkles, please get strawberry poofies instead." He scoffed. "What the fuck is a poofie?"

He checked the address to make sure it was legit, and he found it was a tiny speck in the middle of the forest almost forty-five minutes out of town.

Guess the guy really liked having his privacy.

The rest of the list was full of more weirdly specific items. All of it was food except the faucet, trash can, and lotion. There were a few twenty-four hour markets a short drive away. As long as he was going to be up, he might as well get the shopping done. He got up to leave, touching the Tauri shrine to his parents on his way out.

Tauri was another ancient religion that revered the old gods, though they called them by different names and believed in a cycle of multiple lives. While the ways of the Sages had faded to time, the Tauri faith remained in dominant practice in certain parts of the world like India and eastern Africa. Fred's mother's family had been from India, and she converted to the Sagittarian faith when she married his father.

They kept up with a lot of Tauri traditions like ancestor shrines and morning prayers, and his mother never cut her hair and only cooked vegetarian meals. She had also chosen to honor her father by passing his name onto her son.

She named him Farrokh.

They died when Fred was a teenager, both from complications of heart disease, and Fred became an honorary member of the Fields family with Lynnette and Lochlain. Though he embraced the Sagittarian religion, he never forgot his mother's faith, and he honored her by maintaining the shrine.

He honored his father by taking care of his old truck.

It always took a few cranks to get it going and the engine sputtered and groaned the whole drive over to the store, but Fred wouldn't trade it for anything in the world. He could remember being too small to see over the dashboard, wedged in between his parents as they drove along, going grocery shopping just like he was now.

Damn, that ache was back again.

Fred ignored it, parked, and went inside the store.

It was surprising how much could be learned from doing someone else's grocery shopping.

Fred picked up on his new doctor having quite the sweet tooth, enviously dropping several types of cookies and sugary treats into the cart as he went along the aisles.

He gleaned that the doctor also drank a lot of tea, as there were at least four varieties on the list to pick up. It was clear he didn't cook much since there were also at dozen kinds of frozen dinners, and the lotion spoke of loneliness to Fred.

Or perhaps the doctor really liked to be moisturized.

Maybe he was just projecting, Fred thought glumly. He stared down at his bursting shopping cart and felt a wicked stab of jealousy. He couldn't even remember the last time he'd gone grocery shopping. Probably when he was still alive.

There had been times since his death that Lynnette had asked him to go to the store for tampons or pads, a seemingly squeamish task for mortal men. Fred was always happy to remind her that he was perfectly willing to go even when he had a pulse, and the guys she'd been seeing were just trash.

He also remembered to get chocolate, even if it made him more than a bit jealous he couldn't eat it.

Somehow, that had played into her relationship with Milo. There was a story about him already having a box of tampons from a busted nose and him pledging to buy all the feminine products she would ever need.

Fred thought it was sweet. He liked Milo, and he made Lynnette happy.

Looking into his shopping cart, he wished he was buying these groceries for someone he cared about.

But that wasn't possible.

He'd had his chance to find love while he was alive, and hell, he didn't even know if he could feel those kinds of emotions now. He knew he cared about his friends, but he often wondered how much of that was real and not an echo from his life before.

He cared for Sloane and Azaethoth, he reasoned, and he had met them as a ghoul. It couldn't be impossible, but it felt so far out of reach. After all, who would be interested in dating a big rotten guy? How could they even be together?

Thinking that way led to a lot of fuckin' misery.

Miserable enough to end it all.

He'd heard about other ghouls doing it. They would get so tired of the pain and the rot that they would stop healing and let themselves wither away. It could take weeks for the act to happen naturally, and Fred couldn't imagine that kind of agony.

Being lonely still sucked, though.

He finished shopping and loaded up his truck with the groceries to return home so he could refrigerate what needed to be cold. He was able to find pretty much everything except the faucet. He liked having food in his fridge again, even if it was inside the bags from the grocery store.

It made his apartment feel less empty somehow.

Back to the couch he went, sitting down and turning the TV back on. He let his mind drift, zoning out and trying to relax with a few more episodes of *Legends of Darkness*. When the tape was over, he would wait for it to rewind itself so he could play it again. This was as close to sleep as he could get, and he listened to the familiar creaks and thumps from his neighbors when morning finally rolled around.

The guy on the left would hang around in the kitchen, fighting with his coffee maker for the next twenty minutes before taking a very long shower. The lady on his right had kids, and there was always a rush of loud cartoons and screaming. The people upstairs clomped around like horses, and he never heard a peep from the neighbor below him.

The ache in Fred's arm was getting worse, and the pain made him want to punch something. He needed to move to distract himself from the discomfort. He got up and paced absently around his couch.

Doc had told him to be at the new doctor's house before noon. Maybe he could show up early. The pain was making it hard to concentrate, and he stopped suddenly, staring at the carpet beneath his boots.

He hadn't realized it before, but he'd done this so often that he was leaving a trail of wear in the carpet.

Time to go.

Fred gathered the groceries back up and headed down to his truck. He had to step around a pack of small children as their mother herded them off into the elevator. He whispered their names as he heard the mother patiently fussing at them to hurry along.

"Eleanor, Elizabeth, Vincent."

He could still remember when he used to hear them crying at all hours of the night and was thankful he didn't need to sleep. He felt the corners of his mouth twitch up in a smile when he saw them swearing to their mother that they had done their homework just as the elevator doors were closing.

Fred knew damn well that was a lie because he'd heard the familiar blips of their latest video game when it was supposed to be bedtime.

He opted to take the stairs. It was a little quicker, and he didn't want to scare the kids.

At his size, he was already intimidating. His mother had told him he was built like the mighty god Theros, an amalgamation of the Sagittarian gods Salgumel and Bestrath, who was known for his broad build and big belly. The smell didn't help, and Lynnette had told him he had a serious case of resting bitch face.

Whatever.

Once he got the truck loaded, he punched in the new doctor's address and drove his sputtering truck along. It was definitely a haul, and he took his time navigating through traffic. He was already going to be a few hours early as it was.

Outside of the city, the strain of cars eased, and Fred eventually pulled up to a small cottage a few minutes after nine. There wasn't shit out here except old fences, fields, and trees, and he was instantly wary.

The place looked like it had fallen off a country postcard right down to the lush flower boxes hanging outside the front windows and the white trellis framing the stone path up to the door. He was surprised to see flowers blooming like that so late in autumn, and he wondered if they were fake.

It was too perfect, too quaint, and Fred hated it immediately.

Fred had to duck and turn sideways to step through the trellis on his way to the front door. He knocked a few times. There wasn't an immediate answer, so he tried again.

He heard a noise, a loud grunting, and was immediately on guard.

"*Ignis*," he murmured to himself, summoning a small ball of fire as he slowly crept toward the sound. It was coming from the back of the house, and he stepped around the corner, ready to fight any potential enemy.

What he saw was a skinny half-naked young man digging in the dirt and wrestling with a tree root. He was blond, filthy, and had ear buds in. The music was so loud he could hear the bass thumping through, and the young man hadn't noticed him yet.

Fred dismissed the fire, and he watched for a few moments.

Doc had said this guy was young, but this person looked like he was barely out of high school. His body was lean and steaming in the chilly air. The vision of sweaty pale skin might have been quite appealing when Fred was alive, and maybe it still was, but he didn't think much about it.

He was here on business.

"Hey," he tried.

The young man kept digging, fighting with the stubborn root as he murmured under his breath. He was singing along with whatever was pumping into his ears and remained completely oblivious to Fred's presence.

"Hey!" Fred roared, a bone-shattering shout guaranteed to get some attention.

"Oh!" The boy whirled around, quickly pulling the buds out of his ears. "Sorry! I must have lost track of the time!" His smile was bright, punctuated with a crooked canine, and Fred spotted a long scar across his throat that snaked up to his left ear.

"You the doc?"

"Are you Farrokh?"

"Call me Fred."

"Hi, Fred!" the young man eagerly offered out his hand to shake. "Elliam Sturm! Just Ell is fine. It's so nice to meet you!"

"Yeah," Fred said, accepting the gesture. As he shook Ell's hand, he found that he didn't want to let go. "Thanks for seeing me."

Huh.

Weird.

Ell's hand actually felt warm.

K.L. "KAT" HIERS is an embalmer, restorative artist, and queer writer. Licensed in both funeral directing and funeral service, they worked in the death industry for nearly a decade. Their first love was always telling stories, and they have been writing for over twenty years, penning their very first book at just eight years old. Publishers generally do not accept manuscripts in Hello Kitty notebooks, however, but they never gave up.

Following the success of their first novel, Cold Hard Cash, they now enjoy writing professionally, focusing on spinning tales of sultry passion, exotic worlds, and emotional journeys. They love attending horror movie conventions and indulging in cosplay of their favorite characters. They live in Zebulon, NC, with their family, including their children, some of whom have paws and a few that only pretend to because they think it's cute.

Website: http://www.klhiers.com

Follow me on BookBub

A SUCKER FOR LOVE MYSTERY

ACSQUIDENTALLY
IN LOVE

K.L. HIERS

"A breezy and sensual LGBTQ paranormal romance."
—*Library Journal*

A Sucker For Love Mystery

Nothing brings two men—or one man and an ancient god—together like revenge.

Private investigator Sloane sacrificed his career in law enforcement in pursuit of his parents' murderer. Like them, he is a follower of long-forgotten gods, practicing their magic and offering them his prayers… not that he's ever gotten a response.

Until now.

Azaethoth the Lesser might be the patron of thieves and tricksters, but he takes care of his followers. He's come to earth to avenge the killing of one of his favorites, and maybe charm the pants off the cute detective Fate has placed in his path. If he has his way, they'll do much more than bring a killer to justice. In fact, he's sure he's found the man he'll spend his immortal life with.

Sloane's resolve is crumbling under Azaethoth's surprising sweetness, and the tentacles he sometimes glimpses escaping the god's mortal form set his imagination alight. But their investigation gets stranger and deadlier with every turn. To survive, they'll need a little faith… and a lot of mystical firepower.

www.dreamspinnerpress.com

A SUCKER FOR LOVE MYSTERY

KRAKEN MY
HEART

K.L. HIERS

"A breezy and sensual LGBTQ paranormal romance."
—*Library Journal*, "Acsquidentally in Love"

A Sucker For Love Mystery

It's just Ted's luck that he meets the love of his life while covered in the blood of a murder victim.

Funeral worker Ted Sturm has a foul mouth, a big heart, and a knack for communicating with the dead. Unfortunately the dead don't make very good friends, and Ted's only living pal, his roommate, just rescued a strange cat who's determined to make his life even more miserable. This cat is more than he seems, and soon Ted finds himself in an alternate dimension… and on top of a dead body.

When Ted is accused of murder, his only ally in a strange world full of powerful magical beings calling for his head is King Grell, a sarcastic, randy, catlike immortal with impressive abilities… and anatomy. The two soon find themselves at the center of a cosmic conspiracy and surrounded by dangerous enemies. But with Ted's special skills and Grell's magic, they have a chance to get to the bottom of the mystery and save Ted. There's just one problem: Ted's got to resist Grell's aggressive advances… and he isn't sure he wants to.

A SUCKER FOR LOVE MYSTERY

HEAD OVER
TENTACLES

K.L. HIERS

A Sucker For Love Mystery

Private investigator Sloane Beaumont should be enjoying his recent engagement to eldritch god Azaethoth the Lesser, AKA Loch. Unfortunately, he doesn't have time for a pre-honeymoon period.

The trouble starts with a deceptively simple missing persons case. That leads to the discovery of mass kidnappings, nefarious secret experiments, and the revelation that another ancient god is trying to bring about the end of the world by twisting humans into an evil army.

Just another day at the office.

Sloane does his best to juggle wedding planning, stopping his fiancé from turning the mailman inside out, and meeting his future godly in laws while working the case, but they're also being hunted by a strange young man with incredible abilities. With the wedding date looming closer, Sloane and Loch must combine their powers to discover the truth—because it's not just their own happy-ever-after at stake, but the fate of the world....

www.dreamspinnerpress.com

A SUCKER FOR LOVE MYSTERY

NAUTILUS THAN
PERFECT

K.L. HIERS

A Sucker For Love Mystery

Detective Elwood Q. Chase has ninety-nine problems, and the unexpected revelation that his partner is a god is only one of them.

Chase has been in love with Benjamin Merrick for years and has resigned himself to a life of unrequited pining. But when they run afoul of a strange cult, Merrick's secret identity as Gordoth the Untouched slips out… and so do Chase's feelings. The timing can't be helped, but now Merrick thinks Chase only cares about him because he's a god.

Even more unfortunately, it turns out the cultists want to perform a ritual to end the world. Chase's mission to convince Merrick his feelings predate any divine revelations takes a back seat to a case tangled with murder and lies, but Chase doesn't give up. Once he finds out there's a chance Merrick feels the same way, he digs in his heels. Suddenly he's trying to court a god and save the world at the same time. What could possibly go wrong?

www.dreamspinnerpress.com

A SUCKER FOR LOVE MYSTERY

JUST CALAMARRIED

K.L. HIERS

A Sucker For Love Mystery

Newlyweds Sloane and Loch are eagerly expecting their first child, though for Sloane that excitement is tempered by pregnancy side effects. Carrying a god's baby would be enough to deal with, especially with the whole accelerated gestation thing, but it's not like Sloane can take maternity leave. He works for himself as a private investigator. Which leads him to his next case.

At least this strange new mystery distracts him from the stress of constant puking.

When two priests are murdered within hours of each other, a woman named Daphne hires Sloanc and Loch to track down the prime suspect— her brother—before the police do. Between untangling a conspiracy of lies and greed, going toe-to-toe with a gangster, and stealing a cat, they hardly have time to decorate a nursery....

www.dreamspinnerpress.com